LOGAN'S NEED

THE ESCORT SERIES #3

SLOANE KENNEDY

CONTENTS

Copyright — v
Logan's Need — vii
Trademark Acknowledgements — ix
Series Reading Order — xi
Series Crossover Chart — xv

Prologue — 1
Chapter 1 — 15
Chapter 2 — 26
Chapter 3 — 37
Chapter 4 — 45
Chapter 5 — 58
Chapter 6 — 68
Chapter 7 — 80
Chapter 8 — 105
Chapter 9 — 123
Chapter 10 — 138
Chapter 11 — 147
Chapter 12 — 158
Chapter 13 — 170
Chapter 14 — 179
Chapter 15 — 187
Chapter 16 — 195
Epilogue — 204

About the Author — 207
Also by Sloane Kennedy — 209

Logan's Need is a work of fiction. Names, characters, businesses, places, events and incidents are either the products of the author's imagination or used in a fictitious manner. Any resemblance to actual persons, living or dead, or actual events is purely coincidental.

Copyright © 2015 by Sloane Kennedy

Published in the United States by Sloane Kennedy
All rights reserved. This book or any portion thereof may not be reproduced or used in any manner whatsoever without the express written permission of the publisher except for the use of brief quotations in a book review.

Cover Image: © Kevin Hoover

Cover By: Jay Aheer, Simply Defined Art

ISBN-13:
978-1512271201

ISBN-10:
1512271209

LOGAN'S NEED

Sloane Kennedy

TRADEMARK ACKNOWLEDGEMENTS

The author acknowledges the trademarked status and trademark owners of the following trademarks mentioned in this work of fiction:

Animal Planet
ESPN
Mercedes
SyFy Channel
Seattle Seahawks
Hyatt Hotel
Coca-Cola

SERIES READING ORDER

All of my series cross over with one another so I've provided a couple of recommended reading orders for you. If you want to start with the Protectors books, use the first list. If you want to follow the books according to timing, use the second list. Note that you can skip any of the books (including M/F) as each was written to be a standalone story.

Note that some books may not be readily available on all retail sites

Recommended Reading Order (Use this list if you want to start with "The Protectors" series)
1. Absolution (m/m/m) (The Protectors, #1)
2. Salvation (m/m) (The Protectors, #2)
3. Retribution (m/m) (The Protectors, #3)
4. Gabriel's Rule (m/f) (The Escort Series, #1)
5. Shane's Fall (m/f) (The Escort Series, #2)
6. Logan's Need (m/m) (The Escort Series, #3)
7. Finding Home (m/m/m) (Finding Series, #1)
8. Finding Trust (m/m) (Finding Series, #2)

9. Loving Vin (m/f) (Barretti Security Series, #1)
10. Redeeming Rafe (m/m) (Barretti Security Series, #2)
11. Saving Ren (m/m/m) (Barretti Security Series, #3)
12. Freeing Zane (m/m) (Barretti Security Series, #4)
13. Finding Peace (m/m) (Finding Series, #3)
14. Finding Forgiveness (m/m) (Finding Series, #4)
15. Forsaken (m/m) (The Protectors, #4)
16. Vengeance (m/m/m) (The Protectors, #5)
17. A Protectors Family Christmas (The Protectors, #5.5)
18. Atonement (m/m) (The Protectors, #6)
19. Revelation (m/m) (The Protectors, #7)
20. Redemption (m/m) (The Protectors, #8)
21. Finding Hope (m/m/m) (Finding Series, #5)
22. Defiance (m/m) (The Protectors #9)

Recommended Reading Order (Use this list if you want to follow according to timing)

1. Gabriel's Rule (m/f) (The Escort Series, #1)
2. Shane's Fall (m/f) (The Escort Series, #2)
3. Logan's Need (m/m) (The Escort Series, #3)
4. Finding Home (m/m/m) (Finding Series, #1)
5. Finding Trust (m/m) (Finding Series, #2)
6. Loving Vin (m/f) (Barretti Security Series, #1)
7. Redeeming Rafe (m/m) (Barretti Security Series, #2)
8. Saving Ren (m/m/m) (Barretti Security Series, #3)
9. Freeing Zane (m/m) (Barretti Security Series, #4)
10. Finding Peace (m/m) (Finding Series, #3)
11. Finding Forgiveness (m/m) (Finding Series, #4)
12. Absolution (m/m/m) (The Protectors, #1)
13. Salvation (m/m) (The Protectors, #2)
14. Retribution (m/m) (The Protectors, #3)
15. Forsaken (m/m) (The Protectors, #4)
16. Vengeance (m/m/m) (The Protectors, #5)
17. A Protectors Family Christmas (The Protectors, #5.5)

18. Atonement (m/m) (The Protectors, #6)
19. Revelation (m/m) (The Protectors, #7)
20. Redemption (m/m) (The Protectors, #8)
21. Finding Hope (m/m/m) (Finding Series, #5)
22. Defiance (m/m) (The Protectors #9)

SERIES CROSSOVER CHART

Protectors/Barrettis/Finding Crossover Chart

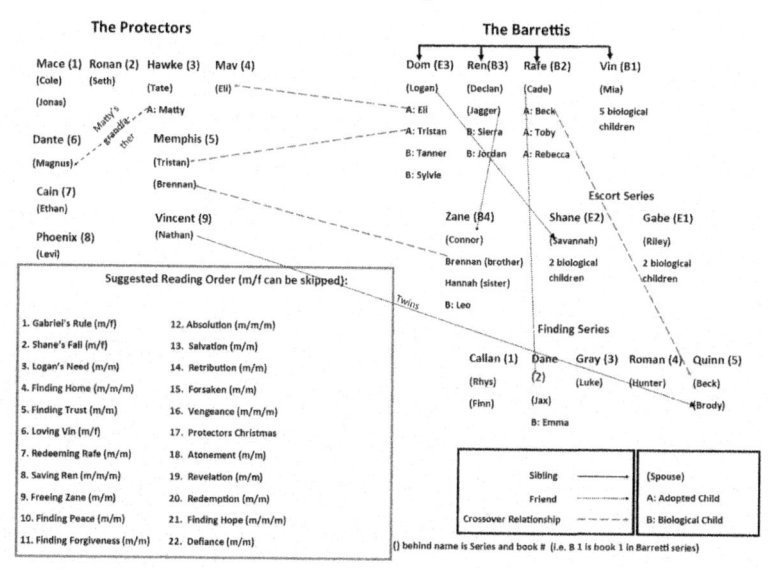

The Protectors

Mace (1) — (Cole) / (Jonas)
Ronan (2) — (Seth)
Hawke (3) — (Tate) / A: Matty
Mav (4) — (Eli)

Dante (6) — (Magnus)
Memphis (5) — (Tristan) / (Brennan)

Cain (7) — (Ethan)

Phoenix (8) — (Levi)
Vincent (9) — (Nathan)

Matty's grandfather

The Barrettis

Dom (E3) — (Logan) / A: Eli
Ren (B3) — (Declan) / (Jagger) / B: Sierra / B: Tanner / B: Jordan / B: Sylvie
Rafe (B2) — (Cade) / A: Beck / A: Toby / A: Rebecca
Vin (B1) — (Mia) / 5 biological children

Zane (B4) — (Connor) / Brennan (brother) / Hannah (sister) / B: Leo

Twins

Escort Series

Shane (E2) — (Savannah) / 2 biological children
Gabe (E1) — (Riley) / 2 biological children

Finding Series

Callan (1) — (Rhys) / (Finn)
Dane (2) — (Jax) / B: Emma
Gray (3) — (Luke)
Roman (4) — (Hunter)
Quinn (5) — (Beck) / (Brody)

Suggested Reading Order (m/f can be skipped):

1. Gabriel's Rule (m/f)
2. Shane's Fall (m/f)
3. Logan's Need (m/m)
4. Finding Home (m/m/m)
5. Finding Trust (m/m)
6. Loving Vin (m/f)
7. Redeeming Rafe (m/m)
8. Saving Ren (m/m/m)
9. Freeing Zane (m/m)
10. Finding Peace (m/m)
11. Finding Forgiveness (m/m)
12. Absolution (m/m/m)
13. Salvation (m/m)
14. Retribution (m/m)
15. Forsaken (m/m)
16. Vengeance (m/m/m)
17. Protectors Christmas
18. Atonement (m/m)
19. Revelation (m/m)
20. Redemption (m/m)
21. Finding Hope (m/m/m)
22. Defiance (m/m)

Legend

Sibling	————
Friend	··········
Crossover Relationship	— — —
(Spouse)	
A: Adopted Child	
B: Biological Child	

() behind name is Series and book # (i.e. B.1 is book 1 in Barretti series)

PROLOGUE

Being shot really sucked, Logan Bradshaw thought to himself as he parked his car. And not just because of the scar that now graced his right pectoral muscle where the bullet had ripped his flesh and nicked his heart, or the other scar that ran down the middle of his chest where doctors had cracked him open to fish said bullet out and fix all the damage it had left behind. No, being shot sucked because now everyone looked at him like they were afraid he would break. His sister hovered over him and forced endless food on him – and not the good kind either. Nope, it was mostly rabbit food mixed in with the occasional exotic fruit that he couldn't figure out what part he was supposed to eat. Logan wasn't sure, but it seemed that Savannah had decided that if he ate a little less red meat and more green shit, then maybe it meant he hadn't actually died twice before even making it to the operating room.

Having someone put a bullet through his chest also meant a stack of medical bills that he couldn't pay, rehab he'd hated with a passion and a physical ache in his chest that still nagged him. But none of that compared to the helplessness he felt at not being able to remember any of it. There was just a dark, empty spot in his life where he'd been alive and well one moment and gracing death's door the next.

Although saying he was alive and well was an overstatement – sure, the alive part was true, but his life had gone completely to hell long before the bullet had ripped him apart.

He was nearly twenty-eight years old and all he had to show for it was endless debt, a burned-out bar that he'd spent more than five years trying to get up and running, and a job that he seemed to be falling back on more and more as his need for money continued to grow. Being a professional escort was something he never would have even thought of doing until a classmate at the university he'd attended had suggested it.

Logan had been finishing up his first year of school when his parents had suddenly died and he'd been left to care for a then fourteen-year-old Savannah. He'd balked at the idea of selling his body for money, but when he'd found out that he could make the same amount in one night as he could in a month bussing tables, the decision had been pretty easy. There'd been too much at stake to let the shame of being a prostitute, albeit a high-class one, to get in the way. As hard as his parents had worked, there just hadn't been enough money to go around after their deaths and he'd faced the very real possibility of losing his sister to foster care if he couldn't figure out a way to make ends meet.

Even all these years later, Logan wouldn't change the decision he'd made. Escorting had let him keep the only family he'd had together and later it had given him the money he'd needed to buy the bar. But the bar was nearly gone now. His sister too, since she'd fallen in love with one of his best friends just a couple of months earlier. Even all his hard work to give Savannah a safe and healthy environment to grow up in had been snatched away. In the cruelest twist of fate, he'd ended up bringing the danger directly into their own home when he'd welcomed his former boss and business partner, Sam Reynolds, into his life. He'd trusted the man as both a friend and a mentor, had even teetered on the edge of considering him a second father. And he'd turned out to be a monster – a depraved force of evil who'd raped Savannah in their own home when she'd been just seventeen. After the brutal assault, he'd forced the traumatized young woman to remain silent in order to save Logan's stupid little bar, a run-down hole in the wall place he'd gambled his future on. And Logan hadn't known any of it. Worse yet, his friends, no, his family, had kept it all from him.

Logan shook off the bitterness as he entered the hotel lobby. He was here to earn a few bucks so he could figure out how to get his life back on track, and to do that he needed to play a role – sexy, confident, sex professional capable of fulfilling any fantasy. Truth was, he was dreading this job. He'd agreed to a request to be the third in a ménage for a wealthy married couple – something he'd never done before. His gut reaction had been to decline, but when he'd heard how much the couple was willing to pay, he'd reconsidered it, then ultimately accepted. It was three times more than he would normally make and the kicker was that there would be no actual sex – no penetration anyway. Apparently, these people just got a thrill out of the idea of him watching and doing some light petting. It was a play it by ear kind of thing, but the one clear message that had him more pleased than it probably should have – no need to stick his dick into a complete stranger. He supposed that was a pretty clear sign that he needed to get the hell out of this business and figure out his shit.

Logan went to the front desk and got the key that had been left for him, then made his way to the room. The hotel was beautiful - one of the most expensive in Seattle - and he'd only been here one other time that he could remember. He'd dressed the part, black slacks and a blue dress shirt, but he still felt like he stuck out. He was blue collar all the way and whenever he put these clothes on, he felt like a little kid playing dress up.

Once he was on the elevator, he swiped the card as he'd been instructed to do by the front desk instead of pressing a particular button. Nothing on the elevator panel lit up, but it began a steady climb. There were no stops in between, no awkward conversations with polite strangers and that somehow made him more nervous. His agency always made sure the clients were on the up and up, but as each floor on the digital display passed and the elevator continued its upward trajectory, Logan couldn't help but feel like he was on some covert operation. When the elevator came to a subtle halt and the doors slid open, he was surprised to find himself not looking at a hallway, but the entrance to the room itself which sported a swanky white and gold front parlor with marble floors and a couple of matching side tables with huge, extravagant flower arrangements on them. A single door on the opposite end of the small entryway was slightly ajar so he stepped off the elevator, gathered his courage and pushed it open.

It was still light out enough that sunlight filtered in through the heavy curtains that hid the view of what he guessed was Puget Sound. It was a large living room with expensive looking, matching leather sofas and a flat screen TV above the fireplace that someone had turned on. The room was quiet in its emptiness, but his eyes had already found his destination off to the left – the bedroom.

As he neared the open sliding doors, he saw a woman sitting on the foot of the bed, her slim form draped in a dark green dress that fell well past her knees. His gut clenched at how beautiful she was – a reaction he hadn't often felt toward his customers. Desire knotted through him as she smiled softly at him, her shoulder length blonde hair shimmering as she tilted her head in greeting. He stopped in the doorway and studied her for a moment, then felt an energy surge through him that almost knocked him to his knees.

But it hadn't come from her.

His skin tingled as he looked to his right and saw dark eyes watching him intently, some emotion glittering in them that he couldn't identify. The husband.

Partial shadows concealed some of the large man's features, but did nothing to hide the confidence he seemed to wear like a cloak. He was built like a football player – wide shoulders, trim hips, muscular thighs. At six feet, Logan was no slouch, but he guessed this guy was a couple of inches taller and significantly heavier, all of it muscle. He could see the outline of a hard jawline and the guy was either bald or had a buzz cut. His burning, intense gaze belied the relaxed way he was sitting in the chair – a king on his throne.

Logan forced his eyes back to the woman and told himself the sparks he'd felt as he took in the hard man's appearance were nothing more than anxiety. The woman had been watching as the two men studied each other and when he turned his attention back to her, she smiled gently at him. He held her gaze as he moved to the edge of the bed, forcing her to tilt her head back to look up at him. She really was exquisite – porcelain skin that most women would envy, bright blue eyes with thick lashes, plush lips that he suddenly and inexplicably wanted to taste. Also another first since he didn't kiss his clients on the mouth – work hazard. It was cliché, but he found it to be true. It seemed harder to keep the emotion out of a kiss then it did sex.

As he allowed his eyes to travel the length of her petite body, he held his hand out to her and gently pulled her to her feet when she accepted it. She seemed a little shaky as she stood and he swore he saw her wince as she steadied herself, but then the beatific smile was back in place and she sighed when he kissed her hand. He still felt the gaze burning into his back and the sensation of being watched made something deep inside of him flicker and then light up. His plan had been to focus on the woman and let the husband call the shots, but something dark went through him when he felt those eyes on him.

In the time the woman had stood, she'd glanced beyond his shoulder at her husband multiple times, not seeking approval necessarily, but seemingly to share what she was feeling with him. Whatever they were about to do, it was clear she wanted her husband's full participation. With that in mind, Logan tugged her forward a few steps and moved behind her so that they were both facing her husband. He saw the man shift his position somewhat, making Logan guess that he hadn't expected to be the focus of their little show.

"What's his name?" Logan asked the woman as his fingers trailed down her side to settle on her hip, the silky green fabric of her dress dragging against his skin.

"Dom," she said quietly as her body quivered beneath his touch. He let his mouth hover against the column of her neck as he asked his next question, his breath stroking her.

"What's yours?"

"Sylvie," she let out in a ragged whisper as he brushed his lips against her skin. She gasped at the contact and one of her hands covered his where it was still gripping her hip.

"Does he tell you how beautiful you are, Sylvie?" Logan asked as he let his other hand drift over her abdomen.

She leaned back against him, her lower body brushing his hardening cock as she said, "Every day."

Logan trailed his lips along her throat and down to her collar bone. She was soft and supple beneath him and he automatically felt the need to be more gentle than normal. As petite and slight as she was, she also seemed to be just a bit too thin, frail almost.

The embers of his own desire were starting to take hold and he had to force back a curse when he felt one of her hands caress his thigh. Even through the fabric of his pants, the contact burned. But he could also still feel that tightening in his gut – the one that had nothing to do with the woman in his arms and everything to do with the man that sat watching them quietly. If Logan hadn't heard his harsh breathing, he would have guessed him to be unaffected. But something was rolling off the man in waves – not jealousy, no. It was need – raw need.

Logan raised his eyes to watch Dom as he brushed the strap of Sylvie's dress aside. There was a harsh intake of breath from the corner when he did the same to the other side of the dress and it slipped off and fell into a silent pool around Sylvie's feet. Logan never took his eyes off Dom as he closed a hand over one of Sylvie's generous breasts. The woman beneath him moaned, but it was the man who held his attention now because Dom leaned forward at Logan's intimate, almost possessive caress.

Dim light brushed over Dom's harshly beautiful features. Strong, straight jaw with just a hint of stubble, broad forehead, nearly perfectly straight nose with nostrils that were now flared as he ate in the sight before him. He was bald, but with a shadow of growth that Logan suddenly wondered would feel like under his fingers.

What the hell?

Logan shook himself of the completely unexpected and unwelcome thought and forced himself to focus on the woman squirming in his embrace as he played with her nipple. He could see that her eyes were open and still on her husband and he felt a momentary pang of envy at the obvious connection that ran between these two people.

"Does he touch you like this Sylvie?" Logan asked as he brought his other hand up to stroke her other breast. A whimper escaped her lips as she nodded and then she was lifting her arms up behind her so she could wrap them around his neck. He knew her position gave her husband an excellent view of the sensuous torture he was inflicting on her breasts. Dragging one of his hands slowly down her abdomen, he stopped when he reached the panties she was wearing, the move holding all three of them there in that moment of anticipation. Dom still hadn't said a word, but he was anything but casual now. He was leaning forward, his body drawn tight, his emerald eyes dark with hunger as they focused on Logan's hand.

"Dom," Sylvie whispered and then Logan's eyes connected with Dom's and the other man tilted his head in an almost imperceptible nod – permission. Logan worked his hand under the panties and brushed over a small nest of curls before he found the bud that was waiting for him. As he circled around it, he felt Sylvie press back against him harder and when he looked down at her, he saw her eyes had finally drifted shut and she was biting her bottom lip. His first stroke on her clit had her crying out and each subsequent press had her undulating against him as she tried to increase the pressure. His eyes returned to Dom and he found the man standing now, although he was still by the chair. Logan couldn't help but admire the huge man, his white shirt open at the collar to offer a glimpse of muscle, his black slacks unable to hide his hardening cock. He really was a good-looking man, Logan thought as he began to mercilessly tease Sylvie with light and hard touches.

"Should I let her come, Dom?" he asked as he used his free hand to pinch Sylvie's nipple.

Still no words, but another nod from Dom, harsh and quick. He was working the buttons of his shirt now and when he finally stripped it off, Logan felt a wave of heat go through him at the combination of olive-toned, nearly hairless skin and rippling muscles. The guy was built like a tank.

"Please," Sylvie begged. Logan forced his attention back to Sylvie, breaking the eye contact with Dom. Her body was grinding against his and it was the first time he was actually worried he wouldn't be able to control himself. Somehow, in just a few short minutes, this encounter had changed to something heavier than he'd anticipated.

"Come baby," Logan whispered against her skin as he worked her clit. "Show Dom how good it feels."

She began crying as her body seized and then started spasming as her orgasm tore through her. Logan stroked her gently as aftershocks quaked through her and then Dom was there in front of her, his lips closing over hers, his hips brushing against Logan's hand as he brought Sylvie down gently. Her arms instantly went around her husband and Logan almost missed the warmth, but something about having Dom and Sylvie pressed against him as they made love to each other's mouths had him fighting back the urge to wrap his arms around them both.

Logan let his hands drift down Sylvie's sides and then froze when she turned in his arms to face him, leaving Dom to focus his attention on caressing her shoulders and back. She looked sated and happy and when she smiled softly at him, he couldn't help but do the same.

"Will you take this off?" she asked as she brushed her hand over his shirt. As Dom's eyes once again connected with his, Logan nodded. While he worked the buttons free, Dom held his gaze, his sharp eyes conveying no emotion. For some reason he couldn't figure out, his fingers were shaking as he undid the shirt.

He opened the shirt, but didn't remove it entirely. Sylvie seemed to notice his hesitation and gently placed her hand directly on his chest, her finger tracing the long scar down the middle. Logan's eyes drifted up to meet Dom's as Sylvie's hand brushed more of the shirt aside so she could also caress the actual bullet scar. Her touch and Dom's unyielding gaze were doing something to him – something that was scaring the hell out of him. At some point between walking through that door and this moment, this had stopped being a job for him and these two people had become his entire focus.

How had that happened?

How had he let it?

"We're so glad you're here, Logan," Sylvie whispered as she continued to caress his scars. It was the first time either one of them had said his name and he both loved and hated it because it was reinforcing the reality that his emotions were seeking out these two lovers – desiring them in more ways than just the physical. Something inside him started to loosen as the couple invited him further into what they felt for each other, even though neither one had moved. God, he needed this – them – for one night. It would feel so good not to be alone anymore.

Before he could stop himself or even think to ask if it was okay, Logan leaned down and kissed Sylvie, his lips worshipping hers as she opened to him. Her hand stayed briefly on his chest before she moved it underneath his shirt to his back. Logan explored every inch of Sylvie's welcoming mouth and then stroked his tongue over hers. At her moan of pleasure, heat flooded his senses, but he forced himself to pull back and then dared to look up at Dom. He expected anger or shock, but what he found had his cock stiffening further and his blood began to boil with lust. Dom was watching him with unadulterated need – *him*, not his wife. His stomach clenched at the realization that this man, this beautiful, powerful man wanted him.

And worse, Logan wanted him back.

The discovery had him stepping back. He wasn't interested in men – never had been. He was just caught up in the moment, he told himself as he tried to take another step back but couldn't. His body was no longer listening to his brain and he stood there motionless, because as much as he wanted what would happen next, he couldn't make himself take that last step.

"Dom," Sylvie said, her voice low, almost pleading. Dom's whole body was ripped with tension, but when his wife gently pulled free of his hold and extricated herself from between the two men, he never took his eyes off Logan. The three hung there in silence for several long, torturous seconds and then Dom was moving.

Logan felt the huge hand clasp the back of his head as Dom closed the distance between them and lowered his mouth. He had precious seconds to stop this – to utter that one word that would put an end to all of it, but when he opened his mouth, it wasn't to speak. Dom's tongue surged past his lips without hesitation and Logan felt only relief as Dom consumed him. There was nothing soft or gentle about the kiss, no tentative exploring or asking permission. It was hard and rough and needy.

And he felt it everywhere.

His whole body exploded with desire as Dom's tongue twined around his and Logan found himself angling his head to allow Dom deeper inside. The hand at the back of his neck tightened as if to prevent Logan from going anywhere, even though that was the last thing on his mind. And when Logan started kissing Dom back, it set something off in both of them and suddenly their bodies were pressed up against each other, skin on skin, hard muscle pressed against hard muscle, cocks seeking each other out.

It was only when Sylvie whimpered that Dom finally pulled free of the kiss. Both men turned to see her sitting on the bed, unashamedly stroking herself as she watched them, her eyes hooded with lust.

"Get her ready," Dom ordered as he stepped back and began working the button on his pants.

Logan was so turned on that he didn't hesitate even for a second before dropping down between Sylvie's legs and seeking out her clit with his mouth through the fabric of her panties. She cried out at the contact and then dropped back on the bed. He pulled the scrap of silk aside so he could reach her skin and then he stroked and sucked her as his fingers searched her soft folds. He knew Dom was watching them both and when he heard a zipper being pulled down, he nearly came in his pants. Leaning back long enough to swipe the panties off Sylvie, Logan spared Dom a glance and tried not to think too much about the rush of pleasure that went through him at the sight of the now naked man standing nearby, his big hand stroking his heavy length.

Logan turned his attention back to Sylvie and returned his mouth to the throbbing bud. As he slowly teased it, he pressed one finger inside her, then two. She arched her back at the intrusion and her body rippled around him, telling him how close she was. He pulled his fingers back out and waited until Sylvie looked up at him. When she did, he sucked his fingers into his mouth, holding her gaze a moment before turning to let Dom watch him lick the rest of her cream off his digits. A harsh breath went through Dom at the sight and then he was grabbing Sylvie by the legs, dragging her closer to the end of the bed and thrusting into her, all in one seamless motion.

Logan shrugged off his shirt and loosened his pants as he enjoyed the sight of Dom working his considerable length into Sylvie's welcoming body. Her ass nearly hung off the edge of the bed as Dom gripped her thighs and angled her so he could hit that perfect spot inside of her that had her begging for relief every time he plunged forward. Logan leaned over her to suck a nipple into his mouth and she cried out at the contact. He was standing so close to Dom that he could feel the man's heat coming off him as he worked his wife's body into a frenzy.

Logan let his hands caress Sylvie's skin as he played with her breasts and then his fingers were working her clit again as Dom pounded into her. Logan turned to watch his own hand and Dom's body work in tandem to bring Sylvie closer to the edge. He bit his lip hard as he realized how close he was to being able to touch Dom's cock as it slid in and out of his wife. When he looked up to meet Dom's eyes, he knew the man was thinking the same thing because he kept looking back down to where their bodies were just inches from being directly connected.

Sylvie began to scream as her orgasm claimed her. Logan reared back so that he was kneeling next to her hips and began stroking his painfully hard cock with nearly vicious strokes. It took him only a few moments to feel the pressure in his balls and the tingling in his spine and he knew he had seconds left before his release would take him. He was stunned when Dom pulled free of his wife's still pulsing body and began stroking his own cock to match Logan's movements. It was too much for Logan and he shouted in relief as he came, his seed spilling down onto the perfect skin of Sylvie's abdomen. An instant later Dom groaned and his release pooled with Logan's. Logan stroked himself a few more times as he watched the lines of white run together and the sight of it caused more fluid to leak from his already spent body. All that was left in the overwhelming quiet were harsh breaths and trembling bodies.

Logan recovered first and quickly pulled up his pants, ignoring the moisture that still clung to him. He stood up and went to the bathroom and easily found a washcloth. He cleaned himself off, then grabbed another and dampened it. His brain was screaming at him to get the hell out of there because this had become more fucked up then he ever could have imagined. He returned to the bedroom with the washcloth and stopped at the sight of Dom laying on top of Sylvie as they kissed and whispered things to one another. Neither seemed to even care that his and Dom's releases were now mixing between their bodies.

A chill went over him as he realized he wanted to join them, to be a part of the kissing and touching that came after – he'd never had that before, hadn't ever wanted it until this moment. He shook it off and hurried to the bed. He dropped the washcloth next to them as discretely as he could, then grabbed his shirt off the floor and left the room. He could have sworn he heard Sylvie call his name as he left, but he was too raw and emotional to stick around to see if they would invite him to join them or just give their thanks and wish him well.

As he neared the door, he came to a stumbling halt when he saw an envelope on the table near the door. It had his name on it and he instantly knew what it was. Finding a tip waiting for him shouldn't have been a surprise and it definitely shouldn't have had him feeling the bile rise in his throat or ice flooding his veins.

It should be the easiest thing to do to - grab it as he walked by. Something he'd done countless times. But just seeing that reminder that this had been a job like any other and that he had failed to remember that for even the briefest of moments had him actually taking a wide berth around the envelope, as if that could prevent the self-disgust that was building inside him.

He'd never exactly been proud of his profession, but this was the first time he ever felt the shame hit him like a physical blow. He was a whore, plain and simple. And not even a good one, because even as he walked farther away from the couple in the other room, he wished with every step that he could turn around and go back to them.

CHAPTER 1

One month later

Savannah Bradshaw watched her brother with worry as he worked on the worn finish of the old wood bar top. Sweat clung to him in the dusty, stilted air and he looked like he was ready to drop, but he pressed on even after acknowledging her presence with a quick nod. She'd been meeting him for dinner every week for the last two months, but it was only in the last few weeks that he'd started standing her up, so she'd taken to dropping in on him unannounced, sandwiches from his favorite deli in tow. Their relationship had been frayed for many years due to her own cowardice and fear, but she'd really hoped that they were making progress. And it seemed like they had shortly after he'd gotten out of the hospital after being shot. Now she wasn't so sure because he was moodier than ever and there was a darkness in his eyes she'd never seen before.

Since he had the sander going, there was no way he'd be able to hear a word she said so she just sat at one of the few remaining tables that had survived the fire and pulled out the food. Minutes passed and she found her irritation growing as he continued to ignore her. Getting up, she made her way around the bar, found the extension cord and pulled it hard. She was rewarded with blissful silence as the sander snarled to a halt.

"Damn it Savannah," Logan said as he released the sander and swiped a dirty arm across his forehead.

"I got your favorite," she said expectantly as she waited for him to abandon his work. He did so with a huff and went to sit at the table, his body dwarfing the rickety chair. He only stayed down for a minute though, long enough to grab his sandwich, and then he was up and moving, pacing. It was very unlike him and Savannah's apprehension grew. He looked physically unwell and she guessed he'd lost at least fifteen pounds.

"Are you sick?" she found herself asking and he stopped abruptly and turned around to look at her.

"What?"

"They found something at your last checkup, didn't they? A complication from the shooting," she said fearfully.

"No," Logan said as he went to sit back down.

She took the seat across from him, but had lost any appetite she had.

"No, everything's fine. I'm fine," he responded distractedly.

Savannah swallowed hard. "I used to say that too, remember?" She saw him tense. "And we both know I was anything but fine."

~

*L*ogan flinched at her words and instantly felt guilty at causing his sister to worry. They'd finally started to mend the rift that had grown between them and here he was tearing them apart again. But how was he supposed to explain the myriad of emotions that had been strangling him since that night in the hotel – the last night he'd sold himself? He'd hoped that if he worked his body into a state of exhaustion, his mind would be forced to stop playing the images of that night on an endless loop and the feelings that went along with them would somehow disappear as if they never were. But it hadn't happened and all he could remember was the taste of Dom on his lips, the feel of his tongue stroking his own, the ache as that hard male body had pressed against his. Even in sleep, his mind and body betrayed him and he was lucky to go even a couple of hours without the endless, burning need that seemed to claw through him now.

He wanted another man.

It made no sense to him at all. Never in any of his years with women had it felt wrong or unnatural. True, he hadn't really gotten off on it the way some men might, but that was because of the circumstances, not the women. At least that's what he'd always told himself. And he couldn't remember a time that he'd ever looked at a member of his own sex and felt the stirrings of desire. But the way his body had responded to Dom, yearned for him even now, it was beyond fucked up and not something he could even begin to figure out how to explain to his sister.

"Do you still hate me?" she suddenly whispered, her eyes downcast, a shimmer of tears brightening them.

Shame lanced through him and he stood and gathered her into his arms. "No," he whispered. He felt her hot tears sting his neck and more guilt washed through him. "I love you so much Savannah – more than anything. Nothing will ever change that, okay?" He felt her nod against his neck. "Do you remember how you told me you needed time to work through some things?"

She pulled back from him and nodded. He hadn't known it back then, but Savannah had been caught in a dark cloud of pain and fear which had caused her to pull away from him in the years after their parents had died.

"I need you to give that to me now – time," he said as he gripped her upper arms. He was glad she didn't flinch away from him like she would have just a few short months ago. It was a testament to the fact that whatever his best friend Shane had done to help her work through her pain was working. She was in love and she should feel only that – not worry or fear from him. Another reason to get his shit together, he thought grimly to himself.

"Okay," she acknowledged. "Whenever you're ready," she added as she dashed away the tears and sat back down. He sat down as well, then took a bite of his sandwich, even though his appetite was gone.

"How's Shane?" he asked, hoping the topic of the newfound love of her life would put that smile back on her face. It did.

"He's good," she said as she picked at her food. "A friend offered him a job at his security firm – he starts in a couple of weeks."

Logan smiled at that. For all Shane's parents' planning to have their youngest son's life turn out a certain way, Shane had gone and blown it all to hell in a matter of weeks. His friend had just started his final year of law school when he and Savannah had begun their relationship. Shane had been determined to stay the course and graduate the following spring and move to Chicago to join his father's firm, but apparently, Savannah had been a game changer and Logan knew his friend couldn't be any happier.

Shane had been in a pretty dark place for a long time and Logan had to admit he hadn't been thrilled to find that his sister was consorting with his friend and fellow escort. But he'd also been kept in the dark about everything by Shane, Savannah and his other friends, Gabe and Riley. The betrayal had stung – admittedly still did – but he understood why he'd been lied to by so many and for so long.

"And the other stuff?" Logan asked carefully.

"It's hard and he's scared," she admitted. "But he's strong."

Logan nodded. It had come as a surprise to find out Shane suffered from the same drug addiction that had ultimately led to his older brother's death. Michael had been only nineteen when he'd committed suicide by overdosing on heroin, leaving sixteen-year-old Shane to step into his shoes and take on the role of the golden boy son. Logan had gotten along with Michael when they'd met as freshmen in college, but he hadn't known him long – that was probably why he'd been able to see that Michael had been battling inner demons. But he hadn't known Michael's other secret – that he was gay – until long after his death. It was something that he was thinking a lot about now though.

"You guys find a place yet?" Logan asked.

She shook her head. "Now that he's got a job, we'll look for something that's between downtown and Queen Anne."

"We need to decide what to do with the house," he said as he polished off the remainder of his sandwich. Up until two months ago, he and Savannah had lived in their childhood home together, but with things changing, he knew it was time to let it go.

"You should keep it for yourself," she said.

He shook his head. "I can't. Not after everything that happened," he began before stuttering to a halt when he saw a flash of pain in her eyes. No, he couldn't live in the house she'd been raped in by the man he'd brought into their lives - the man who'd tried to kill him with a bullet to the chest. He absent-mindedly began rubbing the scar on his chest and then caught himself and dropped his hand back down to the table.

"Whatever you decide is okay with me, Logan," Savannah finally said. She looked like she was going to say something more, but her phone rang and a smile lit up her face when she saw the Caller ID.

Shane.

"Hi," she said softly, adoringly, as she got up and went to the other side of the bar for privacy. Logan chuckled to himself and then began cleaning up the food wrappers. He stopped and stood when a suddenly pale looking Savannah returned to the table.

"What is it?" he said, his gut clenching at the tears forming once again in her eyes.

"Um, a friend of ours - mine and Shane's - died this morning," she said on a half sob.

"Who?"

"Sylvie Barretti."

Logan stilled at the name. It couldn't be. Sylvie wasn't the most common name but...

"Shane and I met her and her husband Dom a couple of months ago," Savannah said, but he barely heard anything else after she said Dom's name because the roaring in his ears was growing louder. Nausea gripped him and his throat closed as it sunk in. The beautiful, vibrant young woman he'd been with less than a month ago was gone.

"What happened?" he managed to ask.

"She was sick for a while. Cancer, I think," Savannah said as she snatched a napkin from the table and dabbed at her eyes. "Shane's just a few minutes away – we're going to stop by Dom's restaurant to pay our respects," she muttered.

Logan couldn't speak. Sylvie was gone and the man who had clearly loved her was alone. How could life be that cruel? Anyone who saw them together would have known they were meant to be together forever. He'd gotten to feel that for the briefest of moments, even if it had been by proxy.

"The funeral's on Monday if you want to come."

Logan snapped his head out of his stupor. "I didn't know them," he nearly shouted, afraid she'd somehow found out about what had happened.

She looked at him strangely and he realized his tone had been harsher than he'd intended. He shook his head in silent apology.

"Didn't Shane tell you?" she said.

"Tell me what?"

"He saved you, Logan."

He froze at that and cold settled like a lead weight in his gut. "What are you talking about?"

She was silent for a moment and he wanted to shout at her to spit it out. "The fire," she began. "Dom was with Shane that day of the fire."

She was talking about the day he'd been shot by Sam who'd then left him for dead in his burning bar as he'd tried to abduct Savannah. She'd been fortunate enough to escape Sam who'd perished in the very fire he'd set. He and Savannah would have died too if Shane and his friend hadn't gotten them out.

"I didn't know his name," Logan muttered stupidly.

"Dom broke the window to get in. He carried you out." He heard Savannah choke up at the memory – a memory he didn't share because he couldn't bring anything from that day forth. "You weren't breathing so Dom did CPR till the paramedics arrived."

Jesus.

Logan felt his knees start to give out and he locked them so he wouldn't fall to the floor. What the hell was happening? His vision actually started to dim as he tried to collect the pieces of truth that slammed into him one by one. Dominic Barretti had saved his life, then hired him to help him fuck his wife. And then he'd blown everything Logan knew about himself apart with one touch of his lips.

Logan was barely aware of Savannah's voice as she talked about the funeral. "I've got to get back to work," he said quietly without looking at her. He gave her a brief hug, ignored her as she called his name and then headed towards the back of the bar. The jingle of the bell above the front door told him Savannah had either left to wait out front for Shane or Shane had arrived – Logan didn't care which one it was because he needed to escape.

Locking himself in the bathroom, he turned on the water with the intent of sticking his face under the faucet, but then his stomach got the better of him and he leaned over the toilet and threw up everything in it. He heaved over and over long after everything was gone, then collapsed on the floor as tears streamed down his face.

Sylvie Barretti was gone.

Harsh sobs wracked his whole body as an image of her kind eyes and gentle touch flashed through his brain and then he curled up into a ball on the dirty floor and let everything else go.

※

Logan enjoyed the burn as the alcohol flooded his system. It was the first time he'd felt warm since Savannah had stunned him with the news of Sylvie's death and the revelation that Dom had been playing a part in his life far longer than he'd thought. Logan slammed down another long drink of the whiskey and then sighed as more heat filtered through his numb arms and legs. He didn't drink often, but as the alcohol started to take away the pain, he began to wonder why he didn't partake more often.

Nothing could have prepared him for today – nothing. The funeral had been soul-wrenching, but it had been the sight of the widower that had done Logan in. He hadn't attended the memorial service at the church, but he had watched the gravesite burial from a distance. It had been cowardly, but he hadn't been able to find the strength to face Dom and try to find some inconsequential words that would somehow lessen the man's pain. But if he'd thought distance would protect him from having to feel too much, he'd been wrong again.

If he hadn't known better, he wouldn't have recognized Dom as the one who'd lost his wife. He'd been stiff and imposing throughout the entire ceremony, his eyes staring blankly ahead, his face impassive. Even a typical Seattle downpour in the middle of the ceremony had failed to elicit a reaction from the man and as others had opened the umbrellas they'd toted along, Dom had stood there, hands clasped in front of him, water streaming down his head and face. He'd been surrounded by people, but he'd been completely alone. Few people had even had the nerve to approach him after the service had ended.

Long after all the mourners had gone, Logan had watched from his perch at the top of the hill overlooking the endless grave markers. Dom had remained standing there, his eyes unseeing as the men had finally given up trying to wait Dom out and had lowered the casket into the ground. When they'd reached for the shovels to start covering the gaping hole, Logan had found himself moving, his intent to force Dom away. But the man had finally turned away on his own as the first shovelful of dirt had hit the gleaming coffin.

Logan had turned to go as well, but had stilled when he'd sensed that gaze on him, the one he'd come to feel in his dreams. Sure enough, when he'd turned, his eyes had caught on Dom's. There still been nothing there though – no acknowledgement or recognition. They'd been dozens of yards apart, but it might as well have been miles for all the response he'd gotten from Dom. And then he was gone and Logan had found himself making his way to the gravesite, the bouquet of fresh flowers clutched in his hands.

The headstone had been simple and elegant, much like the woman it represented. He'd placed the bouquet in front of it and then watched as the men finished their work. Afterwards, he'd sought the escape of his bar and the limitless alcohol it offered, but he'd felt himself easing off after his third swig.

His thoughts drifted to where they always did now and he wondered if someone was there to take care of Dom. He hadn't seen anyone who'd acted like family at the service, but Dom had been so detached that he'd treated everyone the same – as strangers. Savannah and Shane had been there and his sister had tried to offer comfort at one point when she'd reached out to Dom. He hadn't physically rebuffed her, but his silence had spoken volumes and his sister and Shane hadn't lingered.

Logan recapped the bottle and shelved it, then cleaned the glass he'd been using. He heard the bell above the door indicate someone's presence and he cursed himself for forgetting to lock it. The closed sign had been in the window for nearly two months now while he tried to clean the place up, but every once in a while, someone wandered in looking for a party.

He was about to tell the person to get lost, but stopped when he took in the man's appearance – old, balding with a little bit of a pooch, briefcase in hand. Definitely not the standard bar goer.

"Can I help you?" Logan asked.

"Logan Bradshaw?"

Logan nodded and watched in irritation as the guy looked around the bar, the walls still blackened with soot. Clearly the man had a dozen questions, but he seemed smart enough to keep his mouth shut about how shitty the place looked.

"My name is Walter Jessup," he said as he dropped his briefcase on the bar and began rifling through it. He stuck out a business card, then did some more rummaging.

Logan glanced at the card. An attorney – no surprise there.

Walter pulled out an envelope and then snapped his briefcase closed. "This is for you," he said as he handed Logan the envelope.

Logan's name was scrawled on the front and a chill went through him at the obviously feminine handwriting. "What is it?" he asked, handling the envelope like it was a bomb.

"My instructions were just to deliver the envelope, Mr. Bradshaw. I am unaware of its contents," the lawyer declared as he turned to leave.

Logan ignored him and carefully opened the envelope, his fingers shaky. It was a couple of pieces of thick stationary and the second he unfolded it, he saw the initials in gold foil along the top.

SAB.

"Oh, God," Logan muttered as he closed the letter back up and tried to catch his breath. This couldn't be happening.

He should throw it away – shred it, burn it. He knew instinctively that if he read it, it would cost him more than he wanted to give. He sucked in a deep breath and then opened the letter and began reading.

Dear Logan,

I suspect this letter is taking you a bit by surprise. You probably thought you wouldn't have to hear from us again after last night – our amazingly beautiful night. It was more than I could have asked for. But it also told me what I needed to know.

Dom's asleep right now. It's the first time he's slept in a really long time and I'm guessing it will be the last for a while. What happened between the three of us last night has given me something I haven't had in a long time – hope.

So, I have a favor to ask and since you're reading this, it means that if you say no, you're saying no to a dead woman. And if I have learned anything over these past months, it's hard to say no to a dying person, much less a dead one.

My favor is that you just listen.

I told my husband a little white lie when I asked him to indulge my fantasy of bringing another man into our bed for one night. I didn't ask him to do it for me, I asked him for him. I've known for a very long time that Dom gave up a part of himself to be with me and I know he has no doubts about his choice – he's loved me in a way that a person can only dream of being loved. But I needed to be sure about something and that's where you came in.

Your sister may have told you by now that our finding you was no accident. We met Savannah and Shane a couple of months ago. I'll let her give you the details, but we were quite enamored with them – they reminded us of ourselves when we were younger...so much in love, but struggling to find each other. So, when Shane asked Dom for help in finding the man who hurt your sister, he didn't hesitate. It's in his nature to protect the ones he cares about, after all. But digging into Savannah's past meant digging into yours as well.

And that's when I saw things change in Dom, and after he told me what you did on the side to earn money, a plan began to take shape. I am ashamed to admit that I used his obsession with you without giving much thought to how it would affect you and it is something I will have to live (and die) with forever. But when I saw the two of you together last night, it was more than I could have hoped for. You felt it, didn't you? That thing that happens inside when Dom is around. Like he becomes part of you and you can start breathing again.

I don't know anything about your situation Logan, and I don't presume to either. I hadn't planned to reach out to you after last night, but as I said, you've given me hope. Hope that Dom can have a life after I'm gone. Hope that he can let me go even as his love stays with me.

He will hurt, Logan – a man who loves with the passion that he does will hurt in equal measure. I don't want him to be alone. At least not in the beginning. But he will push everyone away and they'll go.

So that's where my second favor comes in. And remember, dead woman asking.

Make sure he's okay, Logan. Don't let him disappear into himself. Even if what I saw last night wasn't what I think it was, I need him to have someone and I think he'll let you in.

Please try, Logan. Please. This is the only way I can fight for him now, but I can't do it by myself. Even if it's just friendship that you can offer – just don't let him be alone.

When you see him, please tell him something for me. Tell him to keep his promise. Thank you, Logan. Thank you.

Sylvie

P.S. – Dom will be at our house in the San Juans. I've enclosed the address and the codes that will get you past the security system. And don't worry about the dog – he's a big old softie...but bring a pack of hot dogs anyway; they're his favorite.

CHAPTER 2

The softie turned out to be a giant Rottweiler and Logan watched apprehensively as it stared at him through the thin glass of the car door window that separated them. The code Sylvie had given him had gotten him through the front gate, so it was reasonable to think that what she'd said about the dog would be true, but seeing the huge teeth that the animal had flashed when it'd opened its jaws to bark at him had him reconsidering. It was yet another sign that he shouldn't be here – that he should have folded that letter back up, stuffed it into the crisp white envelope it had come in and buried it as far down in the garbage can as it could go.

But he'd done none of those things. Instead, he'd read it again, then a third time. By the time he'd reached the end of the last reading, he'd actually heard her broken voice begging him to check on Dom. So he'd gotten in his car, stopped at the store for the damned hot dogs and then driven the nearly two hours to the ferry terminal in Anacortes where he'd just made it onto the ferry that would take him to the islands. He'd had dozens of opportunities to turn around and had done so twice, but something had kept digging at his insides and he'd ended up heading north until he'd finally rolled his car onto the huge boat packed full of vehicles and tourists. And as he'd watched the ferry dock in the small town of Friday Harbor get closer and closer, his anxiety had grown. It was for Sylvie, he'd kept telling himself, but he knew that was a lie. It was for himself…it was for Dom.

Now he literally sat at the threshold of what could be his own personal hell and there was an actual fucking beast guarding the gates. He glanced at the house and then back at the dog. No one had appeared at his arrival a few minutes ago and he figured no one would, so he either needed to bite the bullet and do this or turn tail and run. He wanted to do the latter, but knew it had less to do with the dog and everything to do with avoiding the man who stirred up so many unwanted and unwelcome feelings.

Logan rolled the window down slightly and tore a hot dog free from the package. He dropped it outside, then watched the dog gobble it up, then sit politely on its haunches as if asking for more. Swallowing hard, he reminded himself not to show fear (easier said than done) and reached for the door handle. As he opened it, the dog watched him silently, no growling, no raised hackles, but no wagging tail either.

"Nice dog," he mumbled as he forced himself out of the car, another hot dog at the ready. He tossed it to the animal who was now just a couple feet away, but to his horror, the Rottweiler ignored it, then stood and moved closer to him, its dark eyes watching him. Shit, was he supposed to look away? Wasn't this some kind of play for dominance? Why hadn't he watched more Animal Planet instead of ESPN?

He remained frozen in place as the dog sniffed him and then felt a surge of panic at the thought the dog might take a piss on him to mark him as his territory. He almost laughed.

Almost.

Several long seconds passed before the dog finally nudged the package of hot dogs in his hand and Logan handed him one. Two bites and it was gone. He felt his body relax as the animal leaned into him, nuzzled the hand holding the hot dogs, then waited expectantly. Another hot dog and then he was actually stroking the huge dog's head. Point to Sylvie – the dog *was* a softie.

Logan turned to look at the estate. He couldn't just call it a house because it was so much more than that. The iron gate that no one had answered and he'd been forced to use the code to get past, was almost a mile down the driveway. The house itself sat on at least a dozen acres on the northernmost point of the island and there were no immediate visible neighbors that he could see. Tall pine trees covered most of the property as if protecting the large, contemporary structure from prying eyes. There was what Logan assumed was a guest house off to one side and a monstrous garage on the other that he could only guess could hold several cars at once. The dark waters beyond the house were framed by an endless line of snow covered mountains.

At his inattention, the dog pulled the package of hot dogs from his hand and finished them off, then sniffed around Logan for more. It was only the falling of raindrops that reminded him that a storm was brewing in the turbulent clouds above his head. Logan closed his car door, then hurried to the front door. Within moments of stepping under the archway, the skies opened and rain fell in torrents around him. He knocked, then tried the doorbell, but several minutes passed with no response. He searched out the piece of paper he'd written the codes on and punched the numbers for the house into the keypad by the door. A distinctive click followed and he was pushing the door open. The dog immediately trotted inside and Logan followed, his eyes scanning for any sign of life.

It was an open floor plan on the main part of the house and floor to ceiling glass windows lined the back of the structure. He made a quick tour of the lower level which included dark wood floors with contrasting wood paneled walls. The living room sported plush white furniture along with flashes of colorful accents and artwork – evidence of a woman's touch. A stone fireplace set against the far wall reached all the way to the ceiling. The kitchen was a chef's wet dream and sported double ovens and commercial grade, stainless steel appliances. Any doubts he'd had about Dom and Sylvie's level of wealth were gone in an instant – they were in a stratosphere where few were lucky enough to go.

"Dom," he called quietly as he cleared each room. There were no bedrooms on the first floor, so he began the climb to the second level. Curiously, the dog had stayed with him rather than searching out his owner. He'd passed the dog's food bowl in the kitchen and had noticed that someone had set a huge, full bag of dog food down next to the bowl and just ripped it open rather than pouring a set amount of food into the dish. It didn't bode well that it was apparently too much effort to feed the animal on a regular schedule.

Logan reached the top of the stairs and couldn't help but notice how many pictures there were of Dom and Sylvie and what he assumed were other family members. Other men with Dom when he was younger – brothers maybe – an older couple with four small boys, Sylvie as a teenager, shots of Dom and Sylvie on their wedding day…the photos were endless and seemed to tell a story as he made his way down the hallway and peeked into each room as he passed.

When he reached the last door at the end of the hall, he knocked softly, but heard nothing.

"Dom, it's Logan," he said as he turned the knob. The rain on the roof was nearly deafening now and he heard thunder rumble as he pushed the door open. It didn't get more ominous than that, he thought to himself as he entered the bedroom. It was bigger than the first floor of his own small house and he took in the king-sized bed, seating area across from a massive flat screen TV, dual walk in closets and a door to his left that he assumed was the master bathroom. Glass crunched under his feet and he stopped and then saw the reason. More framed pictures, dozens of them, lay strewn across the floor where they'd been smashed against the wall, glass sprinkled over the hardwood floor. Most of the pictures were of Dom and Sylvie, happy, smiling, in love. Pain lurched through Logan at the sight of Sylvie's bright smile and Dom's devoted expression as he gazed at his wife. The instinct to run hit him again.

The dog trotted past him and Logan began to call it back, afraid the glass would damage the animal's paws, but he stopped when he saw where the dog was headed. The side of the room that faced the water appeared to be several panes of glass that were meant to slide open and fold in on themselves so that the entire wall of glass could be opened. There was a balcony beyond the windows and standing in front of the railing was Dom.

He was still wearing the same clothes he'd been wearing at the funeral earlier in the day, but now they clung to him as the heavy rain drenched him. His back was to Logan so he couldn't see Dom's expression, but he didn't need to either. Pain radiated off him in waves and his entire body was stiff and unmoving. Logan stepped carefully over the broken glass and then went out onto the balcony, his senses on high alert as he noted the blood that dripped from Dom's right hand which was clenched in a fist at his side. The dog went onto the balcony ahead of him, but stopped short of actually touching Dom. He whined and dropped down near Dom's feet, but the man took no notice.

"Dom," Logan said quietly as he gave the man a wide berth and approached slowly from the side. Blood mixed with rain as it pooled next to Dom's foot. He couldn't see the injury itself, but judging by the amount of blood, it wasn't life threatening. "Dom," he said again, a little bit louder. He was standing next to him now and wasn't prepared for what he saw – absolutely nothing. It was like the man was already gone and someone just needed to place his body in the ground next to his beloved wife. Water ran down his skin in rivers and the fabric of his shirt was so drenched that Logan could clearly see the outline of his body. Anxiety went through him as he realized how much worse this situation truly was.

Tentatively touching Dom's clenched, bloody hand, Logan called his name again and was pleased to finally see a reaction. But when Dom just looked at him blankly, unrecognizing, Logan shuddered at the emptiness he saw. A month ago, this man had exuded confidence, desire, passion – now there was just a shell, a mass of bone and muscle and nothing else. His skin was ice cold, his expression hollow.

"Jesus," Logan muttered and his concern turned to all out fear. He ignored the blood and grabbed Dom's hand and tugged. He was shocked when Dom rocked forward at the motion. Quickly recovering, Logan pulled Dom away from the edge of the balcony and into the bedroom. He was glad Dom still had his shoes on because the glass was everywhere and there would have been no way he could have maneuvered the man around it if he'd been barefoot. He flipped on the light as he got them into the bathroom and then reached into the massive shower and got the water going. Warmth – he needed to get Dom warm and then he'd be okay. He'd snap out of this fog he was in.

Logan ignored his own soaked clothes and began working the buttons of Dom's shirt. It was like trying to undress a statue. When he reached Dom's hand to pull the shirt off, he carefully pried open the clenched fist, then stopped when he saw the pieces of glass embedded in his palm. He was torn between tending to the injury and getting Dom warm. Shit, he was so far out of his league here, he thought, as he plucked the bigger pieces of glass from the shredded skin and tossed them into a nearby wastebasket. He finished working the shirt off, then quickly stripped Dom the rest of the way down. As he pushed him into the shower, he hoped the warm water would elicit some type of response, but Dom continued to stand there, blind to everything around him.

Logan hesitated, then began stripping his own clothes off. Hurrying so he wouldn't think too much about what he was doing, Logan stepped into the shower with Dom and forced him to stand under the spray. He didn't need to worry about any awkward sexual tension because the man didn't notice him at all. And Logan was feeling nothing but anxiety at the continued lack of response. Ten minutes passed, then another ten before Logan finally felt some of the cold start to recede and Dom's skin began to flush with the heat. As they stood there, Logan tried to offer comfort by rubbing Dom's back, but if the man felt his touch, he didn't show it. When he was satisfied that Dom's body temperature was starting to return to normal, Logan stepped out of the shower, leaving Dom under the spray. He went in search of dry clothes for both of them. He snagged some pajama bottoms for Dom and some sweats for himself, then hurried back to the bathroom where Dom was still standing just as he'd left him.

Another gentle pull had Dom stepping onto the bathmat so Logan could quickly run a towel over him before working the pajama bottoms on. "Dom, can you hear me?" he asked softly as he worked.

Nothing.

He checked Dom's palm and then rummaged around the bathroom cabinets until he found some tweezers. Dom stood there mutely as he picked out the remaining pieces of glass he could see. As he dug around the wound, he finally saw a response from Dom when he flinched in pain and Logan nearly sighed in relief. It was something at least.

He cleaned the injury as best he could, then wrapped it with some bandages he found in a drawer. He led Dom out of the bathroom and said a prayer of thanks when he saw that there was no glass between them and the bed. He backed Dom up until his legs hit the bed, then forced him to sit.

"Dom," he said again as he touched the man's shoulder. Sighing in frustration at the continued silence, he turned to go back to the bathroom to collect their clothes.

"She's gone."

It was barely a whisper, but Logan heard it and turned back around. Dom was still staring ahead, but instead of emptiness, his dark eyes were filled with agony and realization. Logan sucked in a harsh breath at the sight of the tears welling up.

"I'm sorry, Dom," Logan said as he dropped to his knees in front of him.

"She's gone," Dom said again, his voice hoarse from lack of use.

"What can I do?" Logan whispered, his own throat closing with emotion. "Tell me what I can do, Dom." Dom's eyes finally connected with his and it was like a physical blow.

"Make it stop hurting." Tears fell down Dom's checks. "Please Logan, make it stop hurting," he begged.

Logan shook his head and pressed his forehead to Dom's. "I don't know how." And then he felt Dom's lips seeking out his own. It was brief, barely even a kiss and then Dom was pulling back. Logan knew he should let Dom go. He should put the man under the warm covers and then find someone who knew how the fuck to deal with this because he had no idea what the hell he was doing. But instead of reaching for the phone, he reached for Dom and settled his mouth over the tear stained lips. Dom let out a sigh and then opened to him.

The kiss was the opposite of the first one they'd shared in the hotel, but the desire was the same – instantaneous. And Logan couldn't blame it on the circumstances because he was the one consuming Dom this time. Every gentle thrust of his tongue inside the warm mouth beneath his had his body screaming for more. Luckily, he held on to a shred of sanity and remembered that Dom was at his most vulnerable right now. So he kept the kiss soft, comforting, and used his thumbs to brush at the damp trails of tears that ran down his cheeks.

When Logan started to draw back, Dom's hand closed around the back of his neck and held him there. The larger man's tongue desperately dueled with his and then suddenly they were both on their feet, hands searching, skin burning skin wherever it touched. Things quickly spiraled out of control for Logan when he felt Dom's hand push beneath the waistband of his pants and close around his stiff length. Everything else ceased to exist when Dom stroked him and then fingered the slit on his crown.

"Jesus, shit," Logan cried out as he thrust against Dom's hand. Before he could finish the thought, Dom's tongue was back in his mouth, teeth clashing against his in desperation. Dom's hand released him, but only long enough to push his sweatpants down. Before he could even protest, Dom was stroking him again and when he looked down to watch the rough hand squeeze him, his brain finally registered that somewhere along the way, Dom had rid himself of his own pants.

"Dom," Logan said as he put his hands against the man's broad chest to stop this craziness.

"Please," Dom said as he brought his eyes up to meet Logan's. They both stilled, their harsh breathing breaking the silence between them. He watched Dom reach into the nearby nightstand and shuddered when the man pulled out a bottle of baby oil. Everything was happening too fast, but Logan was helpless to stop it. He wanted this man – it made absolutely no sense, but he wanted him more than he'd ever wanted anyone in his entire life. But Dom was hurting and he needed to be the strong one.

"Dom," he tried again.

"Just for a little while Logan – please take the pain away for a little while," Dom muttered as he snapped the cap on the bottle open.

Dom didn't wait for an answer. He released Logan and turned away and then bent down over the bed, his ass on full display. Lust tore through Logan at the sight of Dom pouring the oil on his fingers and then working those fingers between his cheeks. His cock ached painfully at the sight and he found himself moving closer, his hands parting the globes of Dom's ass so he could watch the man work the oil inside his quivering hole. Any thought of stopping this fled as he imagined thrusting into that tiny opening.

"Now," Dom ordered as he reached behind him and sought out Logan's cock, smearing some of the oil onto his sensitive flesh in the process. Logan realized there was something off in the man's voice and he tried to pull back, but then Dom was impaling himself on Logan's cock and Logan shouted as he was enclosed in the hottest, tightest grip he'd ever experienced.

"Fuck," Logan cried out as he thrust hard and his crown disappeared into Dom's hot body. He felt the powerful man beneath him grunt as he pulled back and pressed forward several more times. Even with the oil, Dom's body resisted him, so Logan grabbed Dom's hips and pushed hard. Dom's groan was muffled by the bedding, but Logan didn't miss how wrong it had sounded. He ground to a halt as he realized that Dom's shouts and grunts were from pain, not pleasure. Horror slammed through him at what he'd done, how thoughtless he'd been.

"Don't stop!" Dom yelled as he tried to push himself back onto Logan's length. But Logan's eyes were open now and he realized what the man was doing. He gripped Dom's hips hard, not allowing him to force any more of Logan's body into his.

"No," Dom cried out as he collapsed onto the bed, his fists clenching the comforter. Sobs wracked him as he realized that he wasn't going to be able to escape the pain inside by using Logan's body to inflict pain on the outside.

Logan knew he should pull out because this was beyond fucked up. His own body was still tight with need, but it didn't compare to what he felt inside as Dom's mournful moans fell from his lips.

"Shhh," Logan whispered as he leaned over Dom's back, careful not to press any farther inside of him. His only goal now was to comfort, so he kissed the back of Dom's neck, then ran his tongue all along the soft skin of his collarbone. He removed one hand from Dom's hip and stroked it up Dom's spine, his fingers gently pushing into each indentation. Dom shuddered beneath him and his moaning stopped. Placing his arm under Dom's body, he stroked the man's tight abdomen and then brushed his fingertips over Dom's flaccid cock. He was pleased when it instantly responded to him, but he ignored it and stroked up Dom's chest. The larger man lifted himself up enough to give Logan the space he needed to stroke and pinch Dom's nipples. He felt the muscles around his cock tighten and Logan smothered his own groan of pleasure against Dom's shoulder.

Logan kissed his way along the muscles of Dom's back as his hand returned to his stiffening cock. When he squeezed, Dom let out a cry, this time one Logan recognized as pleasure. He felt another ripple shoot through Dom's cock as he reflexively tried to push backwards onto Logan's dick. The next time Dom thrust his hips back, Logan let him. It was agony not to pound into him the way he wanted to. But he did start meeting Dom's backward motion with small bumps of his own hips and a hiss of pleasure escaped his lips as he slipped farther past the ring of muscle trying to keep him out. He continued to work Dom's cock to match the rhythm Dom was setting and the pace quickly grew until Logan was fully seated. Pre-come leaked out of the head of Dom's dick and Logan used it to increase his stroking. At the same time, he pulled out of Dom almost all the way and then slid back in.

"Yes," Dom shouted as Logan hit his prostate. So Logan did it again, over and over in long, slow, torturous thrusts. His own body was screaming for release, so he leaned harder against Dom, forcing the man's body back down on the bed so his chest was flat against the mattress. Logan let his weight press Dom down as he began pounding into him while his hand increased the pressure on Dom's cock.

Dom was crying out again, but this time he was begging for relief as Logan sawed in and out of him. Sweat dripped off both their bodies and Logan grasped Dom's hip hard enough to leave a bruise as he fucked him over and over. Logan felt his own balls draw up tight against his body and moaned as his release suddenly ripped through him. Dom shouted beneath him and he felt the evidence of Dom's orgasm coat his hand. Pleasure went through every nerve ending in his body like a flash fire as he emptied himself inside of Dom and then he gave up the fight and dropped all his weight onto the bigger man. Dom's body went lax and collapsed into the soft bedding.

Several long minutes passed as the men fought to catch their breath. Logan finally lifted himself off Dom, then gently pulled free of his body. His limbs felt like jelly and he wanted nothing more than to sink down on the bed next to Dom, but stopped when he looked at the slick moisture coating his cock.

He hadn't worn a condom.

He'd fucked a man for the first time in his life on the same day he'd buried his wife and he'd forgotten the fucking condom! How the hell had this happened?

He stepped back, trying to form the words to apologize to Dom, but then saw that the man had pulled himself farther up onto the bed and had fallen asleep. Logan stood there for several long moments as the realization of everything he'd done started to sink in and he bit back the nausea that swept through him. He'd done an unforgivable thing. Shame crawled through him and he turned to go, but not before he drew up the end of the comforter so at least Dom would have some kind of warmth when he finally woke to the nightmare he'd been thrust into.

CHAPTER 3

Dominic Barretti didn't want to open his eyes. He was still in that blissful state of light sleep where he knew he was on the verge of waking up, but not quite there. Already he could feel the disbelief that she really was gone knifing through his brain. Within seconds he was back to the gut wrenching pain that had him folding his body in on itself in an effort to ease the agony. Tears stung his eyes as he rolled over so he could stare out at the water and mountains beyond the glass door that someone had thought to close last night. Not someone…Logan. He would have thought it was all some twisted nightmare, but the stinging in his ass told him differently. Less than twelve hours after his wife's lifeless body had been placed in the ground, he'd let someone fuck him into the same mattress he'd spent so many nights making love to his wife on. And he'd come harder than he ever had in his entire life.

Dom bit back the bile that rose in his throat and then forced himself to sit up. He swung his legs over the bed and sat there for a moment as he waited for the pain in his head to ease. He'd like to say he'd been drunk last night, but ironically, he hadn't touched a drop of alcohol since his wife had slipped away. It would have been too easy to lose himself in a drunken stupor and Sylvie had deserved better than that. There had been calls to make, arrangements to see to. And when he'd arrived at their vacation home last night, he'd been too numb to even stop at the liquor cabinet. He'd barely remembered to leave out some food for the dog, and that was only because he'd seen a reminder from Sylvie to feed the animal – the note she'd left had been from weeks earlier when they'd come to the house on one of their final trips. It was like she'd known that if she didn't leave it stuck to the fridge, the Rottweiler would have been on the losing end of Dom's prison of grief.

Dom tried to swallow, but his tongue felt too big for his dry mouth. He stood on shaky legs and stumbled into the bathroom. He held his head under the cold water coming from the faucet in the sink, then sucked down several mouthfuls of the liquid. When he finally raised his head, he was startled to see the stranger looking back at him. Red rimmed eyes, pale skin, sunken eyes with black smudges under them. His hair was longer then he'd let it get in a while and the stubble on his face looked unkempt. Sylvie wouldn't be happy to see him in this condition. He dropped his head and then made his way to the toilet so he could take care of business. He finally noticed the bandage on his hand, then remembered that Logan had taken care of that too.

The man had shown up like some fairy godmother, except he'd never heard of any fairy tale where the fairy godmother had fucked her ward into unconsciousness. And God help him, he wanted more.

"Fuck," Dom said as he took a piss, then left the bedroom to hunt down some clothes. He stopped in the doorway of the bathroom and studied the bedroom. All the pictures he'd destroyed last night in his grief were gone, the glass cleaned up. Anger burned through him that Logan had seen to that too. The only one that he needed or wanted to take care of him was gone.

Dom dressed in a pair of jeans and a white T-shirt, then headed downstairs. Everything about the house was wrong now. It was cold when it should be warm, silent when there should be laughter. He'd wanted to escape the endless line of people that had tried to offer him comfort at their apartment in the city, so he'd come running here. It was ridiculous to think that somehow things would hurt a little bit less in this house.

Dom went downstairs, his bare feet silent on the glossy floors. He slowed when an unexpected smell hit him, then came to a stop at the entryway to the kitchen. Logan sat at the island in the kitchen, a cup of coffee clenched in his tight hands. Rage soared through him at the sight of this man being in the place his wife should be. But before the words telling Logan to get the hell out could leave his lips, he saw a flash of moisture on the younger man's face. His head was hung low, but Dom could see tears trailing down his cheeks and falling onto the countertop beneath him.

Logan shifted when the dog noticed Dom and came over to greet him. Dom automatically put his hand on the animal's head, but his eyes never left Logan and when those pale blue eyes caught sight of him, he saw a myriad of emotions run through them. Fear, shame, longing. The man didn't say anything, just wiped his face with his arm. He was wearing the clothes he'd arrived in, not the sweats Dom remembered pushing down so he could get at Logan's beautiful cock. He shook his head at the wayward thought, then moved into the kitchen. He pulled a mug down from the cabinet, then stopped when he saw the full coffee pot. It was too much – another intrusion he couldn't deal with.

With his back to Logan, he fisted his hands on the granite countertop and said, "Get the fuck out of my house."

~

The words should have had Logan moving, not because of the actual words themselves, but the tone with which they were spoken. Hate, rage. But Logan was too far gone in his own confusion to care right now. He'd been sitting here for hours since he'd left Dom sleeping soundly in his bed. There'd been several guest rooms he could have crashed in until it was time to leave to catch the first morning ferry, but sleep had been the last thing on his mind. He'd tried to keep busy by straightening up the mess Dom had made in his room so the man wouldn't cut his feet if he got up in the middle of the night, but that had taken very little time and he'd ended up spending the last several hours just sitting in the quiet kitchen, the occasional shifting of the dog at his feet the only noise to break up the pervasive silence. At least in his own house he had the incessant ticking of his mother's prized Grandfather clock to focus on, but here there was nothing. Even the rain had stopped at some point.

"Why me?" he finally asked, not turning to look at the angry man standing nearby. His voice sounded shaky even to his own ears.

"I told you I want you to leave-" Dom began.

"Why me?!" Logan screamed, his eyes still staring straight ahead through the glass windows.

He sensed Dom turning to face him and he supposed the man was probably caught off guard by his outburst.

"Why did you pick me for that night in the hotel?"

Dom was silent for a long time before finally saying, "What difference does it make?"

What difference did it make? Logan nearly laughed. The difference was that that one night had changed his whole fucking life!

"The difference is," Logan bit out, "that I stuck my dick in your ass last night."

Dom didn't respond. Instead, he strode over to a side table and snatched his wallet off it and pulled out a stack of money. He tossed it on the countertop in front of Logan. "That should cover last night." He grabbed some more and dropped that on the pile too. "And that's to cover what you forgot when you left that night."

Pain and rage mixed within Logan at the sight of the money. The stark reminder of what he was lanced through him and the fact that Dom was so easily able to remind him of that fact made something inside of him die.

"Go to hell Dom," Logan said quietly as he stood, ignoring the money. He grabbed his jacket from the stool. "Sylvie wants you to keep your promise," he added as he turned and headed towards the front door.

LOGAN'S NEED

*D*om dropped the mug at Logan's words and it shattered as it hit the floor. He'd been about to fill it with coffee after tossing Logan the cash and he was lucky he hadn't been holding the coffee pot instead when Logan had spouted his last statement.

Logan was in the process of opening the front door when Dom reached him and slammed his hand on the wood to keep it from opening. Logan was only a couple inches shorter than him, but Dom's bulk played in his favor as he grabbed Logan and spun him around.

"What the fuck did you just say to me?"

Logan stood mutely for a moment, then said, "She wants you to keep your promise."

Tension went through Dom at the words and he wanted to step back, but he suspected if he did, Logan would leave and he couldn't allow that.

"You talked to her?" he finally managed to whisper, the pain exploding inside of him in little starbursts.

Logan shook his head. "She sent me a letter. It arrived yesterday. After..." he said, his words drifting off. "After the funeral," he finally managed to say.

"Jesus," Dom said as he hung his head.

"What promise?" Logan asked quietly.

Overwhelmed, Dom did take several steps back this time. "She made me promise..." he began, but then had to choke back the emotion that suddenly clogged his throat. "She made me promise that after she was gone, I would live. Not just exist, live." Dom felt like his body was going to give out, so he leaned back against the banister of the stairs. "What else did she say?" he asked, hating the begging tone that was so clear in his voice.

"She didn't want you to be alone. She said you would push everyone around you away."

Dom laughed. She *had* always known him best. Now it made sense how Logan had gotten past the security system, how he'd even found the house in the first place. His Sylvie had always given off the impression that she was docile and passive, but she'd been anything but. She'd been fierce when it came to protecting the ones she'd loved most.

"Why me?" Logan asked again, his desperation rolling off him in waves now. He seemed so young like this. Confused, helpless. Dom fought the need to comfort him.

"Why did we pick you for that night?" Dom clarified. Logan nodded. "When we knew she wouldn't be getting better this time, I tried to give her everything she wanted."

"And she told you she wanted to have another man join you," Logan ventured.

"She said it was just to spice things up – she didn't actually want to have sex with someone else."

"She wanted you to watch."

Dom nodded. "I never would have shared her with anyone. I loved her," he said lamely. "I never understood why she wanted that, but how could I tell her no?"

"Why me?" Logan asked again.

"I met your sister and your friend, Shane, a while ago. Shane knew I had some experience in finding information on people who didn't necessarily want to be found. He asked me to try and figure out who had hurt your sister."

"So, you dug into my past and found out what I did for extra money," Logan said.

Dom nodded, shame tingling under his skin. "When Sylvie made her request, I chose you."

"Why?"

Dom didn't have an answer, or at least not one he wanted to share with Logan, so he remained silent. He almost flinched at the way Logan was studying him, like he was trying to pick the answers from his brain.

"She said you were obsessed with me."

Dom couldn't stifle the gasp that escaped him. He shook his head violently. Sylvie couldn't have known that. But Logan didn't take back his statement and Dom knew it was true. Somehow his wife had seen the way he'd lingered on Logan's pictures – the ones he'd found during his research as well as the ones he'd taken during his surveillance. Jesus, he'd betrayed her even before her death and she'd known.

"She said she set up that night for you, not for herself."

"Oh, God," Dom said as he bent over to try and suck in some air. His hand gripped the banister hard. It had never made sense to him that she'd wanted to experiment with another man, but if she'd known about that part of his life, it made complete sense that she would have wanted to give that back to him after she was gone.

"She knew you loved her," Logan said softly. "She had no doubts about you choosing her."

It was too much, Dom thought, as he dropped down to sit on the bottom step. This man was destroying him piece by piece, first by becoming the target of all of Dom's lust, then by sweeping in here and showing him the truth about his relationship with Sylvie. It hurt to know that Sylvie had shared her suspicions with Logan, but not him.

"I knew I was attracted to both men and women at an early age, but I kept it hidden from everyone. I was with a couple of men in college, but when Sylvie and I met, I knew she was the only one for me. I didn't know she knew about that part of me." Dom ran his hand over his head. "She must have seen how I looked at your pictures – the ones I'd collected during my research. I guess I wasn't able to hide my attraction to you," he said quietly.

He heard Logan inhale sharply and saw the man tense up. "I'm not gay," Logan suddenly said, his voice shaky. It was then that Dom finally realized what Logan was struggling with.

"You've never been with a man," Dom said aloud. Logan flushed and then shook his head. "Jesus," Dom said as he understood the shit Logan must be going through. Part of him actually felt a flash of anger towards Sylvie for setting this up – he guessed she hadn't really thought about things from Logan's side when she'd arranged their night in the hotel.

"Logan," he began.

"I have to go," Logan muttered as he turned to fumble with the doorknob. He'd barely managed to get the door open again before Dom was able to close the distance between them. Putting his hand out, he pushed it shut before Logan could escape, then used his bigger body to pin Logan in place, not touching him, but not leaving room for him to maneuver away either.

"Logan, this was our fault. Mine and Sylvie's. You did nothing wrong – you just got caught up in something new and different. It doesn't mean you're gay or that you're even bi," he said gently. God, Dom wanted to reach out and touch the man, comfort him, but Logan was shaking hard now and Dom knew he needed to let him go. "Just let it go," Dom urged. "Whatever she asked you to do, just let it go. You don't owe us anything."

Logan dropped his forehead against the door. "I can't," he said.

"Why not?"

A long pulse of silence. "Because I can't fail her too." He felt Logan step back against him as he forced the door open and Dom moved back to let him. Logan was halfway out when he stopped suddenly, his next words so quiet that Dom barely heard them. "Did I hurt you?"

Logan didn't look at him when he asked the question and it took Dom a moment to realize that Logan was asking about the sex the previous night. "No," he answered gently, truthfully.

A shudder escaped Logan and he nodded, then left. Dom stood there long after he heard the car disappear down the driveway.

CHAPTER 4

He'd fucked a man.
And he'd loved it.

Logan sank further into the deck chair and closed his eyes. It was way too cold and miserable to be sitting out on Gabe and Riley's balcony on a dreary, wet November day, but his only other option was to try to keep it together while he faced his makeshift family inside the apartment as they prepared Thanksgiving dinner. He knew none of them would give him much time out here to sulk though.

It had been only a couple of weeks since he'd been leaning over Dom, fucking him in earnest, that tight ass gripping him like a vise. Dom had told him to let it go, that he'd just been caught up in a moment, but Logan knew it was bullshit. Maybe if it'd happened that first night in the hotel room, he could have used that argument as an excuse and blown the whole thing off. But no, he'd fucked the guy weeks later and the circumstances leading up to it had been nothing even close to what someone would consider a passionate encounter. Dom had been seeking comfort and Logan had used it to his own advantage. It didn't matter if the other man seemed to have enjoyed it at the end – Logan may as well have gotten him drunk or slipped him a drug, because the man had been in no shape to consent.

Logan's body shook as the word *rape* flashed through his mind and he had to put the bottle of beer in his hand down on the side table before he dropped it. He wished he'd ignored his sister's pleas to join them and gone to work like he'd planned. The job he'd taken on a road crew was brutal work. But the physical punishment made his body seek out sleep rather than letting his brain torment him with thoughts of how he fucked everything up, destroyed whatever he touched. Working the long hours also meant he didn't have to interact with the people he cared most about and, even better, he didn't have to come up with lame excuses to try to avoid them. They were a sharp bunch and would have known something was wrong the more time he spent with them. But they readily accepted his excuses that he had to work in order to save up money for the bar. It was bullshit – he hadn't touched the bar in weeks, hadn't even stepped foot inside of it. That part of his life was gone, another failure on the ever-growing list.

He heard a knock on the glass behind him and automatically forced away the perpetual scowl he knew was on his face, then turned to look behind him. His sister was waving at him to come inside. He smiled – she didn't need to know it wasn't what he was actually feeling– and then went inside, snagging his beer on the way. Slamming the rest down, he entered the apartment and went to the kitchen to grab another one. Riley was busy stirring something on the stove while her boyfriend, Gabe, was staring at the turkey, carving tools dangling from his hands.

"I'm telling you Gabe, just start anywhere," Riley said as she glanced over at him. "It'll taste great no matter how pretty the pieces look."

"I want it to be perfect," Gabe said.

"It already is." Riley left the stove and wrapped her arms around Gabe. "Happy Thanksgiving," she whispered and then they did what they always seemed to be doing – kissed. No one deserved to be happy more than Gabe, but seeing his best friend achieve so much despite all the blows life had handed him reminded Logan what a loser he was. And the fact that his self-pity was tied to the envy he felt for his friends made him a complete asshole. He slipped back out of the kitchen and ran right into his sister as she finished setting the table. Before he could even get a word out, she was hugging him, that now ever-present smile on her face brighter than he'd ever seen.

"I'm so glad you made it," Savannah said as she pulled back and then smoothed the wrinkles from his shirt. Two months ago, he would have welcomed her display of affection, but now he was too raw for it. It took everything in him not to pull away.

"Where's Shane?" Logan asked in an attempt to change the topic and get them back on lighter ground.

"He just called. They'll be here in a few minutes."

"They?" he asked, and then felt a chill run through him at the sight of an extra place setting at the table.

Savannah went back to putting the final touches on the table. "Shane and Dom."

"You invited Dom?" Logan croaked as he felt his knees weaken.

"Yeah. Shane found out his brother is still out of the country, so he invited him to join us. Dom insisted that he had to work so Shane went over there to drag him away. Shane says he's been killing himself at the office."

Luckily, Savannah didn't seem to notice his distress as her words sank in. He hadn't been able to keep his promise to Sylvie to be there for Dom, so he hadn't seen the man since he'd walked out of his house a few weeks ago. And now he was coming here? He'd have to sit across the table and play nice with the guy he'd basically raped?

The beer he'd been drinking came back up his throat and he made a quick dash for the bathroom. He heaved into the toilet until his rolling stomach eased. As he washed out his mouth, possible excuses as to why he needed to leave began filtering through his head and he finally settled on the almost truth that he wasn't feeling well. But by the time he got back to the dining room, he knew he was too late because he heard that gravelly voice that made his whole body swim with shame...and desire.

∼

Dom knew it was a mistake to come, but when Shane had shown up at his office an hour ago and insisted, it had been hard to resist. He'd like to think it was because he welcomed the idea of being included at such an intimate event with people he was coming to think of as friends, but the ugly truth was that there was only one person he was really hoping to see. It made no sense to him that his body could ache for Logan even as it continued to mourn Sylvie. The pain of being without her was a living thing and only a few things could make the searing agony of his loss go away for even a few minutes. To that end, he was fitter than he'd ever been because he exercised for hours a day. Work took up the remaining hours and sleep had become a rare luxury that only occurred when his body was too drained from the first two activities to keep him upright. But the memory of Logan inside of him, the feel of those lips caressing his, the tender touch of his roughened palms – those things were always there, whether he wanted them to be or not.

Seeing Logan that morning after he'd betrayed his wife had filled him with a level of rage he hadn't known before. He'd wanted to blame it all on Logan, but the look in the younger man's eyes when Dom had callously dropped that money down in front him had shattered something inside of Dom. His intention had been to hurt, to punish, but when he'd actually seen the result, had heard the breaking of Logan's voice, that had all changed. And the devastating way the young man had asked if he'd hurt Dom had erased whatever anger he'd had left.

"Logan, you've never actually met Dom, right?" he heard Shane ask from somewhere behind him. He tensed up and turned, then felt an almost physical blow at the sight of the man who'd invaded his dreams.

Logan stood in the doorway between the living room and hallway. A white dress shirt was tucked half-heartedly into dark slacks, the sleeves of the shirt rolled up to reveal muscular forearms with a slight smattering of dark hair on them. His hands were clenched at his sides in fists. But when Dom lifted his eyes to meet Logan's, he was caught off guard by what he saw. Horror, guilt, dread. The man was pale – deathly pale – and he looked like he'd lost at least ten pounds since Dom had seen him last. There were dark circles under his pale blue eyes and his thick, black hair was damp from what Dom assumed was Logan running his wet hands through it. His lips – those beautifully soft lips – were slightly parted as if he was trying to say something, but couldn't get the words out.

"No, we haven't," Dom inserted smoothly as he moved across the room, his hand extended in polite greeting. Logan looked at his arm like it was some beast out to drag him into his darkest nightmares. When Logan didn't respond, Dom cleared his throat slightly which finally seemed to knock the other man from his daze. The grip on his hand was cold and brief. Touching Logan had been completely unnecessary, but Dom had needed to feel that connection again. What he felt instead had his gut sinking – the man was a shell of who he'd been those two short months ago in that hotel room.

And it was his fault.

Dom forced himself to turn away and return his attention back to his hosts. He'd only met Gabe and Riley briefly at the hospital after Logan had been shot, but the research he'd done into Logan's past had given him a little bit of insight into Gabe's childhood. Dom thought his own childhood was pretty messed up, but Gabe was the clear victor in the sucky childhood contest. Dom at least had had his brothers to get through shit with. Gabe hadn't had anyone to lean on as he'd dealt with a drug-addicted mother. But the way he clung to his girlfriend made it clear that even the darkest stories could have happy endings. He and Sylvie had had that future once, he mused before shaking off the maudlin thoughts. She'd gone through the effort of sending Logan to remind Dom that he'd made her a promise, and even if it took him the rest of his life, he'd find a way to keep that promise.

He found himself at the head of the table by the time dinner was served – an unusual place for a guest to be, but when he saw how

Gabe and Riley touched and talked softly to one another throughout the meal, it made perfect sense that they hadn't wanted to sit too far away from each other. Savannah and Shane shared one long side of the table, putting Dom kitty-corner to a silent Logan. He was close enough to feel the man's body heat, but his body language was clear – he wanted to be anywhere but where he was. Fidgety and distant even to his sister as she tried to elicit a response, Logan picked at the food in front of him, never actually putting any of it in his mouth.

Dom forced himself to make polite chit-chat with everyone else even though his concern was only for Logan. He knew the man was dealing with a lot when it came to trying to figure out his sexuality after their encounter, but why would that drain him of life like this? Yes, it would be confusing to anyone to find himself with someone of the same sex, but would it beat them down the way it had Logan? He clearly had one of the most supportive groups of friends and family Dom had ever seen – couldn't he have talked through what was going on inside of him with one of them?

By the time dinner was over and dessert and coffee had been served, Dom had reached a decision. As much as his brain was telling him to stay out of it, his gut wasn't going to cooperate and when Logan started saying his goodbyes and searching out his keys, Dom said, "Hey Logan, could you give me a ride home?"

Everyone froze at that and turned to look at Dom, Logan in mute horror, the rest of the group with confused curiosity. "Your sister tells me you've been staying at your bar – that's not far from my apartment and I'm sure Shane and Savannah would like to head home…" he trailed off. He knew he was being high-handed, but at the moment, he didn't really give a crap. Something was going on with Logan – something he and Sylvie had inadvertently started – and he was going to figure out what it was.

"No, it's okay, we don't mind," Shane began as he looked back and forth between Logan and Dom. Dom suspected Shane realized something was going on – the man was too smart for his own good, a trait that had had Dom offering Shane a role in his company after he'd learned the young man was leaving law school.

"I'm sure Logan doesn't mind, do you?" Dom asked Logan brightly, giving the man no valid reason to refuse, especially if he didn't want the others to know something else was up. He was glad when he saw a momentary flash of defiance in the young man's eyes.

Several long, pregnant seconds of silence passed, then Logan finally nodded. "No problem," he managed to grate out. He finished his goodbyes and then left the apartment, not even waiting for Dom. Dom caught up to him by the car, an old SUV that had more rust on it than paint. Before Logan could open the door, Dom grabbed his arm.

"Why don't you let me drive?"

Logan pulled back a few inches so there would be more space between them, his hand gripping the keys so hard his knuckles turned white. Dom wished there would have been anger in those shuttered eyes, but there was nothing. He didn't even get the fight he wanted. Instead, Logan dropped the keys in his hand, then went to the other side of the car, got in and buckled up.

The ride to Dom's apartment was made in silence. Logan stared straight ahead the whole time and only finally started reacting when Dom bypassed the front of the apartment building and pulled into the parking garage.

"What are you doing?" Logan asked in growing agitation as the garage attendant approached them.

"Thanks Jerry, I'll just park it myself," Dom said as he rolled down the window.

"Sure thing Mr. Barretti," the guard responded as he raised the security arm to let the car pass.

He parked in a spot near the elevator, then got out and waited for Logan. The man came around the car and held his hand out expectantly.

Instead of giving him the keys, Dom said, "Come up for a drink."

Logan shook his head and opened his palm, clearly signaling he wanted the keys. "Give them to me," he finally said when Dom didn't budge.

Ignoring him, Dom turned and went to the elevator and pressed the up button. He heard Logan's approach behind him, but wasn't surprised when the man didn't touch him.

"Give me the fucking keys," Logan snapped. Dom was glad to hear that fight in his tone, but he still didn't hand them over.

"We need to have a little talk first."

"No," Logan said adamantly.

When the elevator car came to a stop in front of them and the doors opened, Logan made a move to snatch the keys from the jacket pocket where Dom had stuffed them. Dom grabbed his arm and shoved him up against the wall, his bigger body subduing Logan's instantly. "Upstairs, now."

Dom's intent had been pure when he'd started this whole thing tonight, but now feeling the man tremble against him and the tell-tale evidence of Logan's arousal had him staring at the slightly damp lips just inches from his own. It would be so easy just to lean in a little...

Logan shifted and Dom felt his body harden at the further contact. Desire flashed in Logan's eyes, but it was gone just as quickly and that look of shame was back. It pissed Dom off and he grabbed Logan by the arm and dragged him into the elevator. The man sought out one corner of the small space and watched in silence as Dom pressed in his security code. Dom used the time to get his raging body under control and when the elevator reached the penthouse, he stepped out of the car and waited expectantly for Logan to follow. Which he did – docilely. And that pissed Dom off further. Submissive in the sack was one thing, but Logan wasn't being submissive – he was fucking broken.

Dom bit back a curse, then opened the door leading to his apartment. He motioned for Logan to enter, then shrugged off his jacket and hung it in the closet by the door. Logan took a few steps into the place, then stopped when he saw the Rottweiler trotting up to greet them. If the animal sensed Logan's hesitation, it didn't show it because it happily greeted the still silent man and began sniffing his hands. Dom led him into the living room, fixed them both a drink and then shoved one of the heavy crystal glasses into Logan's hand.

"Sit," Dom said as he motioned to the couch.

"Go to hell," Logan said quietly as he moved past Dom and went to stand by the huge windows that afforded him a view of the sound as well as the lit-up city below. Dom downed his own drink, then went to stand next to him.

"What's going on with you?"

Logan was quiet for so long that Dom didn't think he would answer. He noticed that the liquid in the glass that Logan was clinging to like a lifeline was sloshing around with the man's shaking, so he gently extricated the drink and set it down on a nearby table.

"I can't stop thinking about it," Logan whispered.

"The night you came to check on me?" Dom asked.

Logan nodded, then swallowed hard. Dom could only see Logan's profile because he was still staring out the window, but he was stunned when he saw the man's eyes glisten with unshed tears. "It was just something that happened, Logan. I told you to-"

"Let it go, I know," Logan finished. "I can't."

"Why not?"

"I should have been strong enough to stop it. I knew you were hurting."

"Logan, I asked you to-"

Logan shook his head violently and then the tears did fall. "No, you didn't. I took advantage. Even when I knew I hurt you, I kept going. I didn't give you a choice."

"Jesus..."

"I'm like him," Logan whispered harshly. Dom froze when he realized who Logan was talking about. "I did to you what he did to my sister."

Rage went through Dom at that and he grabbed Logan by the shoulders and spun him to face him. "No, uh-uh. You don't get to do that! You don't get to take what we did and turn it into something ugly!" He shook Logan hard and he knew the man would have bruises on his arms in the morning. "You did not fucking rape me!" he shouted. He felt the dog brush between them as it whined in anxiety, but he ignored it.

Logan shook his head and tried to pull away. He grabbed Logan's face, forcing the other man's eyes to meet his. "If you're going to remember that night, you do it fucking right!" He gentled his hold slightly. "Who kissed who first?"

"You did," Logan said quietly, the tears soaking Dom's fingers.

"Who touched whose dick first?"

"You."

"And what happened when you got inside me?"

"I hurt you," Logan groaned on a sob.

"Why did it hurt?" When Logan didn't answer, Dom did it for him. "It hurt because I wasn't ready. Because *I* forced my body onto yours." Logan tried to shake his head again. "*I* took advantage of *you* – of your inexperience." Dom dropped his hands so they were gently clasping each side of Logan's neck. "What happened when you realized I wasn't ready for you?"

"I stopped."

"Why?"

"Because I didn't want to hurt you."

Dom's thumb stroked Logan's slowing pulse. "Even though that was what I wanted, right? You knew then what I was trying to do."

Logan nodded.

"Why didn't you stop then? Pull out and leave me there like that?"

Logan sniffed, but Dom was glad to see his tears had stopped. "I wanted to make it better."

Dom nodded. "You wanted to comfort me like you'd planned when you kissed me back, right?"

Logan's eyes slid shut and he nodded weakly.

"Open your eyes," Dom ordered. When Logan did, Dom said, "You did, Logan. You took away the hurt. You made me feel so good and I needed that badly…so badly," he whispered. He held Logan's gaze and then said, "I've been with men before, but I never let any of them take me. I never trusted any of them enough."

A sharp breath escaped Logan as what Dom was saying sank in. "Even as messed up as I was that night, I trusted you, Logan. I trusted you to take care of me and that's exactly what you did. Please don't make that first for me into something ugly."

Logan's hand came up to close around one of Dom's wrists and then he nodded. Dom was surprised when Logan leaned in and pressed his forehead against Dom's. "I didn't use a condom. I'm sorry. I'm negative. I get tested regularly," he stuttered.

"It's okay," Dom reassured him and he sighed in relief when he felt Logan's body give in and relax. He forced himself to loosen his hold, then tried not to be disappointed when Logan stepped back to put more space between them. At least that haunted look was gone. It was something.

~

Logan needed to put some space between himself and the man whose body he wanted to cling to. Dom's gentle touch, combined with his quiet strength was turning him inside out and his admission that Logan had been the first to be with him in that way had him reeling with emotion. It was too much to process, but now that Dom had relieved him of the burden that what they'd done hadn't been the horrible act Logan had painted it as, Logan was struggling to come to terms with his wayward emotions. He could no longer deny his attraction to this man, but he needed time to try and understand it. He felt the dog rub up against his hand and he reached out to stroke its large head.

"What's his name?" he asked Dom.

"Bay."

Logan looked up. "What, like Elliot Bay?" he asked, referring to the body of water that made up the part of Puget Sound by the city. Dom hesitated and then shook his head sheepishly.

"It's short for Baby."

Logan laughed out loud and he had to admit that it felt really good. It was the last name he would have guessed for the hulking dog. "Baby," he said softly and the dog leaned against him hard. "Why the hell would you name a dog like this Baby?" he chuckled as he looked back down at the dog.

"Sylvie named him that," Dom said, his voice catching on his wife's name.

Logan stiffened at the mention of Sylvie, then raised his eyes. Dom appeared to be struggling, but then relaxed and let out a little snort. "I shortened it to Bay, but the damn dog only responds to Baby most of the time."

As if knowing his master was referring to him, the dog went over to the big man and settled against his leg, his soulful brown eyes watching Dom quietly. "My brother trains guard dogs. He gave us Bay…Baby as an anniversary present a couple years ago," Dom began as he dropped his hand on the dog's head. "He came with some fancy German name and a pedigree my brother wouldn't stop raving about. Since he was trained for protection, we were supposed to follow all these rules so he'd be an assertive, confident dog. By the first night, Sylvie was calling him Baby, feeding him from the table and inviting him to sleep on our bed. The name stuck and so did all the other bad habits. Vin was pretty mad, but Sylvie had him wrapped around her finger too so that didn't last long," Dom finished with a chuckle.

"Vin is your brother?" Logan asked.

"Yeah, my older brother. I have two younger ones too."

Logan wondered where they were, but figured it was a personal line he probably shouldn't cross.

"You know you don't have to figure it all out in one night, right?" Dom asked.

"Figure what out?" Logan asked, on guard again at Dom's gentle tone.

"The way you're feeling about being with me…about being with another man." Logan took an automatic step back even though Dom hadn't made a move towards him. "I know what you're going through…the confusion. Take it slow – talk it out with your friends." Dom shifted, his hand fidgeting on the dog's head now. "Or you can talk to me. I can't deny that I'm attracted to you, but I can control it. I can listen."

Logan doubted that Dom's control would be the issue – even now, Logan wanted to stride over the man and silence him with a kiss. He wanted to feel those strong arms wrap around him as Dom took control, owned him, showed him the pleasure one hard pressed body against another could bring. But he didn't do any of those things. He just nodded and then looked helplessly around, unsure of what to do next. So he did what he always did – he ran.

CHAPTER 5

"It's too bad you couldn't get the bar open in time for today."

Logan looked up from the tile he was grouting. Shane was admiring his handiwork on the faucet he'd managed to fix. They were nearly done with the bathroom – it wouldn't be pretty, but it would be functional. Might also save him a few bucks since the water would no longer drip incessantly from the leaky faucet.

The apartment over the bar wasn't much, but it met his immediate need to escape the childhood home he and Savannah had spent nearly their entire lives in. She'd been assaulted in the very house that had been meant to protect her – the house he'd struggled to keep for them by selling his body night after night. It hadn't been enough and his own naïve faith in another person had cost his sister her innocence. Staying in that place for even another day was out of the question.

"What are you talking about?" Logan asked.

"It's Black Friday – shoppers galore. Men needing a break from shopping all day with their wives and girlfriends," Shane said as he motioned with his hand.

Logan didn't say anything, just went back to working on the tile.

"So where are you at with things?"

Logan grunted non-committedly, hoping his friend would get the hint and drop the subject.

"Because it looks like things haven't changed much since the last time I was here."

"Been busy," Logan answered.

"Right, the new job." Shane fiddled with the knobs on the faucet. "Fixing potholes," he murmured as he tested the water. "Putting the orange barrels out," he continued.

"What, damn it?" Logan snapped as he turned to glare at his friend. "What's your problem? It's a fucking job and the pay's good."

Shane ignored the outburst, seemingly undeterred by Logan's surly attitude. "Seven years. You busted your ass for seven fucking years to get that place up and running and now you're going to let it go? How much more does that asshole get to take?" Shane muttered as he tossed his tools into the tool bag at his feet. Logan flinched at the reminder of Sam Reynolds and the devastation he'd caused in all of their lives.

"This coming from the guy who drops out of law school in his senior year," Logan replied.

Shane didn't even flinch at the low blow. "Are you seriously trying to pull that shit with me?" Shane asked as he turned to face Logan. "I know you better than almost anyone and you think that crap is going to fly with me? Piss off your best friend so he'll walk away and leave you alone? I fucking wrote the book on that bullshit, you asshole."

Logan leaned back against the shower stall. He was being a dick. His confrontation with Dom had left him a mess the previous night and he'd hurried out of there muttering excuses. The man had extended an offer of friendship and an understanding ear and Logan had pissed all over it, stopping only long enough on his way out the door to grab his keys. He hadn't even managed a proper thank you or even a goodbye. He was a coward and now he was taking all his frustrations out on Shane.

"Sorry," he said.

"Don't do what I did, man," Shane said. "Don't push everyone away. One – they won't go, two – you'll just end up hurting them."

Logan knew Shane was recalling the multiple occasions he had hurt those closest to him in an effort to get them to leave him first. Logan hesitated, then took the leap. "I'm attracted to someone I shouldn't be."

Shane sat on the closed toilet, his hands clasped together as he waited patiently.

Shit, shit, shit. "It's Dom."

That got a reaction from his stoic friend, but amazingly, there was no condemnation – just surprise.

"So, you did meet him before yesterday," Shane said.

Logan nodded. "He hired me to be a third for him and his wife a couple of months ago."

Shane leaned back, his expression confused. Realization dawned. "Shit, he figured out what you did because I asked him to look into your past."

Logan slumped down so that he was sitting on the grimy shower floor.

"I'm sorry, Logan," Shane began. "I asked him to try and figure out who hurt Savannah."

Logan raised his hand. "It's okay." He was silent for a moment, then said, "I was attracted to him that night. Sylvie too. But I felt something for Dom I'd never felt for anyone else. We kissed, but that was it." God, it felt weird talking to his friend about this.

"You didn't see him again after that?"

"Not till the day of Sylvie's funeral." Logan scrubbed a dirty hand over his face. "She wrote me a letter."

"Who?"

"Sylvie. She wrote me a letter telling me Dom was interested in me. She set that night up so that he could explore how he felt about me…about being with another man."

"Shit," Shane muttered.

"She asked me to check on him, so I did. I went up to his house on San Juan Island."

"What happened?"

Logan buried his face in his hand. "I fucked him," he whispered brokenly. "I didn't mean for it to happen...the man had just buried his wife," he said, choking back the humiliation. "He was hurting so bad, he kissed me, touched me. And I just lost it."

He heard Shane move, then felt a comforting hand on his shoulder as Shane kneeled across from him.

"It's okay," Shane said.

"It's not. How can I suddenly want another man? This man?" Logan wrapped his arms around himself. "I like women. I've only ever wanted women."

Shane fell back on his haunches. "Maybe what you feel doesn't need a label."

"What do you mean?"

Shane shrugged. "Maybe you don't need to call yourself straight or gay or bi."

"What else is there?" Logan asked numbly.

"Why does there have to be a name for it? Maybe you're one of those people that looks beyond the rules that society has set. Maybe it's not about man or woman – maybe it's just about how that person makes you feel." Logan fell silent at that, his thoughts turbulent, bordering on painful. "Can I ask you something, Logan?"

He nodded.

"Are you attracted to me?"

God, could this get more humiliating? He shook his head.

"Are you attracted to Gabe?"

"No," he admitted. It was odd because Gabe and Dom had the same build, gave off the same aura of confidence and strength.

"What about Riley? Are you attracted to her?" Logan thought about that. Riley was a beautiful woman. He'd always noticed how attractive she was, but he'd never felt any stirrings of desire.

"No," he answered.

"And your clients...did you want any of them the way you want Dom?"

"No," he said. "So many of them were beautiful and I was attracted enough to be with them, but..." his voice trailed off.

"You didn't really want them?" Shane ventured.

Logan shook his head. "God, I'm so fucked up," he whispered.

"No, you're not," Shane said firmly. "Your brain knows it wants one person in particular. Your body knows it. The package they come in doesn't matter."

"People won't see it that way," Logan said.

Shane smiled and said, "Fuck 'em."

Logan laughed at the typical Shane response.

"Your family will support you no matter who you want to be with."

"I barely know him," Logan began.

"So, get to know him. Or don't. But don't let something as insignificant as gender stop you from finding out."

"Hey, you guys okay in here?" Gabe asked as he appeared in the doorway. If he thought their seating arrangements were unusual, he was smart enough not to pry.

"We're good," Shane answered as he stood, his eyes holding Logan's. Logan nodded, then took the hand that Shane offered him.

"Yeah, we're good," Logan said.

∽

*D*om was just hanging up the phone when he heard a commotion outside his door, then Logan was striding in, Dom's assistant hot on his trail.

"I'm sorry Mr. Barretti. I asked him to wait," she began, but Dom waved her off, his eyes staying on Logan as he stopped on the other side of the large desk, his eyes glittering with rage.

"It's fine Cecile. Can you close the door on your way out?"

Logan slammed down a stack of papers he was holding onto the desk. "I'm not your goddamn whore!" he shouted as he jabbed his finger at the documents in front of him.

Dom took a deep breath and reached out to grab the brightly colored pages, then slowly flipped through them. It only took him a few seconds to realize what he was looking at. "These are your medical bills," he stated as he sifted through each page.

The dollar amounts were staggering and it made sense now why

Logan was working himself to the bone – why he'd accepted the offer from Dom and Sylvie to be their third. He'd known before he hired Logan that the young man had limited the amount of escorting he did, and the few jobs he did in recent years coincided with some large debt usually relating to keeping his bar in business.

"I never called you a whore," Dom calmly responded. He hadn't actually used that ugly word, but he'd tossed money at him that fateful morning at the island house. Saying the words wouldn't have been much crueler than what he'd done.

"But that's what you think of me as, right?" Logan spit out. "You can pay every single one of my debts, but I will never get on my fucking knees for you," he said harshly.

It took a second to understand what Logan was saying. He looked back down at the pages in his hand, then realized the balance on all of them was zero.

"I didn't pay these," Dom said.

"Look at the goddamn name," Logan said as he pointed to a line near the bottom of the first page.

Barretti.

The name was on every page.

Dom sat in his chair, then pulled up a program on his computer. He punched a few keys, then sighed at what he saw. He turned the screen so Logan could see.

"It was Sylvie," he said. "Her grandfather left her and her brother trust funds – sizable ones. We never needed the money so she used it to fund charities that she liked." He regretted his words when he saw Logan go pale at the word "charities."

All the fire went out of Logan and he sank down into a chair on the other side of the desk.

"It looks like she paid these bills a couple weeks before she died. I didn't know anything about it," Dom said quietly as he turned the screen back around.

"Why?" Logan asked. "Why would she do that?"

"She liked you, Logan – a lot. She liked your sister and Shane. It was probably her way of trying to help you get back on your feet."

Logan was quiet for a long time, then finally said, "I wish you'd never picked me."

The comment hurt like hell, but Dom schooled his expression. After Logan had left his place Thanksgiving night, he'd reminded himself that he needed to keep his distance from him, despite his continuing obsession with the young man. Logan was hurt and confused and needed space. His offer to be a sounding board had been genuine, but trying to control the desire that flashed through him every time Logan was near would have been an endless struggle. But to have the man condemn that they'd even met in the first place made his gut burn. His self-preservation instincts kicked in.

"Pay the money back or don't, Logan. I don't give a shit. But don't put words in my mouth again." Dom shoved the papers back across the desk. "You should go. I have a lot of work to do."

"Dom," Logan began, his tone apologetic. But Dom wasn't in the mood.

"Go."

~

Logan had cursed himself the moment he said he'd wished he'd never met Dom and Sylvie. It was a complete and total lie. And he hadn't missed the flash of pain that had coursed through Dom when he'd said the words.

"I didn't mean that," Logan offered. Dom ignored him and focused on the papers in front of him. He huffed in frustration and stood up. But he didn't leave. Instead, he started pacing back and forth in front of Dom's desk. Leaving was the best option – he should end this... whatever *this* was. Walk away. So why wouldn't his legs do what his brain was telling him? He turned to face Dom and saw that the man was quietly studying him. It made him feel exposed, vulnerable...weak.

"Just go, Logan," Dom said again, gently this time. He was giving him an out.

Instead of leaving, Logan said, "I knew that's what I was the first time I did it." He started moving again. "A whore. No one ever says it to your face though. It's always 'escort' because that's classier." He ran his fingers through his hair. "I didn't even fuck the first woman who hired me." He laughed harshly. "She was trying to get back at her husband because he was cheating on her, but in the end, she couldn't go through with it so I just held her while she cried. I even felt kind of good afterwards when she thanked me for being there for her. Then she handed me a wad of cash and I wanted to throw up." Logan went over to the window, not daring to look back at Dom. "I used the money to pay that month's mortgage," he whispered.

He heard Dom shift in his chair behind him, but he kept his gaze on the window. "When you threw that money down in front of me that morning...when I saw your name on those bills-"

Logan wrapped his arms around himself as if he could ward off the cold that was seeping through him. "It shouldn't have mattered. I should have been able to take the money and walk away."

"Why didn't you?" he heard from somewhere behind him. He was afraid to turn and see if Dom had left his chair.

"I never kissed any of them. Never," Logan said harshly. "Not until that night. Not until Sylvie, until you."

"You didn't forget the money that night, did you?" Dom asked and Logan saw his reflection in the glass. Only a few feet separated them.

Logan shook his head. "Fuck!" Logan swore as he slammed his hand against the glass. "I never gave a shit about what anyone thought of me. It shouldn't matter what you think of me."

"Damn it Logan, what do you want from me?" Dom shouted.

Logan turned and leaned back against the window as he watched Dom do the pacing now.

"My wife is dead and instead of mourning her the way I should, I keep thinking about you!" Dom twisted his wedding band over and over in his agitation.

"I'm sorry," Logan began.

Dom flung out his hand to cut Logan off. "Shut up," he muttered. Two strides and he was in Logan's space. "Just shut the fuck up," Dom said again right before he covered Logan's mouth with his own. The force of the angry kiss slammed Logan's head back against the glass, but he barely noticed as he felt Dom's hungry tongue search out his own.

Dom pinned him against the glass with his unforgiving body, something Logan was coming to love. The control this man had over him, over his body, should have scared him, but it only heightened his desire. Dom sucked, nipped and tortured his mouth, each move sizzling through his nerve endings and sending blood rushing to his cock. His arms locked around Dom's lower back in case the man tried to escape, then drifted down to his hard ass. When he squeezed, Dom moaned and then rubbed his pelvis against Logan's.

Logan tried to pull Dom's shirt from his pants so he could touch bare skin, but Dom had other ideas and dropped to his knees. It took the man only seconds to release Logan's aching length from his jeans and underwear and before he could even process what would happen next, Dom's mouth sucked him down to the root.

"Fuck!" Logan shouted as he slammed his hips forward. He heard Dom gag slightly and tried to pull back, but Dom was sucking him intently and he felt hard fingers dig into the globes of his ass to keep him from moving. He'd had a couple of girls in college give him blowjobs, but they didn't hold a candle to this. Within seconds his head felt like it was going to explode and he cried out as his balls drew up. It was too fast, he knew, but he was powerless to stop it. Just as he was ready to let go, Dom released him. "No, please," he begged shamelessly as he tried to force Dom's head back.

"Easy," Dom whispered as he nuzzled Logan's crotch, and then cupped his balls, holding them to prevent the explosion that was so imminent. He felt Dom's tongue lick him from base to tip, then he was teasing the slit on the crown. Logan's limbs felt like they were going to give out so he leaned harder against the glass and locked his knees. Dom teased him over and over until Logan was begging him for relief.

"Look at me," Dom ordered. When Logan did as he was told, Dom swallowed him again, his dark eyes never leaving Logan's. As he bobbed his head up and down Logan's length, he reached into his own pants and started stroking himself. It was the most erotic thing Logan had ever seen. When Dom swallowed around him, Logan gave up the battle and dropped his head back against the glass as he felt the tell-tale tingle in the base of his spine. He moaned as he came and Dom swallowed his release, every tug milking more pleasure from him.

Dom groaned around his cock and Logan looked down just in time to see white jets of come spurt from the head of Dom's swollen length and drip down his hand. He couldn't move and didn't want to as Dom slid up the length of his body as he stood and kissed him, the salty taste of his release still on the man's tongue. They made out like that for several minutes until Dom finally released him and stepped back. He didn't say anything as he went to his desk and grabbed a couple of tissues to clean himself off with. As the languid pleasure from his body ebbed, Logan remembered where they were and quickly straightened his clothing.

"You should probably go now," Dom said as he turned and went towards a side door – a bathroom presumably. A chill went through Logan at the dismissal, but he nodded and watched Dom disappear into the other room. He sucked in a breath, then grabbed the stack of medical bills from the desk and left the office.

CHAPTER 6

Dom tried to steady his breathing as he heard the outer door snick closed. He gripped the sink hard as he stared at his reflection in the mirror. Flushed skin, swollen lips. He could still taste Logan's unique flavor and he knew he should rinse out his mouth to rid himself of the reminder of what he'd just done. He hadn't even had enough sense to lock the door. It was a true testament to his assistant's professionalism that she hadn't come running into the room when Logan had shouted the second Dom had swallowed his thick length all the way down. He just hoped he was paying her enough to keep this little tidbit of information about her boss out of the office gossip pool.

Dom washed his hands, then scrubbed his face for good measure. He searched out the fresh suit he always had on hand on the hanger on the back of the bathroom door and began changing his clothes. As his fingers skimmed over the dampness in his pants, he smiled at the knowledge that he never once would have guessed that his emergency change of clothes would be needed for this situation. Especially since he'd had no plans to do more than send Logan on his way. The man's comments about his regret at meeting him and Sylvie had changed something inside Dom – it had been a harsh reminder that Logan didn't belong in his life. No one did...the only one who was supposed to be there was gone and his physical desire for Logan was just a response to his grief. A way to cope.

But instead of grabbing the man to escort him physically from his office, he'd kissed him and the taste of those lips had had him on his knees before he could even think better of it. It had been rough and fast and part of him wished he could have had the restraint needed to worship Logan's body the way he wanted. Even better, he could have fucked Logan as he was pressed up against that glass, his hot breath steaming up the window as Dom hammered into him from behind, that tight ass clenching his cock in fiery heat.

"Shit," Dom muttered as his dick started to harden again. He pulled the remaining clothes on, then went back to his desk and tried to focus on the screen in front of him. Within seconds of sitting down, his cell phone rang and he looked down and felt relief shoot through him when he saw the Caller ID.

"Vin," he answered, his voice shaky.

"Hey," his brother said, the connection buzzing with static.

"Any luck?" he asked.

"No," Vin said quietly, dejectedly. "But we've still got some leads to work on...some villagers recognized his picture. Said he helped them out before the ambush."

"I've been trying to call you for weeks," Dom muttered.

"I know, sorry. Reception's shitty and the sat phone we had got fucked up."

Dom understood. It wasn't the first time Vin had scared the shit out of him by staying out of contact for so long, but with his emotions already so raw, it was hard to keep from rebuking his brother's oversight.

"She's gone, Vinny," Dom whispered.

Silence, then, "I'm coming home." It sounded like Vin was moving and Dom missed him more than ever in that moment.

"No," Dom forced out.

"I'm coming!" Vin said again and Dom heard shuffling.

"I'm okay," Dom said. "Vin-"

Nothing from the other end, just more shuffling. "Vin!" Dom nearly shouted. The shuffling stopped.

"What?" his brother asked, his voice pained.

"Find him, Vin. Stay there and find him. Bring him home."

"Dom..."

"I have people, Vinny," he said as he remembered Thanksgiving and realized it was true. Between Shane checking on him every day at some point and sweet little Savannah sending him cookies and other sweets via Shane, he wasn't as alone as he'd felt in those early days. And Logan...

"I can be on the next flight out," Vin said.

"I know. Stay. Find Ren."

He could picture his brother's look of frustration as he struggled with which brother needed him more. "Find Ren," Dom said again, then smiled in satisfaction when he heard his brother sigh.

"Yeah. I will."

"I know you will," Dom said as the static crackled and Vin's voice started to break up. He managed a quick goodbye before the line went dead.

∼

"No, no, no," Logan said adamantly as he closed the door in Walter Jessup's sedate face.

He banged his head softly on the door several times, then held it there as he heard the unaffected voice on the other side say, "Mr. Bradshaw, are you declining the acceptance of this latest correspondence from Mrs. Barretti?"

Hell Yes!

Logan absently traced the smooth surface of the doorknob before finally turning it and opening the door. When he'd first heard the knock on his apartment door, a secret thrill had run through him at the thought that maybe it was Dom coming to finish what they'd started in his office. He'd even felt his ass twitch and his cock grow hard at the thought of the larger man's body pressing him down, holding him still as he took him. It was wrong on every level, but there was no denying the disappointment that had shot through him when he saw Sylvie's lawyer on the other side or the dread that'd followed when he'd realized what the other man's presence meant. He'd spent the last two days trying to get the image and feeling of Dom's lips wrapped around his dick out of his head and now the man's dead wife was back to try and drag him back into a life he didn't want or need.

When he opened the door, Walter was holding the envelope up expectantly and Logan snatched it from him. "Always a pleasure, Mr. Bradshaw," the weathered man said as he turned and picked his way down the rickety staircase.

"Right," Logan murmured, his eyes already focused on his name once again scrawled in feminine writing on the front of the envelope. He closed the door, then went to his kitchen table and sat down. It would be so easy to tear it up – rip it into so many little pieces that putting it back together wouldn't be an option. Then maybe he could go on with his life, forget the feelings that had tormented him. His entire life had been about focus and drive and there'd never been a time, even after his parents had died, where he'd lost sight of his future. Success may not have been easy or instantaneous, but it wasn't something he'd ever doubted would eventually come his way if he just put in the effort. And while he hadn't ever specifically thought about a wife or kids being part of that final picture, he'd always just assumed those things would come naturally when it was time.

But one by one things were falling away from him...being torn away, actually. Sam Reynolds had taken most of it – his trust, his faith in others, his belief that he'd done good by his sister, his business and nearly his life. But it was a letter identical to the one in his hand that'd stripped him of his identity. His sexuality had literally been the reason he'd gotten as far as he had, and now even that was in question. Because Sylvie Barretti had seen something in him that he couldn't see in himself. Because one kiss with Dom had lit a fire in him that he knew in his gut would never go away. His feelings for the man were a jumble, but his body would never stop craving Dom's and he knew it.

One fuck and one blowjob would never be enough to satisfy this need that clawed at him now.

Logan carefully tore the envelope open, then unfolded the letter. Before he could even start reading, he noticed how different the writing looked this time. The soft, neat, curvy words were gone, replaced with stark, sharp-edged scrawl that looked jagged against the pretty stationary. Like the writer had struggled to get each word down. He flipped to the second page and checked the name. Her name was there, but the last two letters were nearly illegible. Going back to the beginning of the letter, he sat back in the chair and tried to prepare himself for whatever was to come.

My dearest Logan,

One of the few gifts of cancer is that it gives you time...time to accept that you won't beat it and time to make amends and say goodbye. I called you several times to do the last two, but I always chickened out in the end.

So, I am going to start with the easy part. Goodbye, Logan. You are an amazing, strong, beautiful man and you came into our lives at the perfect time. I have no doubt that if we could have had more time, maybe things could have been different for all of us. I know that Dom was not the only one who was enamored by you. You knew us for one night, but through your sister and through Dom's work, we knew you much longer.

Now the hard part. I wish I could have said these words in person, but I am a coward because I fear you will not forgive me. I'm sorry for the hurt I caused, both by manipulating you into joining us for the wrong reasons and for not being strong enough to let you go. I wrote that first letter only weeks ago and I could easily call Walter up and end all this – you could go on with your life as it was before. But I am selfish and afraid. My desire to protect my husband is stronger than doing the righteous thing and leaving you alone.

I only ask one more favor and it is not forgiveness, because I haven't earned that. By now you may have figured out that I paid your hospital bills. I know you will want to pay all the money back, but my favor is this. Pay it forward instead. When you reach a place in your life where you can, use what you have to help someone else get back on their feet. Someone strong and pure who doesn't deserve the tragedies life has given them. Someone who just needs a helping hand so they can be the person they were meant to be.

Because that's how I see you, not as a charity case, but as someone who has given everything to take care of his family...someone who brings comfort and peace to those around him. Someone who deserves any future he wants.

It's getting late and I find it harder to stay clear-headed when I'm tired. Sorry for the poor handwriting...my mother would be appalled because she always used to tell me that our handwriting was our best first impression. But it's harder to get the words on paper now and I know my fear will keep me from making that phone call I so wish I could have made.

Take care of yourself, Logan.

Love, Sylvie

Tears stung his eyes as he carefully refolded the letter and returned it to the envelope. He didn't want to read it again…didn't need to.

"I forgive you," he whispered as he lowered the envelope to the table. It was the easiest thing he'd done in a long time.

～

Dom unsnapped the leash on Baby's collar and watched the dog trot to his water bowl and start slurping down big gulps, half of it sloshing over the edge of the bowl. He'd started taking the dog for runs with him at a nearby park, but it was clear the animal was out of shape because Dom always ended up having to walk more than run so Baby could catch his breath. The Rottweiler dropped to the floor and rested his chin on the edge of the bowl as he continued to lap at the water. Dom smiled, then turned and headed for a much-needed shower. Even though the December weather was brisk, he'd still managed to work up a sweat. It wasn't enough to knock him into a deep, dreamless slumber like he craved, but it was better than sitting around in the silent apartment missing her voice.

Once he reached his bedroom, he stripped off his shirt and reached for the sweats, but stopped when his phone rang. He didn't typically get phone calls on his home number and when he glanced at the number, he winced.

"Hey Declan, what's up?" he said as he answered the phone.

"I tried your cell," came the clipped voice on the other end. Sylvie's brother, Declan Hale, was an enigma. Big, gruff, quiet – the exact opposite of his little sister. Dom had always gotten along with Declan, but he had to admit that was because the man kept mostly to himself. His only soft spot had been his sister and without her as a connection between them, he'd seen little of Declan since the funeral.

"I was running. I didn't have it with me."

"Something's come up. Can you come down to the precinct?" Declan asked.

"Yeah. Everything okay?" Dom asked curiously. His brother in-law was a detective with the Seattle Police Department.

"How long?" came the response.

Dom felt a chill go through him at the lack of a real answer to his question. "What's going on?" he said firmly, hoping his tone made it clear he wasn't hanging up until he got some real answers.

There was a long silence on the other end of the phone, then Declan sighed and said, "It's about Logan and Savannah Bradshaw."

"Are they okay?" Dom nearly shouted as he reached for his shirt and yanked it on while he fumbled to keep the phone close enough to his ear so he could hear.

"They're fine," Declan assured him. "Some things have come up that I want to go over with you," he said, his voice firm this time as he finished talking and Dom knew he'd get no more out of him for the moment.

"I'm on my way."

~

Logan was bone tired as he trudged up the stairs to his apartment and fumbled with the lock. His too small shower was calling his name after another long night of laying pavement as the endless headlights of speeding cars flew past on the always busy interstate that led out of the city. If he was really lucky, he'd pass out as soon as his head hit the pillow and he wouldn't have the recurring dream of Dom fucking him in every conceivable position. But nothing beat the nightmare that had started after he'd gotten

Sylvie's second letter a couple of days ago. Not only was Sylvie begging him to forgive him as she lay dying in her hospital bed, but it was happening as Dom had him leaning over the edge of her bed as he pounded into him from behind. It was beyond twisted.

"Logan."

Logan spun around at the familiar voice, completely caught off guard at being snuck up on. His surroundings had been something he'd become more aware of since Sam had gotten the drop on him that day in the bar. He didn't remember anything after he'd arrived at the bar, but maybe if he'd been on guard then he wouldn't have nearly cost his sister her life.

"What are you doing here?" Logan snapped, angry that this man was the very reason he couldn't get it together long enough to be aware of what the hell was going on around him.

"We need to talk."

Logan pushed open his door, but placed his body in the entryway. "I don't think that's a good idea," Logan said.

"It's important," Dom said as he took a step forward.

Logan's whole body tightened in anticipation at having Dom in such close proximity, but that only made him angrier. "No," he said as he shook his head. His hand actually came up as if to ward Dom off. His emotions were too raw, his desire too tightly wound to be around this man. If he let him in, he'd be begging Dom to suck his dick again and then fuck him until he was too sated with pleasure to care that he was with a man instead of a woman. He stepped back and started to close the door.

"It's about Sam Reynolds."

Logan froze, his hand tight on the doorknob. He wasn't sure how long he stood there, but he automatically stepped back when Dom gently pushed the door open.

"Let me in, Logan," he urged.

Logan forced himself to release the doorknob that he was still clutching before he backed up into the apartment. His hand automatically went to the scar on his chest.

"The body they found in your bar wasn't his."

Logan shook his head almost violently. "No, Savannah saw him fall into the fire."

Dom closed the door, but didn't move any farther into the room. "Someone at the ME's office fucked up. They released the body for burial before a DNA test was finished and no one at the police department noticed that the testing wasn't done."

"Then how do they know-"

"You submitted a request for a copy of the death certificate," Dom said.

Logan nodded. "I needed it to get the paperwork for the ownership of the bar straightened out. It was the first step to getting him removed as an investor so I can sell the place." He felt numb as he leaned back against the living room wall.

"Someone at the ME's office finally figured things out when they got the request for the death certificate. They took samples from Sam's truck to compare against the body, but never ran them. After your request came in and they realized they'd fucked up, they ran the tests and discovered the DNA from the body didn't match what was found in the truck."

"But someone else was driving Sam's truck that day. Maybe it was his DNA..." Logan faltered, his brain refusing to register what Dom was telling him.

"There were multiple samples in Reynolds's truck including the guy he paid to drive the truck across the border. Bottom line is, none of the samples from the truck matched the body found after the fire."

"He's alive," Logan finally acknowledged.

"He probably got out right after Savannah pushed him. As she was trying to get back to you," Dom said.

"Before you saved us. Me," Logan said quietly.

He saw a flash of something in Dom's eyes at that, but the man quickly stiffened and said, "The body they found in the bar belonged to a homeless man whose friends had reported him missing a couple days after the fire. His age, height and build all matched Reynolds's. They exhumed his body and finally did an autopsy. Reynolds shot him in the head. He was probably dead before you even walked in the door that day."

"He planned to take Savannah with him."

"Faking his death would have bought him the time he needed to get away," Dom agreed.

Fear shot through Logan and he began patting down his pockets. "My phone," he muttered. Every pocket was flat and empty and panic seized at him as he glanced around the room desperately. "Give me your phone," he shouted as he closed the distance between himself and Dom. "I need to call Savannah."

Dom grabbed his arms and held him before he could do anything else. "She's safe, Logan. She and Shane are on their way to Chicago." Logan relaxed marginally and let out the breath he'd been holding. "As soon as I found out what was happening, I contacted Shane. You didn't answer your phone," he added. "We figured it would be safer to get Savannah out of the city, so I had my plane readied for them. The pilot let me know they took off about ten minutes ago."

Logan swallowed hard at the relief that went through him knowing that his sister was safe for the moment. For weeks, they'd walked around unaware that that monster was still out there. It would have been so easy for Sam to grab her. He felt the warmth of Dom's fingers pressing into his arms, the thumbs rubbing tiny circles into his skin in an effort to comfort him. He forced himself to pull free of Dom, then went into his bedroom. There on his nightstand was the cell phone. He grabbed it and went back to the living room, his eyes on the multiple missed call notifications and texts.

"I'm sure she'll be calling you anytime now," Dom said. "She was pretty upset about leaving without talking to you first."

"I always forget the damn thing," Logan muttered as he sent a quick text to Savannah to let her know he was safe and to contact him as soon as she could.

"They'll be safe in Chicago. I've arranged for a security team for them. I have a couple of guys on Gabe and Riley too, but I don't think Reynolds ever had contact with them, did he?"

Logan shook his head. "He met Gabe once or twice, but they never really talked. I don't think he ever met Riley or even knew that Gabe had a girlfriend."

"I want you to come stay at my place," Dom said.

Logan nearly laughed at the absurd suggestion. "No way."

"It's not safe for you to be alone."

Logan rubbed his chest again, then realized what he was doing and dropped his hand. Anger went through him and he said, "I hope that son of a bitch does show up here."

"You think he's just gonna knock on your door so you can kick his ass?" Dom said angrily. "He's a fucking coward and he's going to wait in the shadows and put another bullet in you – one that you won't walk away from this time!"

"It's not your problem," Logan responded coldly.

Dom tightened his lips and Logan saw him shift his weight as if he was preparing to grab Logan. But then Dom stepped away from him and reached for his cell phone. He sent a quick text, then looked back up at Logan. "The police are matching the other DNA samples they collected from Sam's truck. Two of the samples have already been matched to missing women," he said curtly.

Logan reared back at that. "Oh God," he said as he realized the implication. "Who?"

"A nineteen-year old college student who went missing after a frat party last spring and a prostitute who disappeared after being picked up by a john almost a year ago. There are still four more samples that they need to run."

"Jesus," Logan said.

"Both women were about 5'5, late teens to early twenties, slim build, long black hair, blue eyes," Dom said softly. Dread swept through Logan as he realized the women matched his sister's appearance.

"He's more dangerous than any of us could have anticipated, Logan. And he's not going to stop coming after your sister. You're an obstacle and he won't hesitate to make sure he kills you this time."

There was a knock at the door and he watched as Dom opened it to reveal a huge, thickly built man with dark hair. He entered and stood next to Dom, his black T-shirt pulled tight over a sculpted torso. He had a couple inches on Dom which put him at around at least 6'4. His bearing yelled military and his sharp eyes quickly scanned the room, then Logan as if assessing him as well.

"This is Cade," Dom said as he motioned to the hulk next to him. The man nodded at Logan, but said nothing. "He'll be your shadow until Sam Reynolds is found. You don't like it, that's too fucking bad because he works for me," Dom said coldly. "You may be okay with putting your life at risk, but I promised your sister I would look out for you so you can spout as much bullshit as you want about being able to take care of yourself, but he's on your ass for as long as I tell him to be!"

Before Logan could even respond, Dom was out the door. Cade gave him a quick nod, then followed. "Lock this behind us," the huge man ordered as he motioned to the door before pulling it shut behind him. Logan didn't miss the sight of the handgun that was tucked into the back of the man's pants. It was another harsh reminder at how fucked up things had just become.

CHAPTER 7

Dom strode from Logan's building, anger radiating through him. He knew Logan would be pigheaded about staying at his place and hadn't truly expected the man to accept, but it didn't make it any easier. And knowing that Logan was willing to put himself in harm's way to seek vengeance on the man who'd raped his sister and left him for dead had him seeing red.

"You okay, Boss?" Cade said from behind him.

"Don't call me that," Dom sniped as he made his way down the walkway.

"Sure thing, Boss," Cade chuckled.

Dom stopped and swung around, ready to take his frustrations out on the other man. But when he saw the humor in Cade's expression, he forced himself to relax. Cade had lit up a cigarette in the time they'd walked out of the stairwell that led up to the apartment above Logan's bar. The man appeared casual enough, but Dom didn't miss the way his eyes were always searching the environment. His body looked relaxed, but Dom could see the slight tension in his frame – indication that Cade was ready to do battle at any moment if the situation called for it.

"Sorry, I shouldn't have talked like I owned you in there," Dom muttered. He considered Cade a friend and even though Cade did technically work for him – or for Barretti Security rather – he owed the man more than treating him like the hired help.

"Stubborn guy," was all Cade said as he took a drag on the cigarette.

"Yeah," Dom responded.

"Hot though," Cade said mildly.

"Keep your hands off him," Dom growled, then realized what he'd said and how it sounded. He'd known Cade was openly gay, but he'd wanted the best man for the job, so any potential attraction Cade might have had for Logan hadn't even been on his radar. Now, jealousy ripped through him at the thought of Cade pursuing Logan. Cade was studying him so he quickly added, "He's not into men," even though Dom knew that really wasn't true – certainly not after Logan's physical reaction to the surprise blowjob Dom had given him just days ago.

"Right," Cade responded casually, then he stepped around Dom and headed towards his car.

"I'll find someone to relieve you tonight," Dom muttered as he went to his own car and climbed in. His hands shook as he turned the key in the ignition. Driving away was one of the hardest things he had to do, but he forced himself to do it anyway.

~

Logan was on edge as he hurried down the sidewalk, his eyes scanning the face of every person walking towards him. He hated that Sam Reynolds had managed to take his sense of security on top of everything else. When he'd initially heard Dom tell him that Sam might come for him, the desire for revenge had been the only thing that registered and the thought of pounding on the evil man until he no longer breathed the same air or walked the same ground as everyone else, had him blind to everything around him. He'd sat on one of his wobbly, sixties-era vinyl kitchen chairs all day, his eyes trained on the front door as he'd waited for any sign that evil stood on the other side. He'd managed to pull himself away only long enough to talk to Savannah on the phone as she'd begged and pleaded with him to stay with Dom.

It wasn't like he could have told her that if he stepped foot inside of the man's home again, he'd likely crawl into his bed and beg the man to take him until he couldn't feel anything anymore besides the burning pleasure that his body demanded, so he'd lied to Savannah and told her he'd consider it, then had made her promise to keep him posted on how things were going in Chicago. He'd assured her that if things hadn't been ironed out by Christmas, he'd make his way to Chicago so they could be together for the holiday. He'd then spent several minutes being lectured by Shane on staying safe and within minutes of hanging up, Gabe had been calling and insisting he come stay with him and Riley. But putting his friends at risk by being around them was the last thing he wanted to do, so he'd turned him down and lied again by saying he had a safe place to stay and that it was better if he didn't know the details. And it was all bullshit. Truth was, he was scared – it would be stupid not to be. But he was more scared of what it would mean if he sought the safety that Dom was offering.

He hadn't seen hide nor hair of Cade, even though he'd looked for the big man as soon as he'd left his building. But if his bodyguard was there, he wasn't eager to be seen apparently. Taking a walk down to the marketplace probably wasn't the smartest thing to be doing, but Logan was going stir-crazy as he waited for his would-be stalker and sleep had eluded him all day, so getting out and moving around seemed like his best course of action. He would grab a quick bite to eat at one of the small, hole-in-the wall Asian places at the marketplace, then grab a cab home before darkness fell.

The fresh air felt good across his itchy skin as he walked, but he kept his guard up. Someone brushed past him and he nearly jumped, but then calmed when he saw it was a couple holding hands. Something shifted inside him when he saw it was two men and he found his eyes locking on their intertwined hands. A few people gawked at them as they went by, but most didn't seem to notice anything out of place as the young lovers chatted happily, their heads occasionally dipping towards each other.

Logan slowed as the couple entered what appeared to be a small, busy bar. In the doorway were two more men, one pressing the other against the wall as he murmured something in his ear. Another shiver ran through Logan at the sight and he glanced up to see where he was. When he saw the bar's name, he immediately realized it was a popular gay hangout. Ignoring the surge of curiosity that went through him, he took a few steps forward, but then stopped and glanced back at the lovers – or soon to be lovers – as they caressed each other. They were both attractive men, but Logan felt no physical attraction when he looked at them. But as they touched each other, spoke in quiet whispers and shared flirty smiles, Logan turned around and reached past them for the door before he could think better of it.

The bar was noisy and the loud music made Logan's ears ring. Men and women danced around him as he worked his way through the crowd towards the bar at the far end. He felt the occasional seeking hand on his ass, but his brisk pace had him safely at the bar within seconds.

"What can I get you?" asked the heavily tattooed and pierced bartender.

"Scotch and soda," he replied, then took a long drink when the bartender plopped it down in front of him. The alcohol instantly eased his nerves and he looked around. He felt eyes on him from multiple sources, but settled on a man at the end of the bar who was watching him hungrily. A good-looking guy, early thirties maybe, with an expensive haircut and equally costly suit. Some type of businessman, he figured. The man nodded at him, then called for the bartender, his eyes never leaving Logan. Seconds later the bartender was pushing another drink in front of Logan and motioning towards the businessman.

Logan swallowed the rest of the first drink, then started on the second as he turned his attention back to the dancers. Bodies writhed and sweated under the multi-colored lights that flashed overhead and the pulsing bass of the music had Logan wondering if he would need to stop and buy aspirin on his way home. The couples were mostly men, but there were a few women as well. He expected to feel something at the sight of all the grinding and groping that was going on, but didn't. There were a few couples on the edge of the dance floor, some talking, others making out. He had to admit that he was somewhat turned on at the sight of two men who were on each other like they weren't in a public place, but his interest was nothing like the bone-wrenching need that nearly crippled him when he remembered Dom's heat drawing him in, burning him alive. As expected, his cock instantly responded to an image of Dom in his head and he began to shift uncomfortably.

"Hey there, beautiful," the businessman said as he sidled up next to Logan, the man's body brushing his as he ordered two more drinks.

Logan swallowed the second drink down and didn't protest when the man shoved a third drink into his hand. It was too much and he knew he should stop, but another image of Dom bent over, his fluttering hole on display as he waited for Logan's cock had Logan taking a long draw of the amber liquid. The man must have taken Logan's silence as some kind of welcome, because he felt a hand close over his thigh and travel up towards his dick, which was now starting to ache. But not because of this man. Nope, the good-looking man was just more evidence of what was becoming clearer every second.

Just as the man's fingers were about to brush his length through his jeans, Logan stood and pulled away. "Thanks for the drinks," he mumbled as he swallowed the last of what was left in the glass and placed it on the countertop. The man looked pissed, but Logan didn't give a shit and turned to leave. He instantly slammed into a hard body.

"You about done?" Cade asked, his huge hands closing around Logan's upper arms to steady him. The man did not look happy. Logan wrestled free, then pushed past Cade and headed for the door, disappointment driving him to get home and seek out the safety of his bed.

"You find what you were looking for?" Cade asked as he followed Logan out of the bar.

Logan's appetite was gone so he started the walk back home,

ignoring the presence behind him. Cade didn't say another word until they were at Logan's door and he was fumbling with the key. He wasn't drunk, but the alcohol was making him lightheaded. He heard a snort behind him, then felt Cade snatch the keys from him. Logan was still facing the door and he sucked in a breath when he felt the other man's body pin his as Cade carefully worked the key into the lock. But instead of turning the key, he watched Cade's hand drift up until it rested on his waist. As Cade turned him around, warning bells went off in Logan's mind, but he remained silent as Cade pressed him all the way back against the door.

"He wanted you," Cade murmured as his fingers pressed into Logan's waist. "Looks like you wanted him too," he said as his eyes lingered on the hard-on Logan was still sporting.

Cade really was an attractive man – tight muscles, tanned skin, work-roughened hands that knew exactly how much pressure to exert, firm lips, penetrating eyes. He let his eyes drift down Cade's body and noticed he wasn't the only one struggling with an erection. But the way Cade was looking at him made Logan suspect the man wasn't confused by his body's reaction.

"Or is that for someone else?" Cade mused as he continued to stare at Logan's crotch. The man was crude and rough. But instead of pushing him away, Logan stood mute and still as he watched the other man's lips descend. The kiss was demanding and Logan closed his eyes when he felt the tongue slide over the seam of his lips seeking entry. It should be easy to open to this man because he was so much like Dom – big, intimidating, controlling, confident. His goal tonight had been to experiment. To figure out what his body really wanted. And if being at that bar didn't confirm it, this kiss absolutely did. It was a great kiss and the guy kissing him was insanely hot by any man's standard – straight or gay. But it still felt wrong and he pulled his mouth free of Cade's. Even though his eyes were still closed, Logan felt Cade hang there for a moment, likely studying him to see if he truly wanted the kiss to end. Then the other man was releasing him and stepping back. He heard the distinctive snick of the key in the lock.

"You hungry?" Cade asked casually as he pulled Logan away from the door so he wouldn't fall as Cade opened it. Cade entered the apartment first and did a quick look around, Logan in tow behind him.

"Cade," Logan began.

"I know a great pizza place that delivers," Cade said as he locked the front door and pulled out his phone and dialed.

"Cade," he tried again.

"Why don't you go get cleaned up? Take care of that if you need to," Cade smirked as he glanced again at Logan's erection. Jesus, the man had no boundaries.

Too worn out to argue, Logan went into the bathroom and shut the door. He turned the shower on, then stripped out of his clothes and stepped under the hot water. He tried to will his cock into submission, but he was too on edge from the combined exhaustion and stress of the last twenty-four hours. Half a dozen strokes and an image of Dom gliding smoothly in and out of him from behind had him shooting all over the shower tile and he watched in languid satisfaction as his semen collided with the water and disappeared down the drain. He leaned back against the cold tile and let the lingering pleasure loosen his muscles before forcing himself to finish his shower so he could deal with his unwanted guest.

By the time he'd dried himself off and gotten redressed, he found that Cade had made himself at home and was already working on the first piece of pizza that had apparently been delivered in record time. Or he'd been in that shower longer then he thought. He dropped down on the other end of the couch and grabbed a piece of pizza as he watched the man commandeer the remote and start flipping channels.

"Feel better?" Cade asked as he settled on an old black and white sitcom. Logan heard the laughter in his voice.

"Guess this wasn't part of the job description, huh?" Logan finally said as he settled back against the cushion and devoured the pizza.

"What wasn't?"

"Having to watch some guy try to figure out what team he plays for."

"So that's what that was tonight?" Cade asked as he snagged another piece of pizza. "'Cause there's a lot of places with much hotter guys."

"Hotter than you?" Logan said, then nearly choked when he realized he'd said the words out loud.

Cade laughed heartily before taking another bite. "No wonder he likes you," he said as he licked the grease off his fingers. Logan's gut tightened at the obvious mention of Dom. "So, what's stopping you?" Cade asked.

Logan fell silent as he finished off the rest of the pizza slice, then wiped his now clammy hand on his jeans.

"Is it 'cause he just lost his wife or 'cause of the whole team thing?"

"Both," Logan admitted.

"Well, maybe you need to let Dom make his own decision about the first one," Cade said as he started on his third piece of pizza. "And focus on the second part. 'Course, I think for you it's less about teams and more about finding the right teammate."

Logan dropped his head back on the couch and sighed. Never in his wildest dreams did he think he'd be talking sex with some stranger, much less someone who was clearly a friend of Dom's. A man he'd let kiss him just so he could experiment.

"Sorry for using you like that," Logan murmured as his eyes began to feel heavy.

"With that ass and that face, you can use me all you want," he heard Cade chuckle and he smiled. The guy was loud and brash and looked like sex on a stick – and Logan was really starting to like him. That was his last thought before sleep claimed him.

※

*L*ogan awoke in the same position he'd passed out in. His neck ached as he sat up and a blanket fell into his lap from where it had been draped over him. Cade was gone, the TV off. Even the pizza had been cleaned up. Logan stretched as he stood and felt marginally better than he had the night before. At least he'd slept dream free last night. He glanced at his watch and saw that he had less than an hour to get to work. Although he preferred the night shift, a desperate co-worker had asked him to switch, so today would be spent watching rush hour traffic crawl by as he spread hot tar on the always cracked and worn out interstate.

It took him less than fifteen minutes to shower and shave and when he went hunting for something to eat, he was pleased to find that Cade had left him what remained of the pizza. He piled two pieces on top of each other and ate them at the same time as he hunted for his keys, remembered to grab his cell phone, and headed out the door. A quick glance told him the stairwell was empty and he locked his door, his body once again on edge as he went out into the open streets. He automatically searched for Cade, but like the night before, he saw no one. As he drove, he kept his eyes peeled for any sign of Sam, but nothing was out of the ordinary. No cars followed him, there was no feeling of being watched. On his lunch break he called Savannah to check in with her and then finished out the day. The sun had just begun to settle along the horizon when he headed home. This time as he drove, he did notice headlights in his rearview mirror. His tension grew as the car stuck with him and when he took several unnecessary turns to see if it followed, it did.

"Shit," he said as he forced himself to remain calm and used one hand to fumble for his phone. He found the contact he wanted and hit the speed dial.

"Yeah," Dom said when he picked up.

"I think someone's following me and I don't know where Cade is."

"It's me behind you," Dom snapped. "Go home."

Logan was caught off guard by both the fact that Dom was trailing him and at his enraged tone. What the fuck had died and crawled up his ass? Logan hung up the phone and turned on the street that would get him back to his place. Within minutes, he was parked and throwing the door open. Dom had parked behind him, but wasn't getting out of the car.

"What's going on?" he asked Dom through the open driver's side window.

"Nothing. Go inside." The clipped, curt tone was really pissing Logan off.

"Where's Cade?"

"He had another assignment," Dom said, but he refused to make eye contact with Logan.

"What kind of assignment?" Logan asked. Something wasn't right about any of this.

"The kind where he won't be fucking the person he's supposed to be watching," Dom snapped.

Logan reared back in surprise. "What?"

Dom got out of the car, his big body drawn tight with fury. "I don't pay him so he can fuck every tight ass that comes on to him!"

"You think-" Logan began, the confusion just starting to clear.

"I saw you last night! You play a good game Logan, but enough of the 'I don't like dick' bullshit! Your cock looked happy enough last night while Cade was shoving his tongue down your throat."

Dom was nearly in his face as he raged at him. His own anger lit up like a brushfire and he found himself slamming Dom back against the side of his car. "Fuck you, Dom!" he yelled. "You don't know what the hell you're talking about."

"Then explain it to me!" Dom responded as he used his superior strength to turn them around and shove Logan back so that he was stuck between the cold metal of the car and Dom's hot, seething body. "Did you give it up to him? Because I sure as hell know Cade doesn't bottom for anyone. Of course, I never did either until I met you. Did he change his rules for you Logan? Did he let you fuck his ass?"

"Get off of me," Logan said stiffly as he tried to pull free of the bruising hold that Dom had on his arms.

"You're a piece of work, you know that? You don't want me to treat you like a whore, but the second some good-looking guy enters your orbit, you're bending over for him like some street trash. I bet you don't even know his fucking last name, do you? Did you at least get more than your usual rate for letting him ream your virgin ass?"

Pain slashed through Logan at the cruel words and all his anger deflated as his insides turned numb. Dom must have sensed his surrender because he loosened his hold, then released him all together.

"Logan," he said softly, shame tainting his voice.

"Don't," Logan said as he pushed past Dom and went around the car towards the bar and then disappeared into the stairwell. He was proud of himself for managing to hold it together long enough to crawl into his shower, but the second the water hit him, he sank to his ass and cried.

~

*D*om had followed Logan into the building far enough to make sure he got into the apartment okay, then crawled back to his car as the nausea rolled through him. Shame coursed through him as his own words rang in his ears. He'd let his jealousy get the best of him and that volcano of bullshit had come out of nowhere before he could stop it.

A hard body slammed into him from behind and he found himself thrown onto the hood of his car. Instinct had him fighting back, but the body slam had knocked the wind from his lungs so his efforts were pathetic.

"You piece of shit," he heard Cade snarl as Cade released him and he slid to the ground. He waited for a blow or kick, but the enraged man stepped back and studied him as his hands searched his pockets. A cigarette appeared, then a lighter. Cade's eyes never left Dom as he sucked in a long draw from the cancer stick. Dom drew in a couple of short breaths before forcing himself to stand.

"I told you to stay away from him," Dom said as he leaned back against the car for support.

"Yeah big man, I got your text telling me I've got a new assignment," Cade snapped. "What the hell is wrong with you?" Cade leaned back against the car. "The kid didn't deserve that," he said as he took another puff.

Dom nearly laughed at the description of Logan as a kid. The guy was all man, nothing kid-like about him.

"I didn't pay you to fuck him," Dom snapped, his rage building as he remembered the sight of Cade's lips on Logan's, his bigger body pressing Logan into the hard wood of the door.

"Yeah, I heard what you told him…all of it," Cade returned.

Dom quieted. "I saw you guys last night. Outside his door."

Cade took in a deep breath, the cigarette dangling from his fingers for a moment before he dropped it on the ground and stubbed it out. "Yeah, I figured that was what happened when I got your text last night."

"I couldn't find someone in time to relieve you last night so I figured I'd do it myself." Jesus, did he really sound like a whiny kid? Dom forced himself to straighten, then said, "What you do with him on your time is your business." He started back around to the driver's side of the car.

"He went to a gay club last night."

Dom stopped, a chill coursing through him. The idea of his Logan in one of those places…

"Lot of guys were interested," Cade commented casually. "He even let one get handsy with him. The moron actually thought the stiffy Logan was sporting was for him."

Dom wanted to shrink in on himself because hearing about other guys all over the man he wanted was making his ears bleed. It was bad enough to watch Logan with Cade, but to know he'd shopped around beforehand made it a hundred times worse.

"None of my business," Dom managed to force out as he pulled his door open.

"It is if that hard-on was for you." Cade turned so he was looking at Dom over the top of the car. "Because it sure as hell wasn't for me."

Dom sagged against the car and closed his eyes.

"He's got amazing lips. Smooth like silk," Cade said.

"Knock it off," Dom ordered.

"He wouldn't let me taste him though. Wouldn't open those pretty lips and let me in."

"Jesus," Dom murmured as he felt his body harden at the memory of Logan's mouth. If what Cade was saying was true, Dom was still the only man that had tasted that lush mouth, felt that slick tongue slide over his. He remembered the comment Logan had made about never kissing any of his customers.

"He was trying to figure shit out, Dom. About you. About himself." Cade straightened and drummed his fingers on the roof. "I thought he could use someone to talk to so I invited myself in."

Dom closed the door to his car and began pacing. He'd fucked up royally. Had taken a dig at the thing Logan was most sensitive about.

"He's pretty messed up about wanting you…especially since it hasn't been long since Sylvie…" Cade's words dropped off.

Dom closed his eyes at the automatic agony that went through him at the sound of her name, but as sharp as it was, it didn't linger as long as it usually did. Maybe because of the gut-wrenching pain he was feeling knowing that he'd probably just done irreparable damage to whatever his relationship with Logan was.

"I miss her so much," he began as he paced back and forth alongside his car. "But I also want him. I want him the way I always wanted her…maybe more," he admitted as the shame went through him.

"And you think you're somehow betraying Sylvie?" Cade asked.

"How can I be thinking of pleasure? I *just* lost her!" he asked desperately. "How can I have so little respect for her, for what we had?"

"Seeking comfort in the arms of someone else doesn't mean you didn't…don't love your wife. Anyone who knows you knows the lengths you went to for her – they'd never question your love or commitment to Sylvie. And she'd be the first person in line telling you to grab whatever pleasure out of life that you can."

That was true. Sylvie's bucket list had proven that. They'd traveled endlessly to the far reaches of the world, done all the things she'd been too afraid to try before her death sentence, including a skydiving trip that had even had him shaking with fear as he'd stepped out of that plane and watched the ground hurtle towards him. Nothing had been off limits because he'd wanted her to have everything. And she'd already proven that she wanted the same for him by bringing Logan into his life. And he'd gone and fucked it all up with cruel words meant to inflict the same amount of pain he'd been feeling for a betrayal that hadn't actually happened.

"I won't be able to fix this. The things I said," Dom muttered.

"Try," was all Cade said and Dom saw him motion behind him. Dom looked up and sucked in a harsh breath when he saw Logan standing at one of the small windows watching them. He couldn't make out his features, but he felt Logan's eyes on him and a shudder of need went through his body. And then Logan was gone, the curtain falling back into place. The light turned off in the room – Logan's bedroom probably – a minute later.

"Will you keep an eye on things out here?" Dom asked as he hurried towards the building.

Cade just nodded, then went towards his own car which was parked across the street, something Dom had been too preoccupied to even notice.

Dom followed the stairs up to Logan's apartment, then came to a halt when he saw the open front door. There was no damage to the door to suggest it had been forced open and he and Cade certainly would have been aware if Logan had been in trouble. That meant one thing – Logan had opened the door for him. Fear and anticipation warred with Dom as he entered the dark apartment and closed the door behind him. The sound of the lock engaging sounded like a cannon going off. His eyes adjusted quickly as he made his way to the bedroom. The door was open, but the light was off. It didn't matter because he could see Logan's outline as he sat on the bed facing the door. His head was down, his hands clasped together.

Dom entered the room and stopped in front of Logan. He reached for the small lamp on the nightstand and flicked it on. The light was dim, but it was enough that Dom could see a couple of things. The hurt that still lingered in Logan's huddled frame and the bottle of lube and a single condom that sat on the nightstand next to the clock.

"Logan," Dom whispered, but Logan shook his head.

"I can't stop," Logan said as he raised his eyes. Dom felt like he'd been punched in the gut when he saw how red they were. "It's wrong. You just lost Sylvie," Logan murmured. "But I can't stop wanting you."

Dom clenched his fists to keep them from reaching for the tormented young man. "Logan, those things I said-"

Logan shook his head. "It doesn't matter," he said. "I don't need apologies. I need to stop needing you," Logan said harshly. "It consumes me," he spit out. "I need you to make it stop."

Dom wanted so badly to take the pain away that he found himself stepping closer to Logan before he realized what he was doing. "It may not stop after one time, Logan. It hasn't for me."

Logan stood so their bodies were just inches apart and whispered, "Please." Dom gave up the fight and claimed Logan's mouth. It had only been days since he'd last touched the other man, but it felt like years as the hunger slammed into him. Logan's lips opened immediately and he slipped his tongue inside to explore the lushness and heat. He stroked over every surface before he twined his tongue with Logan's. Arms closed around him as the kiss was returned and then Logan was invading his mouth. He heard whimpers of need erupt in the quiet room, but he couldn't be sure if they were Logan's or his own.

His hands skimmed over Logan's muscular body as it tried to memorize each hard angle and plane. Lifting the back of Logan's shirt, he let his fingers stroke over the soft skin of his lower back, then pushed his hands under the waistband of Logan's sweats so he could palm his ass. He groaned at how tight it was and his cock grew uncomfortably hard within the confines of his pants. Logan's hands were busy too as they held his head while Logan continued to plunder his mouth. The man was an expert at kissing and Dom gladly gave up control for the moment as Logan nipped at his lips, then soothed away the sting with his silky tongue. Nimble fingers were working the buttons of his dress shirt and seconds later long, thick fingers were petting his chest, exploring the texture of his nipples.

Dom used his last shred of sanity to grab Logan by the face and force some distance between them. He ran his thumb over the wet, swollen lips, then gasped when Logan's tongue darted out to lick the digit. Dom raised his eyes to Logan's lust filled ones and managed to rasp, "I need you to be sure."

Logan nodded as Dom's thumb continued to trace his mouth.

"I need to hear the words. Say what you want."

"I want you to fuck me, Dom," Logan whispered before opening his mouth in invitation. A thrill shot through Dom as he pushed his thick finger into Logan's mouth and the man clamped down on it and sucked hard, his tongue stroking the tip.

"Fuck," Dom cried out as he replaced his finger with his tongue as Logan pushed the dress shirt from his shoulders. The younger man's hands were everywhere, exploring each muscle and testing how his skin felt. Then Logan had his hands on Dom's nearly bald head and Dom froze at the intimate caress.

"I've been dreaming about this," Logan said as he skimmed over the stubble of hair that had already started to grow. He forced Dom's head down and placed kisses along the top and sides. Dom felt like he was going to explode so he grabbed Logan by the wrists and forced his arms over his head, then pulled the T-shirt he was wearing off. Before Logan could even lower his arms, Dom was kissing and licking his chest, skimming over the nipples. He paused briefly at the raised scar in the middle of Logan's chest, then moved on and followed the trail of hair down past his muscled abdomen. He stroked the outline of Logan's stiff cock through his sweats and smiled when he heard Logan moan. It took just seconds to drop to his knees and pull the sweats down, but instead of sucking Logan down like he had last time, Dom leaned back to study the flesh in front of him. He was long and curved, not quite as thick as Dom, and the purple head was already leaking fluid.

Dom took a quick lick, then used his hands to test the weight of Logan's balls.

"Please," Logan muttered as he tried to push his cock towards Dom's mouth. Dom licked the head, then flicked his tongue over the ridge and followed the thick vein underneath down to the base. He did this several times as his fingers played with the soft patch of skin behind Logan's balls.

"Dom," Logan growled in frustration as he put his hands on Dom's head. Dom bit back a laugh and then sucked Logan in like he wanted him to. He forced his throat to relax as Logan automatically thrust his hips forward. "Yes," he heard from above him as Logan held his head and began fucking his mouth. Dom accepted several hard plunges before he grabbed Logan's hips to force him to stop. He looked up to make sure Logan was watching as he pulled up on a slow, agonizing stroke and let Logan's dick fall from his lips. Logan's mouth was open as he panted at the sight. Dom reached up and forced his middle finger into Logan's mouth.

"Get it really wet," Dom said and Logan did as he was told. When he released the digit, he kept his eyes on Dom's as Dom slid the soaking finger down between his ass cheeks and found the quivering hole that was waiting for him. Logan's body reflexively tightened as Dom rubbed the slick fingertip over the wrinkly skin around the small opening. He pushed in slightly and heard Logan suck in a harsh breath.

Dom closed his lips back around Logan's length and then swallowed him. At Logan's cry of pleasure, Dom pushed his finger into Logan's opening and felt the muscle give way under the incessant pressure.

"Fuck!" Logan screamed as he began pushing back on Dom's finger. Dom sucked him hard as he worked his finger in and out of Logan's body.

"Don't make me come," Logan said as he fumbled to pull Dom back up to him. Dom released him and carefully pulled his finger from Logan's ass. The second he stood, Logan was kissing him and working the button and zipper on Dom's pants. They fell to the floor with a swish and Logan released his lips only long enough to push the underwear down. He felt Logan's hand close around his own aching length, but he knew he was too close to his own release to tolerate much so he forced Logan back several steps until he hit the bed. Then Dom was pushing his body onto the mattress as their cocks rubbed against each other.

"Are you sure?" Dom asked as he pried his lips from Logan's.

"Yes, please," Logan grunted as he continued to hump Dom's pelvis.

"It will be easier the first time if I take you from behind," Dom said as he leaned back. He watched to make sure there was no fear or uncertainty in Logan's eyes, then sighed in relief as the man sat up, turned over, and got into position, his beautiful ass on display.

"Please, Dom," Logan said over his shoulder.

Dom's hands shook as he reached for the bottle of lube and he prayed that he wouldn't fuck this up.

～

Logan tried to concentrate on his breathing as he felt Dom's thick, lubed fingers seek out his hole. He braced himself, expecting Dom to just plunge them in, but he didn't. Instead, he brushed one that wasn't lubed over the opening a couple of times, then the fingers disappeared. Large hands settled on his ass and separated the flesh. Cool air drifted over his entrance and fear went through him that Dom hadn't prepared him enough. Before he could protest, he felt something hot and slick brush his hole, then a shot of pure pleasure went through him as suction was applied.

"Jesus," Logan moaned as he looked over his shoulder and saw Dom's face buried between his cheeks. The man was tonguing him, the hot little appendage stroking and sucking on him. It was an erotic sight to watch, but his body was too overcome with how good it felt and Logan dropped his forehead on the bed. Over and over Dom played with him and moans kept escaping from Logan's lips as he clenched his fists into the bedding. And when Dom's tongue pushed inside him, Logan did scream and he reached for his cock in desperation.

"It's too good!" he shouted as he pumped his hips desperately into his hands. But Dom reached around and grabbed his hand, forcing it away from his length.

"Not yet," Dom murmured against his skin, his breath tormenting his hole further. Dom's fingers returned and this time he did push the tip of one in, the cold lube so different from the hot tongue that had tortured him so briefly. His insides stretched and burned as his muscles tried to accommodate Dom's thick finger and Logan fought through the pain that came with it. But when another finger joined the first, Logan shook his head.

"It's too much," he said even though his body seemed to be sucking Dom's digits in once he got past the outer muscle.

"Shhh," Dom whispered as he lowered his weight down over Logan's back, the heat from his warm body seeping into Logan. The fingers had stopped moving, but Logan felt full…too full. He was about to tell Dom he couldn't do this when Dom suddenly curled his fingers and hit something inside of Logan that had him seeing stars.

"Oh God!"

He felt Dom trailing kisses along his back as he did the move again, then again. Within seconds, Logan was pushing back on those amazing fingers as little firecrackers of delight began to pop under his skin. Dom leaned back and Logan felt more lube dribble onto his hole. Dom twisted his fingers inside of Logan and then pushed a third finger in. Logan bit into the sheets at the stinging that accompanied it, but another stroke of his prostate had the pain fading into the background. He felt hot all over and sweat trickled down his forehead as his body worked to accept Dom's invasion. He heard what sounded like the condom being opened and if he hadn't been too overwhelmed with the sensation of it all, he would have been impressed that Dom could keep him impaled with one hand while he got himself ready with the other.

When the fingers were gently pulled from his body, Logan tried to push back to maintain the connection. But as the last one left his body with a slight tug, he felt incredibly empty and nearly sobbed at the loss.

"Shhh, it's okay, baby," Dom whispered as he leaned over him and ran his tongue along the outer shell of his ear. "I'm going to make it feel so good," he promised before leaning back. Logan nodded and then braced himself when he felt the head of Dom's cock touch his entrance.

Dom watched as the tip of his cock disappeared into Logan's body and the heat that welcomed it was overwhelming. It took everything in him not to thrust forward and claim Logan the way he wanted. His body shook with lust as Logan lay folded over on the bed in complete submission. He'd felt the tension reappear the second his cock had touched Logan's opening, but Logan hadn't tried to draw away or ask him to stop. The trust was humbling and it was the only thing that kept him from forcing his way past the tight muscle that was trying to deny his entry. Instead of pushing his hips forward, Dom let his big hands explore Logan's back and sides, his fingers dipping and following every muscle. He felt Logan shiver beneath him and then the man was pushing back on him. That muscle was still fighting him though, so Dom put his hands on Logan's hips, then pushed hard enough to get past it.

Logan's cry of pain had him stopping and he said, "That's it baby, it'll be easier now."

Logan was panting so hard he couldn't speak, but Dom saw his hand reach behind him and seek out Dom's thigh. The grip on his cock was almost painful, but the touch on his thigh tore something open inside of him. If there was any hope that he'd be able to walk away from this and just consider it another sex act, it was obliterated with that brief contact – that signal that Logan still wanted him there, trusted him, needed him. The only thing that could make this better would be if he could take Logan from the front so he could see those hauntingly beautiful eyes glaze over with newfound passion.

Dom clasped the hand on his thigh, then leaned over Logan and whispered, "I'm going to fuck you so good, Logan." He was rewarded with a moan and then felt Logan's body accept him deeper inside. "Suck me in," he ordered as he leaned down to lick his way up Logan's spine. Another grunt and half his cock was buried. He released Logan's hand and searched out the other man's cock which had initially gone soft at his entry, but was now quickly coming back to life. He began stroking it slowly.

Taking his left hand from where it had been gripping Logan's hip, he reached up and grabbed Logan by the hair, forcing his head back, making sure it stung just a little bit. "The pleasure burns the pain away," he murmured before he reached down and kissed Logan. It was carnal and rough and Logan seemed to revel in it because he fought Dom for control even as his lower half gave up the fight and let Dom sink the rest of the way in. Both men groaned and Dom gave Logan one last kiss before rearing back and slowly pulling his cock out of Logan carefully before thrusting back in. He still had a hold of Logan's hair with one hand, his cock with the other and the knowledge that he now controlled the man in every way had him increasing the pace of his thrusts. Logan grunted at the rough treatment, but the fact that he pushed back against Dom on every upstroke reassured Dom that the other man was enjoying the domination.

"Harder," Logan moaned and Dom accommodated him by releasing his hair and pushing Logan's shoulders down so his chest met the bed. He held him there like that as he began pounding into him and his hand increased its stroking of Logan's erection. Electricity fired through his veins as his pleasure ratcheted up with each plunge and when Logan's inner muscles clamped down on him, Dom shouted hoarsely. His control was completely shattered as he leaned over Logan, uncaring of the weight he was forcing on the man, and rammed him into the mattress. Logan must have locked his knees because he was able to keep enough clearance between his hips and the bed for Dom to keep working his cock.

Dom's balls slapped against Logan's skin over and over and then drew up tight as he felt his impending orgasm. He shifted just enough so that his cock struck Logan's prostate and within seconds Logan was screaming his name as his hot release shot onto the bed below and dripped down Dom's hand. Logan's ass tightened around Dom and he bit down on Logan's shoulder to stifle his shout as his orgasm claimed him. He shot into the condom over and over as the pleasure flooded his system and it was several long minutes before he recovered enough to realize Logan now carried his entire weight.

The young man was completely silent beneath him, save for the ragged breathing. His cheek was pressed against the bed, his eyes closed as he lay limply under Dom. There were red marks on his shoulder where Dom had clamped down with his teeth. Jesus, he'd never lost control to the point that he'd marked another person. Or nearly so, since he hadn't actually broken the skin. He soothed the small marks with his tongue and felt Logan tighten around his dick again at the contact. At some point their hands had intertwined. Dom shifted with the intent of getting his weight off Logan, but the man tightened his grip on Dom's hand and said, "Not yet."

Dom returned to his position, but shifted enough so that his own elbows could support some of his weight. He put his nose against the back of Logan's neck and inhaled the sweet, musky scent of man and sex, then ran his tongue along the soft skin. They lay like that for a few more minutes as Dom laved attention on the few areas he could reach with his mouth, then he forced himself to lift off Logan. He gripped the edge of the condom and carefully pulled free of Logan's body. Standing, he removed the condom and tossed it into the trash by the bed, then went to the bathroom and got a washcloth. Logan was still in the same position so Dom cleaned him up before gently rolling him over so he could do his front. It was then that he noticed that Logan had drifted off to sleep.

Dom went to the other side of the bed to pull the covers off, then went about working Logan's body underneath the blanket. He covered him and went to the bathroom to clean himself off. He grabbed his phone and sent a quick text to the concierge at the apartment asking him to walk his dog, then, before he could think better of what he was doing, he crawled into the bed next to Logan and curled up against him. Emotions were running through him at a hundred miles per hour, but luckily his body was too drained to deal with them and he was out within minutes.

∽

Logan knew he was alone when he woke up, but the tingling in his ass was an instant reminder of the night before. Flopping onto his back, Logan stared at the ceiling as images, sounds and scents went through his head. Dom's commanding voice and dirty words, his gentle petting as Logan had been coming down from an orgasm that had taken away even his ability to move, the sound of Dom's flesh slapping against his as his thick cock burned Logan from the inside out. He wouldn't lie – it had hurt like a son of a bitch at first and he'd been sure it would be over before it had even really started, but then Dom had stroked his back, caressed his sides and he'd focused on that instead of the pain. And when Dom had pushed past that final barrier of his body, Logan had felt like he was being ripped apart. But that rough voice in his ear calling him "baby" for the second time had taken the sting away and left him with the overwhelming feeling of being filled so full after being empty for so long. That emotion had had him reaching out to Dom so he could hold onto the connection for as long as possible. Pinned to the bed like he'd been, there hadn't been much he could reach, but Dom's thick, muscled thigh had been his anchor when he'd needed it.

And then the man had worked him over until everything but the need for release had disappeared. He'd loved the way Dom had mixed pain with pleasure and those crude words had made his body seek more of Dom out. By the end, he'd had no control whatsoever as Dom had pounded him into the mattress – it had been rough, almost animalistic – and he'd loved every moment of it. And those teeth sinking into his skin had made the aftershocks of his orgasm feel like rockets going off in his head.

He reached over his shoulder to touch the abrasions he knew were there, then in a curious need, he climbed out of bed and walked naked to the bathroom and turned his back to the mirror so he could see what they looked like. Small, red marks in the shape of twin, mirror-opposite arches. Dom hadn't broken the skin though, and Logan was almost disappointed that there wouldn't be a scar. As he started to turn, Logan noticed bruising on his hips, then smiled when he realized what they were.

"Sorry about those," he heard Dom say from the bathroom door where the man was leaning, fully dressed. Except he didn't look sorry at all, and his hungry eyes traveled up and down Logan's body. His traitorous cock hardened and before he could even say anything, Dom was on him, his mouth stealing any protest he might have made. Which he wouldn't have. That sinful tongue swept into his mouth and he felt the hard sink bite into his lower back as Dom pressed against him. Greedy hands explored him, then settled on his cock. Logan reached for Dom's shirt, but Dom grabbed his hand and forced it behind his back. "I have to get to work," he muttered. "I left some breakfast for you on the stove," he said as he licked over Logan's lips. But instead of leaving, Dom dropped to his knees and sucked Logan's cock into his sleek mouth.

Logan reached behind him to grab the edge of the sink with his hands as Dom wasted no time and started sucking him hard and deep. The man truly must be in a hurry because he had Logan coming within a minute and he swallowed every drop of his release before he stood and kissed Logan again, the taste of his own come exploding on his tongue. "Mmmm, breakfast of champions," Dom said as he kissed Logan one last time, brushed his fingers over the bruises on his hips, and then left the bathroom. An instant later the front door closed. Logan slumped against the sink, then finally sank to the floor – his body too weak to support him anymore. A smile passed over his lips as his own flavor, along with Dom's, lingered there.

~

"Not a word," Dom said as he neared his car and saw Cade leaning against it, a satisfied smirk on his face. "I'll find someone to relieve you once I get to the office," Dom said.

"Thought I was reassigned," Cade drawled.

Dom bit back a smile and searched his pockets for his keys. "Just keep your eyes off his ass."

Cade laughed, then sobered. "I've got someone in mind to relieve me. He's a good guy...could use the work."

Dom studied him for a moment, then nodded. "Fine. Have him contact Cecile to get set up."

"Just like that?" Cade asked, almost suspicious.

"Yeah, just like that." Dom got in his car and drove off, another smile ghosting his lips as he watched Cade standing where he'd left him. He saw his own reflection in the rearview mirror and was surprised how much lighter he looked. And the smile that lingered looked foreign. He tried to force it away, but the taste of Logan that loitered in his mouth had him remembering the moans and gasps that had come from the young man as Dom had sucked him off in that tiny bathroom. When he'd first seen the bruises on Logan's skin, he'd been horrified by his own aggressiveness, but then the look of wonder in Logan's eyes as he'd fingered the marks had made Dom instantly hard and unashamedly proud that he'd left something of himself that Logan would see and feel for days to come. Rushing through the blowjob had been a necessity, since he knew if he lingered in bringing Logan his pleasure, he'd have had him bent over that sink in no time, sore ass be damned.

That image had him smiling again and before he could think better of it, he picked up his phone and dialed.

"Hi," Logan said softly. Dom couldn't help but be thrilled at the notion that Logan had put his number in his phone and recognized the Caller ID. Even better, whatever awkwardness was bound to be between them hadn't stopped Logan from answering.

"Have lunch with me today," Dom said.

A long beat of silence, then a simple, "Okay."

"Do you know where my restaurant is?" he asked.

"Yes."

"Noon work for you?"

"I'll be there."

"Bye Logan."

"Bye Dom."

Dom disconnected and smiled again, then forced his attention to the thickening traffic as he headed for his office.

CHAPTER 8

Logan knocked on the door and waited. Cade was standing at the end of the alley, his eyes darting around as he kept vigilant watch. Logan had been surprised to see the man waiting outside his apartment. He'd worried there would be some awkwardness between them, not only because of their own near intimate encounter, but because he knew Cade was aware of what he'd done with Dom last night. He'd been drawn to his window as he'd gotten ready for bed by the shouting between the two men. There'd been no doubt in his mind that he'd been the cause and when he'd seen Dom looking up at him through the window, the hunger in his eyes mirroring his own, Logan had gone to the front door to open it. Having Dom come to him had been a foregone conclusion; it had been what he'd expected and needed Dom to do. Dom's cruel tirade may as well have left welts on his body, but hadn't changed his need for the man. One hard fuck. That was all he'd needed to get the other man out of his system and then things would go back to normal.

Well, he'd gotten the hard fuck he'd wanted, but life would never be normal again...at least not the version of normal that had been driving him his whole life. The question was, could he build a new normal for himself – one that included Dom? Or was what was happening between them some freak chemistry thing? In reality, he knew next to nothing about the man. So when he'd gotten the invitation to lunch, it had been easy to accept. And when he'd told Cade where he was going, the man had nodded and then opened the door to his own car. If the other man resented him in any way, he was damn good at hiding it.

The door opened and he felt a smile tug at his lips at the sight of Dom. "Hey," he said as Dom motioned him inside and then sent Cade a wave.

Once he was in and Dom had closed the door, they were all over each other, both struggling to control the kiss that flared to life between them. Dom finally forced them to separate when he muttered, "Shit, my garlic!"

Logan laughed at the strange comment, then followed Dom to the kitchen where the man was trying to save a pan of something that was sizzling on the gas stove. Logan had worked in professional kitchens before, but Dom's was clearly top of the line. *Barretti's* was a high-class place and reservations were often hard to come by, at least for the prime dining times.

"Where is everybody?" Logan asked as he looked around the empty kitchen. Stainless steel gleamed everywhere and not a speck of dust or stray food lingered on any surface. Every dish, pot and pan was in its proper place. Logan sat on a stool near the island, his eyes enjoying the view of Dom's ass as he worked with whatever he was cooking.

"We're closed on Mondays. Gives us a chance to restock inventory, plan the menus, stuff like that. I asked the staff to come in a bit later today so we could be alone."

Logan felt a pang of disappointment go through him at Dom's words.

"Don't do that," Dom whispered and Logan raised his gaze to see Dom watching him intently.

"What?" he asked, trying to be nonchalant.

Dom sighed and then turned the stove off. He wiped his hands on a dishtowel, then closed the distance between them.

"You're thinking I don't want people to see us together." Logan dropped his eyes and studied his hands. He felt Dom's hand stroke his hair. "I didn't mean those awful things I said to you last night," Dom said quietly.

"Then why did you say them?" Logan heard himself ask, even though he'd intended to keep his mouth shut.

"Because I'm an asshole and seeing you kiss Cade did something to me," Dom said as he stepped back and ran his hand along his head. "I wanted to hurt you back."

It was a tough admission to hear and probably harder for Dom to say. But Logan got it – if the situation had been reversed, who knows how he would have reacted to seeing Dom with someone else. "He kissed me, but I let him. I wanted to know if it was just you." His eyes lifted to meet Dom's. "It *is* just you."

Dom seemed to tense at his honesty, then stepped between Logan's legs. "I wanted it to be just us today because I didn't think you'd be comfortable being with me around other people." Dom leaned down, his lips hovering over Logan's. "And I knew I wouldn't be able to keep from doing this," he whispered as he brushed a soft kiss on Logan's mouth.

Logan wanted more, but Dom stepped back, his fingers grasping Logan's neck, forcing him to tip his head back so he could look Dom in the eye. "I'm not ashamed of you. I don't think you're a whore and I don't care what you had to do in the past to protect your sister. And I will be forever grateful for what you gave me last night, no matter what happens between us."

Logan nodded and saw some of the tension drain from Dom's body.

"Okay," Dom said as he turned back to the stove and started working on the food again.

"How long have you had this place?" Logan asked.

"Sylvie and I opened it about ten years ago," he began, his voice catching slightly on Sylvie's name. "But it really didn't take off until about five years ago and since then it's been tough to give it as much attention as I would like."

"It's a strange mix – restaurant and security firm."

Dom nodded. "The security firm came first. Sylvie thought the restaurant might be a good hobby," Dom said, laughing. The sound sent a wave of warmth through Logan. "Neither of us had any idea how much work went into starting up a restaurant. She ended up taking on most of the responsibility," he said, a hint of sadness dulling his voice.

"Why security?" Logan asked as he watched Dom add some pasta to water.

Dom stirred, then lowered the flame on whatever he was sautéing in the pan. He turned to face Logan. "It kind of became a family business," he began.

"With your brothers?"

Dom nodded. "Vin and I started the business after I got out of college and he was discharged during his second tour in the Middle East." Dom sighed. "We have two younger brothers that we had to look out for after our parents died so I think it just became second nature to go into a business where our protective nature would work for us."

Logan wanted to ask the obvious question about Dom's parents, but didn't. He felt like it was too personal – like they weren't there yet. But Dom took away the issue by saying, "Our father killed our mother, then took his own life."

"Dom," Logan said on a gasp, then shook his head as the rest of the words escaped him.

"Vin was eighteen, I was fifteen. Our brothers were just ten and seven. Vin was old enough to get custody, but we struggled to keep our family together."

Logan was stunned into silence. He never would have guessed that he and Dom shared such a similar past.

"I joined ROTC so I could get enough money to put myself through school. I was in my senior year when the towers were attacked and my unit was deployed to Iraq. My specialty was computers – it was what I was studying in college so they had me working in intelligence. Our younger brother, Ren, had just turned eighteen. He joined the army the day after his birthday and eventually made it to Special Forces."

Dom reached behind him to stir the pasta, then turned his attention back to Logan. "Vin joined the military too, but he ended up becoming a SEAL. He was honorably discharged after he got shot four years later. The bullet caused a lot of damage to his left arm – not enough that he can't use it, but enough to end his career." Dom increased the burner under the skillet and started putting together some type of cream sauce. Logan was glad that he kept talking while he did it.

"I was only in for a couple of years. I came back here and finished school. I decided to get my master's degree and that's when I met Sylvie. She was a freshman and I was twenty-four." Dom laughed. "I met her at a party and immediately dismissed her because she was way too young for me. But she wasn't having that and we've been together ever since." Dom stopped what he was doing when he realized his use of the present tense and Logan froze. He watched Dom take a few deep breaths, then visibly relax as he reached for the pasta to drain it.

Several minutes passed as Logan watched Dom prepare the dishes and then the man was sliding a huge plate of Fettuccine Alfredo in front of him, the scent making his mouth water. "My mother's recipe," Dom said as he sat down next to Logan and handed him a fork. The pasta melted in his mouth and he groaned as he licked his lips to collect some of the sauce that clung there. His breath caught when he saw Dom staring at his mouth. Lust flared in Logan at the other man's hungry gaze and he considered pushing the food aside and eating Dom's mouth instead.

"What about your other brother?" Logan forced himself to ask. The spell was broken and he saw sadness pass through Dom.

"Rafe," he whispered as he poked at the food in front of him, but didn't eat any. "He was only seven when we lost our parents. We lost custody of him just after he turned eight."

"Did the state take him?" Logan asked softly, remembering his own fears of losing Savannah to the system when his parents had been killed.

Dom shook his head, then put the fork down. "The reason our father killed our mother was because he found out that she'd been cheating on him and that Rafe wasn't his. When she finally admitted it, he stabbed her to death, then shot himself with the gun he kept in the house for protection. Rafe saw and heard the whole thing."

"Jesus," Logan said.

"Rafe's real father showed up one day with a court order. All it took was a cheek swab and Rafe was gone. We went to lawyer after lawyer, but none of them would help us. We don't even know where his father took him. He kept begging me and Vinny not to let them take him," Dom said as he choked back a sob.

Logan stood and pulled Dom against him, the other man's head pressed against his stomach. "I'm sorry Dom," he whispered as he bent down to kiss Dom's head.

"I can't find him," Dom managed to say. "I've been searching for almost fifteen years, but I can't find him. Ren's gone too – his unit was ambushed last year just outside Kabul. Vin's convinced he's alive and goes back there every time there's a new lead, but I just don't know anymore. We were supposed to protect them both…"

"Shhh," Logan said as he bent over Dom. There was no point in trying to come up with some set of words that would take the pain away, so he just held Dom until he quieted. He hadn't meant for their conversation to get so heavy, but he was glad that Dom felt comfortable enough to share his past with him.

"I know what it feels like – that sense that you failed someone," he admitted. Dom sat back and Logan reached for his stool and dragged it closer.

"You didn't fail your sister," Dom said as he used his arms to wipe at his damp face.

"We both know that's not true," Logan said. "Even if I couldn't have prevented the rape, I should have seen what was happening afterwards. I know why she didn't tell me, but in my gut, I knew something was off. I just thought it was related to losing our parents."

"I guess it's easier to blame ourselves then it is to forgive our mistakes," Dom said.

Logan smiled at that. Everyone always told him it wasn't his fault – excused him. This man was accepting that Logan couldn't just let himself off the hook and he loved that.

"Thank you," he found himself saying as he brushed a kiss over Dom's lips. He pulled back, then handed Dom his fork before pulling his own food closer and digging in.

"You're a fucking genius with food, Dom," Logan managed to say around the pasta he crammed into his mouth. Dom laughed, then followed suit.

"What is with you?" Gabe said as he bit into his burger.

"What?" Logan asked as he glanced at his watch again.

"You can't sit still for even a second," Gabe mused. "You haven't even touched your food," he commented.

"Who hasn't touched their food?" came Nell's voice from somewhere behind him. Logan snagged up a fry and shoved it into his mouth. If the diner's owner caught him just picking at the food her big bear of a husband, Pete, had prepared, Logan would never hear the end of it. Nell came to a stop at their booth and studied both his and Gabe's plates intently.

"Got any of the blueberry pie today?" Logan asked in an attempt to divert her attention. The bulky woman smoothed back a stray gray hair, her features drawn tight as she looked between him and Gabe. She finally smiled and said, "You know I do, darlin.'" She looked at Logan's plate expectantly and Logan grabbed the tuna melt sitting in front of him and took a huge bite.

"Be right back with your pie," she said happily.

"Me too," Gabe called out. Nell gave him an impatient look as she turned and headed for the dessert carousel at the end of the counter. The old-fashioned diner was as busy as ever, but it shouldn't have surprised him that Nell was always nearby, her sharp ears focused on her favorite customers. He, Gabe and Shane had been coming to this place since they'd discovered it in school and Nell and her tattooed, food-loving chef husband had taken them all under their wings.

"Bastard," Logan muttered at Gabe when the man smirked at him.

"Seriously, how are you holding up?" Gabe asked, all humor gone now.

"It's easier knowing Savannah is safe. All this time we thought he was gone – he could have gotten to her so easily."

"Have you talked to her?"

Logan nodded. "She's spending a lot of time with Shane's mom. Dom has an office out there so Shane's been doing some work here and there as he learns the business. It sounds like his relationship with his parents has improved a lot," he mused.

Gabe chuckled. "His dad actually called me last week. Invited me and Riley to come stay with them for Christmas."

Nell interrupted them with their pies and a fond look at them both before she meandered off again.

"I was worried about you there for a while," Gabe said as he ignored his lunch and started inhaling the French Silk pie Nell had placed in front of him.

"What do you mean?"

"You've been so withdrawn since the shooting. I mean, we expected it would be a long road to recovery, but it was like you'd given up or something. You were like a fucking zombie at Thanksgiving."

Logan dropped his eyes. So much for his acting skills. Apparently, everyone had seen through him anyway.

"And you haven't done anything with the bar since the fire. You worked so hard for that place and now it's like you don't care what happens to it."

Logan shrugged, then forced a couple more bites of his sandwich down. He glanced at his watch again.

"What the hell is with you and that watch? You said you didn't have to work again till this weekend," Gabe said in frustration.

Logan drummed his fingers on the table in agitation, then blurted out, "I'm meeting someone this afternoon."

"Okay. And?" Gabe asked, Logan's explanation clearly not enough.

He wasn't about to tell Gabe that in a few short hours he'd hopefully have Dom's dick deep inside him, so he hedged and changed the subject.

"I'm thinking about selling the bar."

It was enough to get Gabe to stop shoveling pie into his mouth. He leaned back in the booth.

"Why?" he asked, his tone even, non-judgmental.

"All I see is him and me working there, talking strategy, business. The way he encouraged me, supported me. But I can hear her screaming," he whispered. "I can hear Savannah screaming in the background and she's begging me to help her, but it's like I'm watching myself. I see myself standing there talking to Sam while she's calling my name. I can't warn myself about Sam. I can't help her. I can't do a fucking thing," he admitted. "I hate everything about that place now. It took everything from me, from her."

Gabe sat silently, his dark eyes sharp and probing.

"Shane says I shouldn't let Sam take anything else, but the truth is I lost that bar the moment he came into our lives. I put Savannah in his sights. She chose to hurt herself to deal with her pain rather than risk me losing that place. I wish it had burned to the ground," he said with more venom then he'd intended. He pushed the food away and fumbled to pull his wallet from his pants. He felt raw and vulnerable admitting the ugly truth to his friend and he just wanted to get the hell out of there.

"You didn't let me finish," Gabe said.

Logan looked at the nearly empty plates in front of Gabe. "Then finish. Or order something else," he muttered as he pulled some money from his wallet.

"You didn't let me finish what I was saying about you."

Logan stilled, then remembered Gabe's comments about him being a zombie at their last family get together.

"Finish," Logan said.

"You look lighter today, happy. You smile when you check your watch and I've seen you check your phone a couple of times too." Gabe leaned forward, his voice dropping slightly. "Is it because of this 'someone' you're meeting?"

Logan scrubbed a hand through his hair and nodded. Why was this so fucking hard?

"You don't owe me anything, Logan. I just like seeing you this way. It's been too long."

"I don't know how to tell if it's just a physical thing or something more," Logan finally said. "I thought if I acted on it, I would have my answer, but I don't."

"Yeah, our heads have a way of fucking things up, don't they?" Gabe said as he began picking at Logan's pie. The man ate like a horse, but had the physique of a heavyweight boxer. "Maybe you don't need to figure it out right away."

"Maybe," Logan mused and then glanced at his watch again.

"Go," Gabe said as he stuffed the last bite of Logan's pie into his mouth. "And tell Dom I said hi."

～

Dom watched Logan get off the elevator and walk towards him. When the Concierge had buzzed him to let him know that Logan had arrived, Dom could have easily just unlocked the door and opened it a crack so Logan could let himself in. It probably would have looked a lot less desperate. But instead, there he stood, a grown man with a sizeable bank account, hundreds of employees, three homes, two jets at his disposal and an investment portfolio that would make most people drool – but what had he been reduced to? Standing at the door like a little girl waiting for her first date. It had been less than twenty-four hours since he'd seen the other man and yet he was overwhelmed with insecurity and nerves. He knew Logan was still on shaky ground regarding their relationship and that every time the young man walked away from him, it could be for the last time. It was something he knew he had to accept, but doing so was proving to be harder than he thought.

Logan flashed a smile at Dom which had his insides doing cartwheels and then the man was pressing him back into the doorframe, his expert lips stealing Dom's breath. He opened automatically for Logan and settled his hands on the other man's hips as his mouth was taken over.

"I need to be inside you again," Logan whispered against his lips before he flicked out his tongue to trace their outline. "I want you to fuck me till you come, then I'm going to fuck you so hard that you come again."

Dom couldn't speak, so he just nodded. Logan grabbed his hand and led him into the apartment. Baby was there to greet him and Logan gave him a quick pat as Dom slammed the door shut.

"Where's your room?" Logan asked, his voice firm, dominant. Dom's dick twitched at the commanding tone and he pointed down the hallway to their left.

"First door on the left," he managed to say. Logan rewarded him with another kiss before pulling him in that direction. But when they got to the room, Dom skittered to a stop, his eyes on the king-sized bed in front of him. His bed. His and Sylvie's.

Logan seemed to sense his hesitation. "Do you have a guest room?" he asked gently as he started to pull Dom back out of the room. Dom took a deep breath and held his ground.

"It's okay," he said as he lost a little bit more of himself to Logan. He tugged Logan into the room. The other man studied him for a moment as if considering if he was telling the truth, then nodded and kissed him.

Logan made quick work of their clothes, his mouth leaving Dom's only long enough to get them both naked. Then things slowed dramatically as Logan examined Dom's body, his long fingers drifting all over him. It was sensual torture and by the time Logan had finished his exploration, Dom's cock was aching.

"Lie back on the bed," Logan ordered.

Dom did as he was told, his body on fire. Logan climbed up next to him, but settled closer towards his feet and then just watched him some more. His perusal was like a physical stroke and Dom found himself touching the places Logan's eyes lingered – his chest, his abdomen, his thighs. But when he reached for his cock, Logan said "No." His fingers hovered just above the head of his dick as his eyes clashed with Logan's. Dom had nearly always been in control in the bedroom, so giving it up was hard…and a big turn on. He pulled his hand back and settled it on his chest as he watched Logan smile in satisfaction.

"Do you know how perfect you are?" Logan asked as he finally shifted so he could lean over Dom and kiss him. They were soft, gentle kisses that had Dom begging for more. But Logan was on a mission and his tongue tormented Dom as it licked and sucked its way down his body. But it bypassed the part that needed his attention the most. More kisses all the way down to his feet before Logan returned to his side.

Anticipation went through him at what would happen next. Logan shifted, then did something Dom hadn't expected. He straddled Dom, but did it in reverse so that Logan was facing Dom's feet. The position had their cocks touching and Logan rubbed them back and forth against one another. Dom groaned and closed his eyes. Logan shifted his body back towards the headboard and Dom immediately missed the feeling of their dicks mashed together.

And then that tongue was back, stroking his length tentatively. Dom shuddered at the contact, but remained still. Logan took his time tasting every ridge and vein before he sucked the crown into his mouth.

"Shit!" Dom cried out as his back arched. Logan seemed to be ready for him though, and he grabbed Dom's base to keep him from pushing further in. He felt Logan's thighs on each side of him and it was a reminder of Logan's position. When he opened his eyes, he groaned at the sight of Logan's ass nearly in his face. He immediately sought out Logan's hole with saliva coated fingers. Logan's attention on his cock faltered for just a moment, then he was hungrily sucking Dom in as far as he could. Logan's cock brushed Dom's chest as he began humping against him and pre-come leaked onto his skin. Dom worked his finger farther in and matched the rhythm Logan was setting.

"Oh, God," Logan muttered as he released Dom. "Get me ready," he said as he looked over his shoulder. Dom fumbled in the nightstand for the lube he'd been smart enough to buy earlier today and praised his good sense to have removed all the protective wrapping before he'd stashed it in the drawer. He placed a generous amount of the cool liquid on his finger, then used one of his hands to open Logan's ass. His tongue ached to flick the tiny opening, but Logan's mouth was back on his cock and he knew he'd never last long enough, so he focused on slicking up the hole instead, his finger pushing easily past the resisting muscle. Logan moaned, but kept up his pace of sucking and stroking. Dom added another finger and found that spongy spot that he knew would drive Logan wild. And it did. The man pulled off his cock and cried out as a tremor went through him. He quickly pulled off Dom's fingers and turned around, smashing his lips down on Dom's.

As Logan's tongue dueled with his, Dom fumbled for a condom in the drawer. He snagged one, but before he could open it, Logan was grabbing his hand to stop him.

"I want you inside me. Just you," he said.

The thought of being bare inside Logan nearly had him coming on the spot. He managed to nod and say, "I got tested last week. I'm negative," before Logan was kissing him again and rubbing their cocks together once more. Logan drew back before snatching the bottle of lube from the bed where Dom had dropped it and worked some down the length of Dom's dick.

He tossed the bottle aside and moved forward. He reached behind him and pulled Dom's nearly purple cock away from his stomach. Logan rose up on his knees and fumbled to get Dom's cock in the right position, then began lowering himself. Dom nearly snarled at the sight of Logan with his head thrown back in passion as he worked himself down onto Dom's thick length. It was tight and slow-going and it took everything in Dom's power not to thrust up into the other man. He saw Logan wince as Dom finally breached him and then Logan sighed as he sank all the way down until his ass brushed Dom's thighs.

Logan hung there for a moment, his head still bent back and then his bright eyes met Dom's and he smiled. Dom shuddered at how young and beautiful he looked and he couldn't help but reach out and rub his palms on Logan's thighs. The hair was rough under his hands and he felt Logan's muscles flex as he began lifting and lowering himself on Dom in small increments.

Without a latex barrier, Dom could feel everything and the heat was like a furnace. When Logan began tightening his muscles on Dom as he pulled up, Dom quickly sat up and wrapped an arm around Logan's waist. No longer able to remain passive, he thrust up to meet Logan as his body dropped down. Logan groaned and increased his pace as his mouth sought out Dom's. They kissed desperately as their moves became more frantic. Dom reached for Logan's cock, but Logan grabbed him. "No, I need to be inside you when I come," he managed to get out between harsh pants.

Dom nodded and wrapped his other arm around Logan and soon they were pressed against each other everywhere. Logan wrapped his arms around Dom's neck and slid his palms down Dom's back, the tips of his fingers biting into his too tight skin. Logan's heartbeat was pounding against Dom's ear where he was pressed up against Logan's chest. Dom tried to hold on, to drag the contact out as long as possible, but then his hole fluttered as he remembered that Logan would be inside him soon and he came just like that, his semen flooding Logan's smooth, inner walls.

"Logan!" he shouted against Logan's damp, warm skin. His orgasm continued as spurt after spurt of come left him and burned them both. Sparks shot through him as the pleasure flooded his system and it took several long seconds before the tension began to drain from him and the warmth bathed every nerve and cell inside him. As he fell back on the bed, Logan following him down, he felt like he was floating. Soft kisses bathed his face and neck and he nearly cried out at the loss when Logan pulled himself off Dom's cock. He looked up and caught his breath at the sight of his come leaking from Logan's ass.

"Jesus," Dom said as he pulled Logan down and rolled him over, mindful of the raging hard-on that Logan had managed to maintain. Dom reached between their bodies and rubbed his fingers in his own come that was slipping from Logan's body, then brushed the sticky substance on Logan's mouth. "Beautiful," he muttered before he kissed him again. Logan began to squirm as he rubbed his hard dick against Dom's abdomen. Lust sparked through Dom again and he rolled them back so Logan was on top of him once more. "Fuck me, Logan. Fill me up," he said.

Logan's eyes darkened with need and he grabbed the lube. "I can't go slow," he said, his voice shaking.

"Then don't," Dom responded. Seconds later he was moaning as Logan's fingers breached him. He pulled his legs higher to give Logan better access and sighed as his hole collapsed and Logan's fingers sank deep inside of him. The burn was intense and when Logan added a third finger, he nearly cried out at how good it felt. He used his arms to draw his legs further apart and back and then looked down to watch Logan working him. Each pull on his body had him trying to follow, but Logan was holding him in place, controlling the rhythm. His cock started to harden again and he watched as Logan leaned down and licked the length, his saliva coating the flesh with glistening moisture.

"Please," he heard himself saying and then Logan was sucking him in as his fingers increased their tempo. Suddenly Logan hit his sweet spot and Dom cried out, releasing his hold on his legs as his back arched and he slammed his dick down Logan's throat. The other man gagged, but didn't let up on his sucking. Another strike on his prostate had him grabbing Logan's hair to try to keep him there. Logan gave him another few seconds of ecstasy, then grabbed Dom's wrist, forcing him to release his hold. He pulled his fingers free, but before Dom could protest, that long cock was pushing into him. He wasn't even sure at what point Logan had lubed up his length, but it didn't matter because it took only three hard thrusts for Logan to be completely seated inside him.

Logan reared back and thrust inside him again, then used his arms to press Dom's legs back onto himself. The position made his muscles burn in protest, but the angle had Logan going deeper as he rammed into Dom mercilessly. Sweat dripped off Logan's forehead as he lunged in and out like a mad man and Dom had to put his hands above his head to keep himself from slamming up against the headboard. Each powerful thrust had Dom's whole body rocking up and Logan grunted as he grabbed Dom's shoulders to hold him in place. There was nothing sweet or gentle about what was happening – it was pure, raw fucking and Dom felt tears sting his eyes at how good it felt.

Logan shifted again in a way that had him hitting Dom's prostate and it took only a few more seconds before come shot out of his dick and all over his chest and abdomen. Logan didn't even have to touch him this time. Logan continued to saw in and out of him for several long, torturous seconds, then he shouted as he shoved in as deep as he could one more time and hung there, his fingers biting into Dom's shoulders. Heat flooded his passage and set off another mini-orgasm which had Logan moaning as he pulled back slowly and thrust back in, drawing out the sensation.

It could have been minutes or hours that passed before Logan pulled free of him. He felt the quickly cooling come drip from his ass, but he didn't care. Logan didn't seem to either because he dropped down on Dom's chest, ignoring the sticky residue there. There was no kissing or talking – just labored breathing. Dom was stuck somewhere between the realization that it was the best sex he'd ever had with anyone and that he was quickly falling in love with the man on top of him. Dom waited for that stinging reminder that he was betraying his wife, but it didn't come. She'd want this for him – he knew it in his gut. He felt Logan sigh against him as he started to drift off and Dom smiled, then wrapped his arm around the other man in case he got any bright ideas about trying to escape.

*L*ogan knew he needed to turn off the water and get out of the shower – not because he'd soon be out of water because he guessed that in a place as nice as Dom's, something like running out of hot water just wasn't an issue. No, he needed to get out because his skin was starting to prune and he'd already caught himself nodding off. He was sitting on the built-in bench in the massive shower, numerous shower heads pelting him from all angles. He'd been there since Dom had bent him over the bench, rimmed him till he'd been sobbing and begging for relief and then slammed into him from behind. He wasn't sure what it said about him that he'd loved the burn of that slick cock sliding home in one powerful thrust. And he'd tried to pretend that he hadn't begged Dom over and over to grant him his release as the big man had held him down and tortured him with slow, shallow strokes.

That heavy, smoky voice had said filthy things to him and long, hard fingers had gripped him by the hair till it hurt. And not once had Dom needed to touch Logan's cock. He'd added to his torture by not letting Logan touch himself either. In the end, he'd come only when Dom had ordered him to and then Dom had kissed the shit out of him and said he was going to make breakfast. Standing hadn't been an option after that, but sitting on his stinging ass wasn't feeling great either – he wondered if he'd find relief if he had one of those blow-up rings to sit on. But what frightened him more than anything was that he wanted it again already. His body ached from the aftermath of sex, but it still wanted more. And he wanted more of last night too – the stuff that had happened after the mind-blowing orgasm that had left him unable to do even the basic things like climb off Dom's body after he'd collapsed.

At some point, he'd ended up curled against Dom, his head using Dom's chest as a pillow. Two steel bands had been wrapped around him and Dom's even breathing had ruffled Logan's hair. Sometime in the middle of the night, he'd awoken to gentle kisses along his neck and back. It had been like he was being worshipped and when Dom had rolled him onto his back and pushed inside him, it had felt like he was home. The lovemaking had been just that...making love. There'd been no rush, no desperation. Just a slow, steady burn that Dom had stoked with probing kisses and encouraging words. And when he'd gone over the edge, Dom had been right beside him.

Whatever illusion he'd had that he could get past his craving for Dom was gone – completely and totally blown apart. The man gave and took in equal measure. When he'd arrived the night before, Dom had given him complete and utter control, something he knew hadn't been easy for someone so naturally assertive. And then he'd cherished him in a way Logan hadn't known he needed. And a few short minutes ago, he'd changed things again by making sex raw and dirty and fun. It just couldn't get better than this, he thought to himself as he forced himself to get up and turn the shower off.

He toweled off and then went back to the bedroom to find his jeans, finally locating them on a floral chaise in the corner of the room. The feminine piece of furniture was a stark reminder of where he was and the circumstances that had brought him here. He brushed the darkness that sifted through him away and yanked up his jeans, forgoing his search for wherever the hell is underwear had ended up. He could smell something cooking in the kitchen and his growling stomach didn't give a shit what Dom was throwing together.

As he neared the kitchen, he slowed at the sound of an unfamiliar voice. Cade had followed him last night, but he figured the man would have taken off for the evening. His plan had been to text him to let him know when he was leaving Dom's that morning.

"I think they'd be more open with you," someone was saying as Logan entered the living room. The floor plan was open so there were no barriers between where he stood and the kitchen where Dom stood in a pair of sweats next to another man. Two sets of eyes looked up at him and then the stranger said, "What the fuck?"

CHAPTER 9

Dom took in the sight of Logan shirtless, hair still damp from their shower and his cock thickened in his sweats as he remembered the smooth arch of Logan's back as Dom had bent him over the shower bench. Declan's harsh curse snapped Dom out of it and anger went through him when he saw Logan flinch.

"Declan," Dom warned, but the man was clearly too upset to pay him any notice.

"Sorry, Dom, I didn't know…" Logan said awkwardly.

"It's okay, Logan," he said. "Come have some breakfast." Logan glanced at him, then back at Declan and he saw a shadow pass over his features.

"Logan?" Declan whispered. "Logan Bradshaw?" he said, horrified. He swung around to face Dom, the file folder in his hand forgotten.

"Logan, this is Declan Hale. Sylvie's brother," he said on a sigh, knowing what was coming next.

The gasp that Logan let out tore through Dom and he saw Logan's instant withdrawal.

"Are you fucking him?" Declan shouted. "In my sister's house? In her bed?"

"Enough," Dom said coldly. "Logan," he called, but the man was heading back towards the bedroom.

"Answer me, damn it!" Declan yelled as he shoved Dom hard.

"Back off!" Dom returned and circled around the island. Logan returned before Dom could get to the bedroom. He'd managed to get his shirt on, but was carrying his shoes and socks. He tried to push past Dom. "Logan, don't do this," Dom said.

"Let me go," Logan said as he pulled free of the hold Dom had on him. "This was a mistake," he whispered. "A terrible mistake." Hurt lanced through Dom at the finality in his tone and he watched Logan leave the apartment.

He ignored Declan and went to the island and grabbed his phone. He dialed a number, then waited until Cade answered. "He's on his way down." If Cade had anything else to say, Dom didn't hear it because he hung up and turned his attention to Declan.

"Get the hell out!" he said coldly.

Declan ignored him and came around the island and got in his face. "Did you fuck around on my sister while she was still alive too? With a fucking male prostitute?" he shouted.

Dom punched him hard and Declan hit the floor. Baby, who'd tried to follow Logan as he'd left, whined and came over to the two men and pushed between them.

"Get the fuck out of my house!"

Declan rubbed his jaw as he stood. He tossed the file folder he'd been holding down to the ground and the contents spilled out all over the place.

"We're done, Dom. We're fucking done!" Declan stormed out.

~

*L*ogan's skin crawled as he watched the last of the tables and chairs being carried out. Most had perished in the fire, but there'd been a few that could be saved if refurbished by the correct person.

LOGAN'S NEED

"Thanks man," said the happy new owner as he carted the last chair through the back doorway.

"No problem," Logan muttered as he leaned back against the wall to study the now empty bar. Soot still clung to the walls and windows, but at least the floor was somewhat free of debris. He'd take a huge hit when he sold the place. But the sooner it was out of his life, the better. Maybe then the nightmares would stop.

"When are you going to re-open?" he heard a voice say from the back entrance. He didn't need to turn to see who it was. That voice haunted him in a whole other way.

"Not going to. I'm putting it on the market tomorrow," he said. He forced his eyes to look at Dom who was leaning against the doorframe, his white dress shirt crisp and slightly open at the throat, the sleeves rolled up to reveal corded forearms. Even after this morning's humiliating encounter, he wanted him.

Dom's footsteps sounded hollow as he moved closer.

"It won't work, Dom," Logan said. Dom stopped in front of him, his fingers tucked in his pockets.

"Why not?"

"You know why," he said, suddenly feeling very tired.

"I know that a couple hours ago we were happy – that what we had felt good, right? What's changed?"

"Life," Logan muttered. "Reality. The shit that exists outside our little fuck bubble."

Dom slapped one of his palms next to Logan's head as he closed the distance between them. "So that's all we have between us? All you want is my dick and my ass?"

He forced himself to remain still as Dom stuck his nose against his neck and inhaled. It made him think of a stallion preparing to mount a mare. And it fucking turned him on. "Which one do you want more right now?" Dom whispered as he brought his pelvis in closer and brushed his cock against Logan's. "Or is it my mouth you want?" God forgive him, but he did want that. But then the word *whore* flashed through his mind and it was Declan Hale's voice saying it.

"How did he know my name?" Logan asked.

Dom stiffened and pulled back slightly. He seemed to put a lid on any desire that had been building and stepped back.

"He's working the Reynolds case."

"He's a cop?"

"Detective. He got pulled in when they discovered the link to the missing women."

"Does he know about me?" Logan asked.

Dom was silent for a moment, then nodded. Logan's heart lurched. Not only had Declan discovered his brother-in-law with another man, he knew Logan was an escort.

Logan laughed. "This just keeps getting better." Hysteria started twining through him. "I guess everyone knows fucking everything about me now."

"Logan-" Dom interjected.

"Your wife somehow knew just by looking at me that I wanted you. Shane figured out something was up; Gabe seems to know now too. Cade knew within minutes of meeting me!" he shouted. He slammed his fist against the wall. "My own sister knows I fucked strangers for cash and never told me! You've all been lying to me from day one!"

"I never lied to you!" Dom countered.

"Yeah, but you weren't exactly honest with me either, were you?"

Dom stilled.

"How long did you watch me for? How many hours did you spend "researching" me? How many others did you consider before you chose me for you and your wife's little games?" Logan straightened. "You joined right in when everybody decided to play the 'Let's Keep Logan In The Dark' game. And you used it to your advantage!"

Dom's features hardened and he went quiet for a long time. Logan knew he'd overstepped, but he refused to wish the words back. Instead of responding, Dom reached into his pocket and pulled out a picture and handed it to Logan. "His name is Elias. He's the younger brother of the prostitute who went missing – the one whose DNA was in Reynolds's truck. Declan seems to think he's more likely to open up to someone who isn't a cop."

Logan was caught off guard at the abrupt end to their argument with the change of subject.

"I thought you might want to come with me because I know how shitty it is to feel helpless," Dom said coldly.

"Yeah, okay," Logan replied wearily. It would have been so easy for Dom just to walk out of there and look for the kid on his own. There was absolutely no obligation to include Logan – he'd done it because that's the kind of guy he was. And Logan had shit all over that.

"He's been arrested in the past while working International Boulevard near the airport. We'll start there tonight. I'll pick you up at your place at ten." Dom took the picture back as he turned to leave. His voice was empty as he said, "And don't worry about our 'little fuck bubble.' It just burst."

"Stop doing that," Logan heard Cade mutter from behind him.

Logan turned. "Doing what?"

"That twitching thing you're doing," Cade said as he lit up a cigarette.

"Don't smoke that shit in my place," Logan said as he snatched the cigarette from Cade's fingers before he could take a draw of it. He ignored the startled man's look and went to the kitchen where he doused the cigarette under running water before tossing it in the trash. "And I'm not twitching," he said as he went back to stand in front of the window. It wasn't a complete lie – he wasn't twitching, but knew he wasn't far from it either. It was hard to stand still as his stomach rolled with anxiety. Something in Dom's voice had been so final this morning and even though that was what Logan had wanted, it was now burning a hole in his gut. For the first time since meeting Dom, he was less focused on the physical desire that had been haunting him and more concerned that he'd pushed away the one person who understood him best.

"He'll be here," Cade assured him.

"I know." And he did – he had no doubt whatsoever that Dom would show up. "How much did you hear this morning at the bar?"

"All of it."

Logan kept his eyes focused on the street below him. "You think he'd forgive me for what I said?"

Cade was silent for a while, then said, "I don't know. Are you going to ask him to?"

Logan shook his head and was surprised when he felt the sting of tears. "It's better this way."

"For you or for him?"

"He's just trying to deal with losing Sylvie," Logan said.

"And what are you trying to deal with?" Cade asked, his voice even, casual, as if they were talking about the weather. He detected the tiniest Southern drawl and wondered if that meant Cade was more agitated then he let on.

"Where are you from?" Logan asked distractedly.

"Alabama."

"How do you know him?"

"We met in the army. Hung out a bit after he got out and before I was redeployed."

"Were you...?"

"Lovers?" Cade interjected for him since he couldn't get the word out.

Logan nodded.

"No."

He shouldn't be relieved, but he was. "Why not?"

"I like 'em a bit softer, submissive," Cade said. "He did too. Two tops don't a bottom make."

Logan remembered the feel of Dom's ass encasing his dick. Dom definitely liked being in control, but he'd proven that he could give it up too. For him. Logan felt another hole open up inside of him.

"You said some pretty shitty things to him."

He nodded. What else could he do? It was one hundred percent true. He'd lashed out at Dom unfairly, taking the trust issues he had with his friends and family out on the one man who hadn't actually lied to him.

"That's why he shouldn't forgive me. And why I won't ask him to."

∼

*L*ogan twisted his hands in his lap to stop the twitching he was now actually guilty of. It had started when he'd climbed into the passenger seat of Dom's Mercedes sedan. There'd been no greeting, no polite head nod, no nothing. Dom had nodded at Cade though, before he'd pulled away from the curb and somehow that had stung. He hadn't even been demoted to "friend" status after their blowout. Even acquaintance would have meant some type of acknowledgement, but the deadly silence he was getting was a cruel reminder that he'd gotten exactly what he'd wanted – he didn't exist in Dom's world anymore. Less than twenty-four hours ago, Dom had been worshiping him and now this.

The silence was broken by a ding on Dom's phone and Logan glanced at it where it sat on the console between the two seats. Dom picked it up and briefly glanced at the notification on the screen, then put the phone back down. The only hint that something was wrong was the almost imperceptible tightening of Dom's hands on the steering wheel.

"Everything okay?" Logan asked, knowing he was completely out of bounds. Considering that he really wanted to reach over and take one of those clenched hands into his own, he figured asking the question was the more appropriate option.

Dom didn't answer and long, slow seconds ticked by. His jaw was locked, the tension obvious. "Vin's on his way home," Dom finally said.

Logan would have been relieved to even get a response, but it was what Dom hadn't said that had his heart catching.

"Ren?"

Dom shook his head and then brushed his arm across his eyes. "He didn't find him."

This time Logan did grab Dom's hand. "I'm sorry, Dom," he whispered as he enfolded the shaking hand between his own. But Dom quickly pulled free of him and put his hand back on the steering wheel.

"If we find the kid, let me do the talking," Dom said, his voice once again even.

Logan wanted to fold in on himself, the pain was so intense. There'd been a little speck of hope that maybe he could still have something with Dom – some contact that would let him keep feeling some of the good things Dom brought out in him. But the Dom who trusted him, needed him, was gone. The man next to him didn't even hate him – he just no longer gave a shit. "Yeah," he responded dully as he carefully put his hands back in his lap, the twitching gone now as the coldness inside overtook him. "No problem."

※

Dom steeled himself against the need to grab Logan's hand. He'd been weak for just a second and the other man's touch had brought all the emotion back to the surface. Knowing Ren was still out there made him want to seek comfort in Logan's arms, but that wasn't an option anymore – never would be again. He was alone again. Sylvie had left him. Logan had left him. Even his brothers had left him. A dark image of himself lying alone in the bed that he'd only ever loved two people in flashed through his head.

It would be so easy to lay down top of the expensive duvet his wife had painstakingly picked out and imagine Sylvie on one side of him, Logan on the other. He could drift off to sleep and be with them forever. He wouldn't have to choose who he loved more or justify that he'd found love again so soon after Sylvie. And he wouldn't have to feel the cruelty of Logan's words tearing him apart over and over again. It had only been twelve fucking hours since Logan had devastated him – how would he get through a lifetime of this?

"Can I see the picture again?" he heard Logan ask.

He pulled the picture from his jacket pocket and handed it to

Logan. He turned on the dome light, then turned his attention back to the road.

"He looks young," Logan said quietly.

"Fifteen." He saw Logan glance at him briefly.

"What's his name again?"

"Elias Galvez. He goes by Angel when he's working."

They reached the busy stretch of International Boulevard and Dom turned off the light. Logan handed the picture back, then started searching the faces of the men and women striding up and down the heavily trafficked area.

Dom pulled over and lowered Logan's window. A heavily made-up woman with big boobs in a tiny top stuck her head into the car and smiled, a bit of her bright red lipstick painting her teeth. "You boys looking for a little bit of fun tonight?" she said coyly as she plopped her substantial assets on the window frame.

"We're looking for Angel," Dom said as he held out some money.

And so it went for more than an hour. They got a couple of tips, but it wasn't until an incredibly tall transvestite in a purple mini dress and silver five inch stilettos leaned into the car that their luck changed. They only had to travel a couple of blocks to find their quarry.

As Dom pulled over to the curb, the kid came out of the dark alley. He was wiping his mouth on the sleeve of his jacket, but when he saw Dom's car he slowed, then pulled his jacket off and sauntered towards them. Behind him, a heavy-set man hurried out of the alley and disappeared down the street. He heard Logan take in a sharp breath as it registered what had just transpired.

Elias was wearing a super tight T-shirt that rode up to reveal his flat stomach. Leather pants showed off his pubescent figure and he'd put some type of eyeliner around his dark eyes to enhance the effeminate look he naturally had.

"Hey sugar," he said to Logan as he looked him up and down. Then his eyes shifted to Dom. The voice had the right mix of innocence and femininity he suspected helped the kid sell what so many men were willing to shell out big bucks for, but his eyes looked wary and haunted. Dom pushed back the sick feeling that lurched through him knowing what this boy had been through – what he went through every night because there was no one to look out for him.

"How much?" Dom asked.

"To do you both?" he asked, forcing excitement into his voice that he clearly wasn't feeling. Dom nodded and he felt Logan tense up next to him. But he remained silent, his eyes on the kid. "A hundred bucks to blow each of you. Two hundred and I blow him while you fuck me. Three hundred and you can both fuck me."

Logan did make a sound this time and Dom reached out to grab his hand, hoping he'd play along. He didn't want to touch Logan, but he needed this kid to buy into the whole act. He felt Logan's fingers tighten on his. The kid saw the contact and something flashed in his eyes so quickly that Dom couldn't figure out what it was. "Deal. Get in," he said as he motioned to the backseat. Part of him was glad when the kid showed some sense and hesitated at getting into the back of a strange car with two men, but his desperation for cash won out and he climbed in.

Dom tried to pull free of Logan's grasp, but he could tell Logan was on the verge of freaking out so he let him hold on to him as he maneuvered the car back into traffic. It took him only minutes to get to the hotel he had in mind.

"Shit, ain't never been fucked in no Hyatt before," the kid said from the back. His tone was cocky, but Dom could see in the rearview mirror that the kid was tense. He pulled into the garage and found a spot, forgoing the valet parking that was available.

"Baby," he said to Logan. Logan seemed like he was in a daze so Dom gripped his hand hard until Logan finally looked at him. "Go get us a room while I wait here with our new friend," he said calmly as he handed him a credit card. He gave Logan another squeeze, gentler this time and Logan finally nodded.

"He's hot," the kid said after Logan got out. "Can't wait to suck that dick," he announced. The kid absolutely could not sit still and he guessed that his own silence was spurring the kid to try to convey his confidence in what he thought was about to happen.

Logan returned within minutes and they made their way to the room. He knew the kid stuck out like a sore thumb, but his only concern was getting them into the privacy of the room. Once they were inside the simple suite with the king-sized bed, the kid tossed his jacket on one of the side chairs and said, "Cash first."

Dom ignored him and went to the phone and dialed room service. When the attendant came on the line he said, "Yeah, give me one of every entrée you have and a couple of Cokes." He hung up the phone and turned to face the boy.

"Sit down, Elias."

~

Logan wanted nothing more than to go into the bathroom and throw up everything he'd eaten today. From the second he'd realized what he was seeing as the teenager came out of that alley, the contents of his stomach had been churning. And now when he saw the look of abject fear in the boy's face, he felt a hollowness settle in his chest. He could've been this kid. If his parents had been just a couple notches down on the socioeconomic totem pole, this would have been him.

"What the fuck?" Elias shouted as he tried to get to the door.

"Sit. Down," Dom said firmly as he blocked the only way out.

The kid ignored Dom and looked around frantically.

"Elias," Logan said gently.

"How do you know my name?" His voice was shrill as the panic threatened to overtake him. Suddenly, he whipped out a small knife and waved it at them. "Stay back or I'll cut you. I swear I will."

Dom was on in him in two strides and with one quick move, had him disarmed. Elias didn't even realize what had happened until Dom closed the switchblade and tucked it into his pocket.

"Sit," Dom said once more and the boy finally did it. "Elias," Dom began.

"Eli," came the quiet response. The kid was scared shitless, but managed to say, "Only my mama and sister call me Elias."

"Eli," Dom began again. "We have some questions for you about your sister."

That got Eli's attention and he sat up straighter. "Elena? Did you find her?" he asked hopefully. Logan felt his heart break for the kid. He saw Dom glance at him briefly before he pulled out a chair and sat across from Eli who remained seated on the bed, his earlier fear pushed to the back as he waited for good news.

"No, we didn't," Dom said. "We don't know where she is, but we're trying to find someone who might know what happened to her."

"It was her boyfriend, wasn't it?"

"She had a boyfriend?" Logan asked.

"Yeah. That's what she called him anyway. I think he was just one of her regulars though."

"You saw him? Do you know his name?" Dom asked.

"He had a weird name. Sy or something like that. I remember because that's my favorite channel. SyFy."

"What did he look like, Eli?" Logan said as he pulled up another chair.

"Kind of fat. Old. Older then you," he said, looking at Dom. "Bald like you too, but some hair on the side," he said as he touched his hand to his own head to show them what he was talking about.

Logan sucked in a breath. The description matched Sam's.

"Did he take her?" Eli asked.

"Maybe," Dom said. "Do you know where he was from?"

Eli shook his head. "She used to bring him home and I'd have to stay in the closet while they fucked. Sometimes he'd tell her after they were done that he was gonna take her back to his place – that he had a special place picked out for her on the hill behind his house. She was excited because he said it had a pretty view of the lake."

Jesus Christ. Logan did go into the bathroom this time and stuck his hand under the cold water and then wiped it on his face.

"You okay?" Dom asked from the doorway, his eyes darting back to the other room to make sure Eli didn't try to take off.

"A special place picked out for her? It sounded like he was describing..." He couldn't even finish the thought.

"A grave," Dom supplied.

"Christ," he said as he gripped the edge of the sink.

"It could be nothing."

"She's been gone a year. We know what he's capable of. He killed her," Logan whispered so Eli wouldn't hear him.

"I know." There was a knock on the hotel room door. "That's room service. We need to see if we can get him to remember anything else."

Logan nodded. "I'll be right out." He scrubbed his face, then dried off with one of the numerous bright white hand towels. When he left the bathroom, he saw Eli sitting cross-legged on the bed, a plate of food in his lap. The kid was practically inhaling the burger, pausing only long enough to suck down some fries and take a swig of one of the two sodas on the nightstand. There were at least six other plates full of different types of food on the dining cart in front of the teenager.

Dom was watching him in silence and Logan could see he was trying to work through something in his mind. He glanced up at Logan and motioned to the food. "There's plenty," he said quietly.

The last thing Logan wanted to do was eat, so he sank back down into the chair next to Dom and tried not to notice the heat coming off the other man. He wished Dom would take his hand again like he had in the car. He knew the move had been Dom's attempt to keep Logan from giving away the horror that had been running through him as Eli had propositioned them, but Logan hadn't been able to let Dom go once they were on the move again. He'd known the plan was to question Eli, but he hadn't considered what they'd need to do to get the kid to a place where they could do so. And what was an act for them was something Eli dealt with every day. Fifteen fucking years old.

"You okay?" Dom asked him once again and Logan snapped his head up. He nodded and swallowed hard. Dom watched him for another long moment and Logan thought he saw longing in the other man's eyes. Wishful thinking, he figured, because Dom's eyes hardened again and he turned his attention back to Eli.

"Where's your mom, Eli?"

Eli stopped chewing as sadness passed over his features. "She got deported last year."

"To where?" Logan asked.

"Mexico. It was just me and Elena...then it was just me," he said as he shoved another fry into his mouth.

"Do you have your mom's number?"

Eli shook his head. "The agents took her away so fast that we didn't get to say goodbye."

"What about your father?" This from Dom.

Eli just shook his head again. Logan took that to mean he didn't have a father in his life...maybe never had.

"Elena said she could make enough money so we could find Mama. She said Sy loved her and was gonna take care of us someday and then we'd be able to bring Mama back."

"Did Sy know about you?" Dom asked.

"No. Elena said she'd tell him about me when he asked her to move in with him." The rest of the burger disappeared and Eli dropped the plate next to him on the bed and reached for a plate with a huge T-bone steak on it.

They let Eli work on the food for a while, then Dom leaned forward and took the plate from him and set it aside.

"Eli," he said, his voice low. "Do you have anyone that can take care of you?"

The kid looked confused. "I take care of myself."

"So, no family? Aunts? Uncles? Cousins?"

Eli shook his head again and then hungrily eyed the steak.

"Look at me," Dom commanded softly. Eli did as he was told. "I need you to make a choice right now. We can drop you off where we picked you up and you can go back to the way things were," he began. "Or you can come home with me and I'll make sure you never have to do what you've been doing to take care of yourself again."

"So, you're the only one who will fuck me?" The hope in the kid's voice made Logan want to vomit and he saw Dom tense up.

"Jesus," Logan said before he could catch himself.

"No one will ever touch you again. Not me, not him," he said motioning to Logan. "No one. And I'll do what I can to help you find your mom."

Now the kid was suspicious. "What do I have to give you?"

"Nothing."

Eli shifted uncomfortably and then looked at Logan. He tried to reassure the kid with a nod.

"You'll find my mom? You won't put me in jail?"

"No jail."

"They always put me in jail. Then they stick me with some people that don't want me," Eli said mutinously.

"No foster care either. You stay with me for as long as it takes to find your mom," Dom said.

"What about Elena?"

"She may not be coming back, Eli," Dom answered. "I'll try to find her, but I may not be able to bring her back to you."

"'Cause she's dead," Eli said. A statement, not a question. Dom didn't answer and Logan guessed that Eli wasn't really expecting one.

"Okay," he finally said. "But I get to leave whenever I want," Eli insisted. "No cops."

Logan had to wonder what kind of shit he'd been through with the judicial system to already have such a deep-seated fear of the police and child protective services.

"Agreed. Finish your food and we'll go."

Dom leaned back in his chair as Eli snatched up his fork and knife and started sawing away at the meat. Logan felt pain sear through his chest and he reached up to rub the scar there. But the pain had nothing to do with the physical damage that had been inflicted. No, it was in that instant that he realized he was in love with Dominic Barretti and it was too late to do anything about it.

CHAPTER 10

"He what?" Dom said into the phone, sure he'd heard wrong.

"He fired me," Cade drawled.

"Tell me you're still with him," Dom said as a flash of panic went through him.

"Seriously, Dom?" Cade asked, sounding mildly offended. "He's at his parents' house."

"Damn it," Dom cursed as he pinched the bridge of his nose. He was too tired for this shit. He sighed and said, "If I bring the kid, will you keep an eye on him?"

Cade was silent before he said, "I don't like kids."

"Jesus, Cade, can you give me a fucking break here?" Dom shouted.

"Fine, sure."

Dom hung up and resisted the urge to throw his phone across the room. He'd already run himself ragged between trying to keep up with Eli's mini panic attacks and keeping his promise to find the kid's mom. To make matters worse, his concern for Logan had been nagging him for days, even though he'd promised himself he'd walk away with a clean break.

Logan had been surprisingly quiet when they'd gotten back to his apartment three nights earlier. Eli had fallen asleep in the back seat and Logan had been unnaturally still since they'd left the hotel. It had taken everything in Dom not to pull the other man into his arms and tell him everything would be okay.

"Eli?"

"What?" came the shouted response from the guest room Dom had set him up in.

"We're going for a ride," he yelled back.

"Where?" The kid still didn't make an appearance.

"Get your ass out here," he ordered. The kid was turning out to be a typical teenager – moody and mouthy. And Dom liked him a lot. He was surprisingly smart, despite his limited formal education, and the way he talked about his mom had Dom remembering the special bond he'd had with his own mother. But it was the way the teenager doted on Baby that'd had Dom seeing what a good heart he had. Eli had dropped to his knees the second he'd set eyes on the dog and had started talking to the animal like he was a person. He'd showered the Rottweiler with praise and attention and had talked to him like he really was a baby. It had reminded him of Sylvie, but instead of the sharp pain and automatic sting of tears that usually accompanied one of his many memories of her, he'd felt warm inside.

As was the case now, boy and dog were inseparable as proven by the big dog trotting behind Eli as he came running out of his room.

"What?" he said again. Dom was amazed by how comfortable the kid seemed to be since he had no problem talking to Dom with that exaggerated exasperation that only kids seemed to know how to do. Baby sat down next to Eli and his big head settled under the kid's fingers.

"I need to run an errand and you're coming with me."

"I'll just stay here," Eli said.

"No. Get your shoes."

"Fine," Eli snapped as he sullenly went back to the room. It wasn't that Dom didn't trust Eli, it was the panic attacks that worried him. The first one had happened in the middle of the first night and it had only been Baby's incessant barking that had told him something was wrong. Eli had been frantically trying to figure out how to get out the front door and hadn't realized that the deadbolt required a key to open it. At first, Dom had thought Eli was having a nightmare or sleepwalking, but the kid had been wide awake and screaming that he needed to leave.

He'd pounded and scratched at the door until Dom had been able to grab him and hold him still so he wouldn't hurt himself. Then he'd collapsed onto the floor in tears. Dom had tried to comfort him, but his touch had seemed to make things worse and it had ended up being Baby who'd solved the problem. The dog had climbed right into Eli's lap and licked his face until the tears had stopped and Eli had fallen asleep. Dom had been able to carry him back to bed, but when he'd brought it up the next morning, the kid had played dumb and said he'd had no idea what Dom was talking about.

The second meltdown had come when Dom had taken him shopping to get some new clothes to tide him over until they could get back to the apartment he'd shared with his sister to get his stuff. His plan had been to take him to a couple of the shops near the marketplace, but when he'd seen the busy streets full of tourists, Eli had started shouting at Dom that he wasn't going to let him pimp him out. He'd accused Dom of lying to him and had tried to get out of the car while it had still been moving. Without Baby there to act as a buffer, it had been a struggle to get Eli calmed down enough to get them both home in once piece. Eli had settled once they'd reached the apartment, but once again he'd refused to talk about it. Other than those two times, he'd acted relatively normal, considering the circumstances.

He knew the kid would need some professional help at some point, but he'd have to earn his trust first if he ever hoped to get Eli in front of a doctor. Dom hadn't really considered what would happen long term if he couldn't find Eli's mother. He'd struggled with the idea of how to deal with that as he lay awake at night, wondering if he could really take on the responsibility of being a surrogate father to a fifteen-year-old boy. That was when he missed Logan the most – not just having his warm, hard body pressed against his side, but having someone that would help him face his fears. Logan made him feel safe and strong and needed. Logan would have known what the right thing to do was – he would have known how to comfort Eli in those dark moments.

"Can Baby come?" he heard Eli ask.

"Yeah," he automatically said. If the kid needed a hundred and ten-pound security blanket to feel comfortable, then so be it. Cade would just have to babysit them both while he dealt with his pain in the ass former lover who he missed more than he ever would have thought possible.

～

"You said you needed me to just watch the kid," Cade said as he stared at Baby and his drool covered jaw in disgust. His cool eyes shifted to Eli who stiffened and crossed his arms defensively.

"Eli," Dom said.

"What?" he responded, his eyes still on Cade.

"I'll be right in that house if you need me," Dom said as he pointed to the small Cape Cod style house where Logan's car was parked in the driveway. "Stay with Cade."

Eli nodded, then leaned back against Cade's car, his position mimicking Cade's. Dom didn't see any fear in the boy's eyes, so he looked back at Cade. "Watch him," he ordered firmly. He saw Cade start searching his pockets for his beloved cigarettes. "And don't smoke that shit around him."

He heard Cade curse behind him as he crossed the street and went to the house. He knocked on the side door, but there was no answer. He tried the door, found it unlocked and let himself in and looked around. The house was outdated, but clean. There was a feminine touch just about everywhere, probably Logan's mom since the décor looked like it was from the eighties. He looked around the lower level of the house, then went upstairs to where he assumed the bedrooms were. He found Logan in the first bedroom, his tall frame sitting on what was clearly a girl's bed. Savannah's room. He was holding a framed picture in his hand.

Logan jerked around when he heard Dom behind him, then relaxed.

"Dom," he said, clearly surprised to see him. "What are you doing here?"

"What did you think would happen?" Dom said, angry that Logan looked so vulnerable. "Did you actually think Cade would walk away because you told him to? He works for me!" Dom shouted.

Logan stood warily. "What are you talking about? I didn't-"

Before he could stop himself, Dom closed the distance between them and slammed Logan hard against the wall. Before Logan could speak, Dom was crushing his mouth down on the other man's. He poured all his anger, frustration and loss into that kiss. He wanted to punish Logan, wanted him to hurt the way he was hurting, wanted him to want the same things he wanted.

If he thought Logan would fight him, he was wrong. Dead wrong. But the man didn't go soft and submissive beneath his mouth either. No, Logan did what he always did – he turned everything on its ass and surprised Dom by spinning them around so it was Dom's back pressed against the wall. Powerful hands grabbed him by the neck and he felt Logan's leg push between his own. He brought his hands up to grab Logan's arms so he could regain control, but then one of Logan's hands was somehow down his pants and closing around his throbbing cock. He needed to stop this, because it would end the way it always did and he'd lose yet another piece of himself to this man. But when he opened his mouth to speak, Logan's tongue was there to answer him.

"Don't," Dom managed to rasp a few long seconds later as he tore his mouth from Logan's. He felt Logan's hand still on his cock and he fought the urge to grind into the rough, hot palm that held him. "I can't do this again," Dom said as he pulled free of Logan. The other man released him and stepped back, his eyes wide with confusion. "I know, I started it. I'm sorry."

Logan shook his head, then rubbed the hand that had been down

Dom's pants on his jeans as if trying to rid himself of the reminder of what had nearly happened. "I didn't fire Cade," was all he said as he retrieved the picture that had ended up on the floor during their tussle.

"He said," Dom began, then muttered, "Son of a bitch," as he sought out his phone and went to the window that overlooked the street. The fucker's car was gone, along with the kid and the dog. He pulled out his cell phone to dial, but stopped when he saw the message on the main screen.

Took the kid for ice cream. Talk to him – he's pretty messed up about something.

Dom swore to himself before tucking the phone back into his jacket. He turned to see Logan still studying the picture in his hands. Dom knew he needed to walk away. He couldn't keep his sanity if he continued to put himself through the ups and downs of being with this man. The hurt they caused one another was as brutal as the pleasure their bodies gave each other.

"Your folks?" Dom heard himself asking as he motioned to the picture.

Logan looked up at him as if surprised to still see him there. He nodded, then dropped the picture on the bed. Dom picked it up and studied it.

"How old were you here?" he asked, intrigued by how young and happy Logan looked.

"Seventeen. I'd just gotten my driver's license." A self-deprecating smile passed over his lips. "Took me two tries."

Dom chuckled. "What happened?"

"The guy doing the testing thought I should be able to parallel park on 2nd Avenue…during rush hour." Logan laughed, but it sounded empty. "It was the first time I'd ever failed at anything." Logan went to the closet and pulled out a couple of empty cardboard boxes and put them on the bed. "I hated that feeling," he said. "Letting everyone down." He began emptying the closet and putting the contents into the boxes. "How's Eli?" he asked.

"Settling. He has moments where he panics. Baby helps settle him down a lot which is good because I sure as hell don't know what to say to him."

"Maybe he doesn't need words. I'm sure he's heard a lot of those from a lot of people."

Dom nodded. "I want him to go talk to someone – a professional."

Logan glanced up at him briefly. "Gabe and Savannah see the same therapist. They both seem to like him…I'm sure one of them can give you his number." He went back to his packing.

"Shane says you're thinking about selling the house," Dom said.

"Yeah. Savannah's moved in with Shane and they're looking for a new place. I'll stay at the apartment until the bar sells."

"Too many memories?" Dom asked.

Logan stopped what he was doing, but didn't turn around. He seemed lost in thought as he stared into the dark closet. He finally shook his head. "No, just one really bad one." Dom knew Logan was referring to Savannah's assault.

Logan resumed his packing. "I'm worried about you," Dom finally admitted. No response. "Cade sends me reports every day. He says you haven't left your place since the night we found Eli." Still nothing. "What about work?"

"I quit."

"Why?" Dom asked.

"Why not?" came the clipped response.

"Logan-"

"What do you want from me, Dom? Why are you here?" Logan finally asked, more sad than angry.

"I need to know you're okay."

"But why, Dom? You don't owe me anything," he insisted. "Not after the things I said…"

They stared at each other for a long time because Dom didn't have an answer – at least not one that he had the strength to admit. If he said what he wanted to say, he'd be opening himself up to more pain, more loss.

Logan came up to him and took the picture. He stepped back around the bed and carefully packed it. "You know, when I woke up in that hospital bed after the fire, I hated you for just a minute. I didn't even know who you were then, but I cursed you for not leaving me in that place."

"Why?" Dom heard himself manage to ask.

"Because I was a fucking coward and didn't want to face the truth," he said easily. Too easily.

"What truth?" Dom asked carefully, still stinging from the thought that Logan had hated him for even a second.

"That I'd failed. Failed Savannah, my parents, my friends. I didn't want to remember all the times I'd sat across from Savannah at breakfast or dinner and ignored the hollow look in her eyes, dismissed it as the normal sadness that comes when you lose your parents. I didn't want to have to think about the nights she sat in her room at school and used a razor blade to try to bleed away some of the pain that was consuming her." Logan swiped at a stray tear. "I didn't want to admit that I'd failed her in every possible way."

Logan began grabbing knick-knacks from the shelves by Savannah's bed. "And then I met you and Sylvie. That one night took away that last few things I thought I knew about myself."

"Logan, if we'd known what it would do to you…" Dom began.

Logan paused in what he was doing, his eyes downcast. "I don't regret it. I wouldn't change any of it," he said vehemently and Dom believed him. Then his voice dropped to a near whisper when he said, "I feel like I've been wearing blinders for my entire life and now they've been ripped off and everything's too bright – too harsh. Part of me wants them back so I only have to see what's right in front of me."

Dom watched him carefully put the figurine he'd been clutching in the box. "What does the other part want?" he asked, refusing to acknowledge that twinge of hope that curled inside his chest. But Logan shook his head, the refusal to answer leaving Dom frustrated. He was finally beginning to realize that loving Logan was slowly destroying him, the wounds deeper even than the ones Sylvie's death had left on his soul.

"I have to stay away from you," Dom said softly.

"I know," Logan nodded, his eyes studying the remaining items on the shelves. His voice sounded empty and hollow. "Find Sam. Please. I need Savannah to be safe."

"I will," he said as he left the room. His promise hadn't been about Savannah, even though he cared a great deal for the young woman. No, it was for himself. Because he wouldn't be able to completely walk away from Logan until he knew the man was safe, so even if it took every penny he had, he'd find Sam Reynolds and send him back to the hell he'd come from.

CHAPTER 11

Logan was packing up the last of the items in the bar's storeroom when he heard raised voices in the alley behind the bar. He stepped outside and saw Cade standing toe to toe with Declan Hale.

"Fuck off, Detective," he heard Cade say.

"Cade," Logan called out and when the other man looked at him, he shook his head. Cade stepped back to let the other man pass.

Declan Hale was a big guy like Dom, but had light hair and his features were less harshly beautiful than Dom's. Logan expected to see animosity in the other man's gaze as he drew closer, but he didn't. What he saw almost looked like regret.

"Can we talk inside?" Declan said, as he motioned to the doorway leading into the bar.

Logan nodded and as he followed Declan inside, he saw Cade walking towards them, clearly intending to follow.

"I'll be fine," he said to Cade as he drew near.

"I don't trust him," Cade responded as he reached for his phone.

"Don't, Cade. Please," Logan said, knowing who Cade was planning to call. The other man must have heard the pleading in his voice because he put the phone away. Logan realized then how lucky he was to have found a friend like Cade.

"I'll be right here," Cade muttered as he leaned next to the doorframe. He grabbed a cigarette which Logan promptly took away from him.

"Enough with these," he said as he dropped it to the ground and crushed it under his work boot. Cade grumbled, but didn't reach for another one.

Logan went into the bar and found Declan waiting for him just inside the main room, his eyes studying the darkened windows.

"Heard you were selling," Declan said.

"What can I do for you, Detective?" Logan asked, already on the defensive.

"There's been some progress on your case," he finally said as he turned to face Logan. Excitement went through Logan at the thought that maybe this would all be over soon, but that hope was quickly dashed when Declan said, "It's not much, though."

"What is it?"

"Once we realized the body we found here wasn't Reynolds's, we started to check with area hospitals to see if any of them treated burn victims. It seemed unlikely that he got out of here without some kind of injury that day," Declan said as he moved around the small space. His fingers drifted over the bar that Logan had started stripping the finish from so long ago, but never finished.

"We didn't find anything locally so we expanded the search. There was a hit in Spokane. A man with a badly burned arm showed up at an ER there with some story about an accident with his grill. They admitted him and treated him for a couple days before they realized the name and address he'd given them was fake. He also had some injuries that couldn't have been from the fire. Mainly scratches on his neck and face and there was some minor trauma to his eyes. Your sister's statement indicates she used some self-defense moves on him that she'd learned."

Declan pulled a picture from his pocket and handed it to Logan. It was grainy, but the man in it was definitely Sam. "He took off before cops could question him, but we got some good pictures off the security footage."

Logan handed the picture back. "So, you really don't have anything, do you? He could be anywhere by now." He couldn't help but be angry, but he wasn't sure how much of it was pointed directly at Declan for more personal reasons.

"I said it wasn't much," Declan grunted.

"Yeah," Logan said, then stepped away from the doorway and crossed his arms, sending a clear message.

Declan turned his back to Logan again as if he was once again studying the bar. "She was my baby sister," he heard him say brokenly. "She was all I had left."

Logan was surprised by the amount of pain in the words. He softened his stance, but didn't move from where he was. "She was amazing," he finally said and he saw Declan look over his shoulder at him.

"You knew her?" the other man asked.

Logan wasn't about to discuss the circumstances of how he'd come to meet Sylvie, so he simply nodded, then said, "She gave me something I didn't know I needed."

Declan studied him and Logan wondered if he knew he was talking about Dom.

"She was twelve when she was diagnosed the first time. Leukemia. I took her to all her treatments, held her when she cried from the pain, carried her when she was too tired to walk, celebrated with her when she went into remission," Declan said painfully.

"Where were your parents?" Logan asked.

Declan snorted. "The same place they are now. Overseas somewhere. Probably attending some party or political function. Being ambassador to some hole in the wall country is more important than childhood cancer – especially if the prognosis for recovery is more than fifty percent." Logan saw Declan's fists clench. "They made sure to ask for prayers for their little Sylvie during their speeches though. Sent a nice big flower arrangement for her funeral too." Declan seemed to finally notice how much anger was radiating off him, and he took a deep breath as if forcing himself to calm down. "It came back in her twenties, but she beat it again."

But not the last time. Declan didn't need to say the words. Logan felt a wave of sadness go through him at how much Sylvie had suffered – how all three of them had suffered.

"She was lucky to have you," Logan said softly.

Declan shook his head. "I couldn't handle it – not the last time. Not when the doctors told her there would be no more remissions. She was a rock though. Dom too," he said. "I knew he loved her, but the things he did for her..." Declan's voice trailed off.

Pain went through Logan at the reminder of the man he'd lost his heart to.

"The things I said that morning," Declan began, his tone uneven. "I had no right and it was none of my business," he said, his head hanging low with shame.

"You were looking out for your sister. Like you always did."

"She would have been ashamed of me for how I acted – the things I said."

"Declan," Logan said softly and was pleased when the other man looked up at him. He hated to see the torture this man was putting himself through. "We're good," Logan said. "We're good," he repeated firmly.

Declan hesitated, then finally nodded. He moved past Logan towards the back door. "I'll keep you posted if there are any more developments," he said.

"Thank you," Logan responded and watched him disappear. A shadow fell over the doorway and Logan looked up to see Cade studying him. "All good," Logan said. Cade nodded, then disappeared again.

"I changed my mind," Eli said as he shifted uneasily in front of the door.

"It'll be fine," Dom said as he heard footsteps approaching on the other side. Even though he had two guys covering both the front and back of the apartment complex, he still kept his eyes on the hallway.

The door opened and Riley smiled brightly at him. He didn't even get the chance to greet her before she was hugging him. "Dom, it's so good to see you. I'm so glad you called," she said, then turned her radiant smile on Eli. He had expected the kid to shrink back, but he stood stock still when she said, "You must be Eli," then pulled him into her arms as well.

Gabe appeared behind her in the doorway and he felt Eli nudge closer to him. "Eli, this is Riley and Gabe," he said.

"Come in," Riley said as she dragged Eli into the apartment, the kid's eyes wary as they looked Gabe up and down.

"Hey Eli, nice to meet you," Gabe said as he stuck out his hand in greeting. Eli hesitated for a long time, but Gabe was patient and Eli finally shook it. Then his eyes widened in delight at the sight of the pit bull sitting next to Gabe, its long tongue lolling out of its wide jaws.

"This is Bella," Gabe said as Eli dropped down in front of the dog and began crooning over her, just like he'd done with Baby. He was seeing a theme with this kid.

"Thanks for keeping an eye on him for me," Dom said as he watched Bella roll on her back so Eli could rub her belly.

"We're so happy you asked us," Riley said before she sat on the floor next to Eli and the dog and began chatting about how Gabe had rescued the dog.

Gabe motioned to the door and Dom followed him. "Sweetheart, I'll be right back, okay?" Riley smiled at him and nodded.

Gabe led him into the hallway and pulled the door closed. "Any more leads?" he asked.

"They've identified another one of the women. She worked as a prostitute in Portland. I'm heading down there now to see if I can find out anything else. The cops couldn't find any family so I'm hoping some of the women she worked with might talk to me."

Gabe nodded. "Logan going with you?"

Dom recoiled at that, but forced his features to stay expressionless as he shook his head. It had been two long weeks since he'd seen Logan, heard his voice. And it was fucking killing him. Gabe seemed to be studying him, his dark eyes too perceptive for Dom's liking.

"How's it going with Raul and Trevor?" Dom asked, referring to the two men he had watching the couple.

"We're glad they're here, but it's been hard on Riley. She's still trying to deal with her piece of shit ex's attack."

The young woman had been lucky to escape with her life after her ex-fiancé had tracked her to Seattle and threatened her with a gun.

"Maybe we'll get lucky and Portland will turn something up." He turned to go.

"And what happens then? What happens after you find him and he's behind bars where he belongs?" Gabe asked.

Dom sighed because he knew what Gabe was really asking him. "Things will go back to the way they were," he finally said.

"You're okay with that?"

Dom studied the other man for a long time. He motioned to the apartment door. "You love her more than anything, right?"

"Yes," Gabe responded without hesitation.

"She knows what you used to do for a living?" Dom asked.

"She does," Gabe responded.

"She doesn't care, right?"

Gabe hesitated briefly, then said, "She says it doesn't matter to her."

"Do you think she's lying to you?"

"No," Gabe said firmly.

"But there's still something there for you. Regret? Shame?"

Gabe sighed and said, "A little bit of both."

"Multiply that by a thousand and that's where Logan is. How do I take that away from him? How do I give him back the trust that Sam stole? How do I convince him that what happened to his sister wasn't his fault? That he can trust his friends again even though they kept things from him? How do I reassure him that it's okay for him to have feelings for a man after a lifetime of only ever wanting women? What do I say to take away the guilt he feels for wanting someone whose wife of more than a decade died less than three months ago? Tell me that, Gabe. Please."

Gabe leaned back against the wall and remained mute, the frustration that he didn't have an answer clear in his expression.

"Thanks for watching the kid," Dom said quietly. "I'll let you know when I'm on my way back. If he freaks out, use the dog to bring him back," he said.

"Be careful," Gabe said.

Dom nodded and left.

~

Logan watched the waters of Lake Michigan lap at the shoreline as snow fell softly around him. Everything was blanketed in white except for the green-blue water. He'd expected Shane's parents to have some ritzy apartment downtown, not a sizeable Tudor style home north of the city. They'd had an excellent view of Chicago when they'd arrived in Dom's plane earlier in the week, but it had only reminded Logan how far he was from where he wanted to be.

When he, Riley and Gabe had gotten to the Seattle airport, he'd been stunned to learn that Dom was lending them his jet for their flight. It hadn't even occurred to him as a possibility when Riley and Gabe had told him they'd take care of the travel arrangements that would take them to the Midwest to spend Christmas with Savannah, Shane and Shane's parents. So when he'd stepped onto the luxurious airplane, it had instantly felt wrong. Dom should have been on that plane with him. He should have been sitting next to Logan as they'd looked out the window and admired the view of the snow-capped mountain ranges below as they'd flown east. It should have been Dom's hand he'd clung to instead of the armrest when the plane had bumped and shaken as it'd touched down in Chicago.

But Dom was back home where Logan couldn't hurt him anymore. He'd ached when Dom had said he needed to stay away, but the man had been right. Their physical attraction was just too undeniable to even be in the same room together. And since he couldn't give Dom what he deserved, it wasn't fair to expect him to maintain any kind of connection. He'd hoped that the agony of not seeing or talking to Dom would start to fade if enough time passed, but instead, it grew worse and he was finding it harder and harder to get through each day.

"Logan?" he heard his sister say from somewhere behind him.

"Yeah," he said without turning, needing those few seconds to try to collect himself.

"You forgot your jacket," Savannah remarked as she appeared beside him on the beach.

He couldn't tell her that the frigid air on the outside made it feel a little less cold on the inside, so he thanked her and took the jacket. As he shrugged it on, he felt her reach up to straighten his collar. He couldn't stop himself from flinching away from her and he saw her startled look as he fixed the collar himself.

"You guys get the tree done?" he asked with a smile, hoping she'd ignore what had just happened.

She nodded, but blinked her eyes rapidly and he knew she was fighting back tears. But what could he say? How could he explain that he was so raw that one touch would have him coming apart at the seams? That his wounds ran so deep that nothing she said or did could fix them.

"Dinner's almost ready," she said quietly. He nodded and watched her return to the house. Darkness was just starting to seep over the edges of the cloudy skyline and he saw the Christmas lights that Shane's parents had covered the house in light up and twinkle in celebration. The Christmas tree inside the bay window came on too, a plethora of bright colors and shimmering tinsel. He saw Gabe and Riley admiring it, his big arms wrapped around her smaller frame. Shane was there too, his arms opening to Savannah as she walked back into the house. He turned away from the homey scene and glanced back over the water. He wondered what Dom was doing. Hopefully, Vin had made it home by now so Dom wouldn't be alone tomorrow. But then again, Logan was surrounded by the people who loved him most and he'd never felt more alone.

~

"Merry Christmas everyone," John Matthews said as he lifted his glass high. "Or Merry Christmas Eve rather," he chuckled. "I want to thank my lovely wife for this amazing dinner she's put together for us tonight," he said as he smiled at the woman beside him.

"And to Savannah and Riley for the beautiful job they did on the tree," he said. He glanced at Shane before saying, "We're so blessed this year to have you all here." He looked around at each of them. "You've been my son's family for so long and he couldn't have picked a better one. We hope that maybe you'll all consider us your family now too. And as your own families grow, we hope you know you'll always be welcome here. It would be good to hear the pitter patter of little feet in this house someday," he added with a wink.

Everyone laughed and raised their glasses. Logan took a sip of the champagne in the delicate glass that had been placed in front of his plate, but it may as well have been water because he couldn't taste a thing. Food started appearing in front of him, but he couldn't remember if he'd put what ended up on his plate there or if someone else had. Silverware clanged as everyone dug in and he looked up and to his right to see Gabe and Riley laughing about something. He'd ended up at the head of the table across from Shane's father while Savannah sat to his left on the corner. Shane was next to her and he saw his hand close over hers briefly as they shared an intimate look between them.

He dropped his eyes back down to the plate in front of him and picked up the fork and knife. Then time just seemed to stop as his eyes focused on the sharp knife in his right hand. The light caught it and reflected off the serrated edge.

"Logan?"

The voice sounded far away as he ran his thumb over the sharp little indentations and felt each one drag and catch on his skin.

"Logan!"

Savannah's frightened voice broke through and he looked up at her. Her eyes, so much like his own, were filled with a mixture of fear and confusion. Everyone else was looking at him too.

He turned his attention back to Savannah. "I understand now," he said quietly as he glanced back at the knife. "I understand why you did it." He heard her sharp intake of breath. "I didn't really get it before – I didn't understand how much you must have been hurting inside," he said. He saw Shane clasp her hand again.

Logan lowered the fork first, then fingered the knife once more before he lowered it as well. "God, I wish you had come to me," he whispered.

"Logan," Shane said in warning.

"No, Shane, don't," Savannah said as she squeezed his hand. She turned her attention back to him, tears swimming in her eyes.

"I should have," she agreed.

"Maybe I couldn't have fixed it," he said. "But I would have tried."

She nodded, but couldn't force any words out.

"I hurt like that now, Savannah."

"Please tell me why," she begged.

"I pushed him away," he said, the words catching in his throat. "I can't tell what's real anymore and what's not. I don't know if he can love me the way he loved her. If he can forgive me for the choices I made." He looked up at her, tears blurring his vision. "But it's like I can't breathe without him," he said as he wiped his hand across his eyes to clear them.

"Are you talking about Dom?" Savannah asked gently. He nodded.

"Son," he heard from the other end of the table and he looked up at Shane's father. "Life changes in an instant," he said solemnly as he gripped his wife's hand. He knew they were remembering the son they'd lost to suicide after they'd pushed him away in an angry moment. "If you love this man, you need to tell him so. Second chances aren't guaranteed."

Savannah grabbed his hand. She pulled it up to her lips and kissed the back of it. "I love you so much. I wish I could go back and change things. I wish I could find a way to earn back your trust," she said softly.

He shook his head, but she spoke before he could. "I know you've forgiven me...us for keeping things from you," she said as she motioned to everyone else at the table. "You've forgiven us, but you haven't forgotten, have you?"

"No," he admitted. "I'm sorry," he said softly. It was a brutal truth to have to admit to.

"It's okay," she said, tears streaming down her face. "We're going to prove to you that you can trust us again. It doesn't matter how long it takes," she said emphatically. "That's what family does."

He nodded, then pulled his hand free so he could wipe the tears from her face.

"I love you," he said as he stood up and kissed her forehead. He looked around the table and saw that Riley was clinging to Gabe, silent tears streaming down her face. Shane's parents were holding hands as they watched him with concern and Shane was rubbing Savannah's back as she dabbed at her eyes with a napkin. When he asked, "Can someone give me a ride to the airport?" he smiled at the sound of every single chair scraping against the floor as they were pushed back. He really did have the best family a guy could ask for.

CHAPTER 12

Dom stepped back to check if the picture was straight. It was one of his favorites of Sylvie, taken days after her terminal diagnosis. She had asked him to take her to the Olympic Peninsula and they'd spent the day exploring the jagged rocks along the beach near the Cape Flattery Lighthouse. They'd taken Baby with them and he'd managed to snap a picture of Sylvie as she'd sat on the beach watching the sunset, the loyal dog sitting protectively next to her. The picture was from the back, so her face wasn't even visible, but the setting sun had cast a mix of light and shadows that showed the strength in Sylvie's small frame.

"It's beautiful," he heard behind him and he closed his eyes at the combination of need and relief that went through him at the sound of one of only two voices that could bring him to his knees. He steeled himself against the emotion that went through him and stepped back from the picture, his fingers briefly skimming over the glass.

He turned and faced Logan who was standing near the doorway of the bedroom. Seeing how beautiful and broken the younger man looked had him taking a step forward before he realized what he was doing. He covered his weakness by moving to the nightstand and putting down the hammer.

"What are you doing here?" he forced himself to ask.

Logan stepped further into the room, his ragged features drawn tight as he drew his arms around his body as if he were cold and was trying to warm himself. Dom automatically reached to flip the switch that would close the glass panel door behind him that he'd opened earlier when he'd arrived at the island house. It wasn't particularly warm outside, but the air had been soothing somehow.

"Where are the rest?" Logan asked as he motioned around the bedroom.

"Still in my study where you left them," he said. "I'll find other places for some of them and put the rest in a photo album," he answered flatly. He hadn't given the pictures much thought after he'd smashed them the night of the funeral. The night he'd welcomed Logan into his body for the first time. Silently cursing himself, he shook off the memory.

"Where's Cade?" Dom asked.

Logan shrugged. "I'm not sure. I didn't let him know I was coming back early." He flinched when Logan stopped next to him and studied the picture. The proximity was brutal on his senses so he pushed past Logan and went to the other side of the room to close the box of nails he'd left sitting on a chair in the corner.

"Why are you here?" he asked again.

"You weren't at your apartment so I figured you'd be with your brother or you'd be here," Logan said quietly.

"Vin's not back yet," he said, his anger growing. "Answer the fucking question. Why are you here?" He tossed the nails down on the chair and turned to study the other man.

"Where's Eli? And Baby?"

Dom bit back a growl and said, "I found Eli's mom and pulled some strings to get her a green card. She arrived this morning. I put her and Eli up in a hotel 'till I can find them something permanent."

"And Baby?" he asked.

"I gave him to Eli. He needed him more than I did." Logan nodded. "I don't want to see you, Logan," he said, his need knotting in his gut.

Logan turned to face the water, his back stiff. "Tell me how to stop and I'll go."

"Stop what?"

"Loving you," Logan whispered. He turned to face Dom, his expression pained. "Tell me what I have to do to stop this endless ache I feel for you."

Dom's world shattered at the words and he stepped back. "No," he said automatically, angrily.

Logan closed his eyes. "I kept waiting for another letter from her," he said, motioning to the picture of Sylvie. "I kept waiting for her to tell me it was okay to love you."

Dom felt like his chest was going to explode. His knees started to buckle and he put his hand on the wall to keep himself upright.

"You have to go, Logan."

Logan ignored him and continued. "I kept thinking I needed other people to approve of what I felt for you because I didn't trust myself anymore. I couldn't see past my mistakes and choices to see what you see in me. I couldn't believe that maybe you could love me the way you loved her."

"Jesus," Dom said, his body starting to shake.

Logan was looking directly at him now. "But you did, didn't you?"

"Yes," Dom managed to rasp out.

"But I'm too late. I hurt you too much," he said quietly.

"Yes, damn it!" Dom shouted.

Logan turned away as a small gasp of breath escaped his body, then he nodded and walked towards the door. A few seconds and this would be over for good. Dom knew there would be no coming back from this. He just had to hang on for a few more seconds.

～

*L*ogan bit down hard on his lip as he walked past Dom. He'd known this was a possibility and had accepted it when he'd boarded the commercial flight earlier tonight. His encounter with his family had left him drained, but the hope that he could get

Dom back in his life had kept him moving forward. Walking away was probably one of the hardest things he would ever have to do in his life, but he owed Dom that. His fear and lack of trust had destroyed any chance of a relationship and it was unfair to ask Dom to take yet another risk on him. He forced his eyes to stay on the floor as he passed Dom, and he was proud of himself for holding the tears that threatened at bay.

As he reached the door, he heard shuffling from behind him, then felt himself being pulled back.

"No," he heard Dom say as the man closed his hand around his arm. "No, no, no," Dom repeated before he turned Logan around and covered his mouth with his own. Logan cried out at the feel of Dom's lips against his, then let the tears fall as Dom's tongue stroked his in greeting.

"I love you so much," Dom whispered against his lips. "So much," he said again as he pulled Logan against him, his grip around his waist almost painful. And then his lips were on his face, those heavy hands holding his head as he kissed away the dampness at his eyes, then found his way back to Logan's mouth.

Logan tore his mouth free and reached his arms around Dom's neck and just held him. "I love you, Dom," he said as he clung to him and buried his face against Dom's skin. His whole body shook with how close he'd come to losing this and he felt Dom soothing him with long strokes up and down his back. "I'm sorry it took me so long to tell you."

"Shhh," Dom said as his lips peppered his forehead with light kisses. His anxiety melted under Dom's calming touch and he reached up to fasten his mouth on Dom's. They kissed languidly, like they had all the time in the world. But the desire kept building to that familiar ache and he heard Dom groan against him as their cocks brushed against one another.

"I need you, Dom," he whispered as his hands searched out the warm skin of Dom's abdomen.

"Yes," Dom said against his lips and then reached for the hem of Logan's shirt.

*D*om's eyes settled on the round scar on Logan's chest before he dropped the shirt he'd taken off him to the floor. He stroked the scar with his finger over and over, then locked eyes with Logan.

"That was one of the worst days of my life," he admitted as he caressed the raised skin. "There was so much blood," he said softly. "And I leaned down to listen to your heart and there was nothing." His voice caught as he remembered the terror that had gone through him. He felt Logan hold him tighter as if trying to comfort him.

"Your lips were cold when I gave you my breath." He traced Logan's lips with his thumb and smiled when Logan pressed a small kiss on it. "I was so scared. And then you took a breath." He leaned down and kissed him hard and fast before he pulled back again. "And when the doctor came out and said you were going to be okay…" He shook his head, unable to finish the sentence.

Logan pulled Dom's head down so their lips were almost touching. "Make love to me, Dom," he breathed and Dom trembled when those perfect lips brushed his. He grabbed the back of Logan's neck and held him there as he poured all his emotions into their kiss. His tongue played with Logan's before he tilted Logan's head back and ran his lips along the hard jaw before settling on Logan's rapidly beating pulse. His hand skimmed down Logan's strong back and rested on his lower back and he heard Logan moan when their hips came together. He found that sensitive spot at the base of Logan's neck and sucked hard, then soothed the area with a lick. Logan's skin was hot beneath his tongue as he kissed and licked his way across the well-defined pectoral muscles, stopping briefly to give extra attention to the bullet scar.

Logan's hands were on the move too as they reached under his shirt to dig into his upper back. Dom released Logan long enough to pull his own shirt off and the other man took full advantage of his distraction by latching his mouth onto one of Dom's nipples. Lust spiked through Dom at the sensation and then his hands were on

Logan's head as he found the other nipple and gave it the same treatment. "I need to taste you again," Logan muttered as he surged up and walked Dom backwards till his legs hit the bed. Logan followed him down to the mattress and made love to his mouth for several heart-stopping moments before he slid to his knees on the floor. Soft lips fluttered over his abdomen as Logan worked off his shoes.

Stretching his arms above his head, Dom reveled in the feel of Logan's lush lips loving and teasing his tight skin, alternating between light kisses, wet licks and the occasional nip that had Dom's cock pushing at the confines of his jeans. Logan's hand rubbed the hard length through the fabric before working the button and zipper free and pulling his pants and underwear off. Dom tensed as he waited for those magic lips to touch him, but they didn't. Before he could look up, he felt Logan capture his thighs and push his legs up. Hands separated him and he felt the cool air waft over his hole before Logan's hot tongue covered it and licked softly.

"Oh God," he yelled and he shifted up and grabbed his legs so he could watch what Logan was doing to him. The position was awkward and he could only hold it long enough to watch Logan flick his tongue back and forth over the wrinkly skin a few times before he collapsed back on the bed, his hands biting into his legs as he pulled them farther up to give Logan more room to work. His body trembled and twitched with every brush of Logan's mouth. Then he felt slick liquid land on his hole – Logan's saliva he guessed – and his whole body tightened at what would come next. But it wasn't the long fingers he had expected. No, Logan's curled tongue was pushing against him, working the saliva inside with each nudging probe.

"Open for me," Logan whispered before he was pushing again and Dom forced himself to relax and then he was bearing down and he felt Logan's tongue breach him. He shouted as he was licked from the inside and then grabbed the comforter in his hands as Logan began fucking him with his mouth. It was agony and ecstasy combined and he cried out at the loss when Logan pulled free of him. And then the heat was back, wrapped around his dick as Logan sucked him down and swallowed. He lowered his legs and leaned up on his elbows so he could watch that beautiful mouth work up and down his length. Spikes of pleasure went through him as Logan hummed around him before drawing off so he could dribble more saliva onto Dom's length.

Logan's eyes found his before he sucked him in again, and this time those pale blue eyes held him as Logan bobbed up and down on him. The sensation was too much and Dom began thrusting into that hot, lush mouth over and over. Logan didn't try to even stop him as he slammed against the back of his throat once, twice. It was only his need to be inside Logan in another way that had him stopping and sitting up. He grabbed Logan by the neck and pulled him up so he could reach his lips. Their tongues battled as Logan climbed up his body and settled onto his lap. But kissing wasn't enough for Dom and he stood, taking Logan with him, before he flipped them so Logan's hard body was beneath his.

He pinned Logan's wrists to the bed and held him there as he rubbed his cock against the steely hardness that was still trapped beneath the fabric of Logan's jeans. He kissed and licked his way down Logan's body and stopped when he reached his hips. Straddling Logan's lower half, Dom reared back so he could study the man beneath him.

"You've lost weight," he muttered as he ran his fingers over the slightly protruding ribs.

Logan watched him quietly, solemnly, his hands still resting beside his head. His eyes were open to Dom completely, no longer shuttered or haunted or unsure. God, he loved this man. Not just his stark beauty, but the strength and kindness in him, the selfless love he had for his sister and the friends he'd made into his family.

Dom leaned back over Logan and kissed him softly. "I'm going to take care of you," he said softly. "We're going to take care of each other."

Logan smiled, then kissed him back. The passion that had slowed came back in full force and Dom pulled back and worked the rest of Logan's clothes from his body. He popped off the bed and scrambled around the nightstand drawer until he found the bottle of baby oil he was looking for. He turned back to Logan who had already pulled his legs up to give Dom access to what he needed. Dom felt his whole body go hot at the sight of that little hole waiting for him and fumbled to get the baby oil open.

∽

Logan watched with a mix of amusement and desire as Dom worked the cap on the small bottle open and slicked up his finger. But all his humor fled when those fingers touched him and Dom's mouth closed around the head of his dick. He wasn't sure which he wanted more – the probing fingers or the suction that threatened to blow the top of his head off. He felt Dom lick the slit on the head of his cock and then his tongue trailed down to his base. The tip of a finger rubbed over him as Dom sucked one of his balls in, then the other. Logan groaned when he felt oil being directly applied to his opening and then the fingers were back. Dom kept alternating the torture on his balls before one finger slid all the way inside him.

"Fuck," Logan muttered as the finger pulled out, then plunged back in. On the next pass, a second finger joined the first and Dom's tongue drifted down to lick the skin around his hole as the thick fingers fucked into him over and over.

"Hold yourself open," he heard Dom order and Logan instantly reached down with his hands to separate the globes of his ass. Dom used his now free hand to grab Logan's cock and stroke it as his mouth and fingers worked in tandem to loosen him. Logan pushed and squirmed around the digits that twisted inside of him and he shouted when a third finger was added. And then Dom finally brushed his prostate and Logan nearly wept at the shockwaves that went through him.

"Please, Dom," he heard himself begging. "I need more."

That sinfully hot mouth returned to his cock and swallowed him as the fingers continued to work him, but stopped just shy of hitting that spot inside of him again. Logan released his ass and grabbed Dom's head to hold him while he fucked into his mouth. On every down stroke, he pushed against Dom's probing fingers as hard as he could. He was close…so fucking close. He felt his body start to tingle, but before he could get the relief he needed, Dom pulled off him, releasing his now leaking cock with a pop. The fingers disappeared and Dom's big body was covering his again as a tongue thrust into his mouth. But before he could protest the loss, Dom's cock was pushing into him in one long thrust, the slick oil letting him slide all the way home as Logan's body readily accepted the intrusion.

"Yes," Logan moaned as he closed his fists over Dom's muscled back. But Dom only gave him a few shallow thrusts as he continued to explore his mouth with his tongue and Logan groaned in frustration.

"Fuck me," he said as he panted against Dom's lips as he pushed his hips up to get Dom deeper inside of him.

Dom stopped all his movements and hung over Logan, his dark eyes glittering. "I'm going to, baby. I'm going to fuck you until you beg me to stop. Then I'm going to do it harder. And when you think you can't take any more, I'm going to start all over again," he promised.

Logan shook at the words and then watched as Dom lifted off him, but kept their lower bodies connected. His hands closed around Logan's ankles as he spread his legs wide and high and then he looked down to where they were joined. He thrust in and out in slow, even moves, enough to keep Logan's desire burning, but nowhere near what he needed to get the release he craved. He tried to shift his body enough so that Dom would nail his prostate, but Dom guessed his intent and stopped moving all together. Logan cried out, but he got the message and didn't move again once Dom finally resumed his previous pace. His inner walls rippled and ached with each pass, but it wasn't enough.

"Dom," he moaned and when their eyes connected again, he saw Dom smile in satisfaction. Bastard was enjoying this too much. But before he could do anything, Dom suddenly slammed into him. One hard thrust that had him as deep as he could go. Then a long draw as he slowly slid out. Another slam that pushed Logan back as his insides tried to keep Dom there. Over and over Dom rammed into him, long and hard, deep and slow. So fucking slow. Sweat began to gather on Logan's forehead, but he was afraid that if he moved even a little bit,

Dom would stop again. He dug his fingers into the bedding as Dom slowly increased the frequency of his thrusting. The force of Dom ramming into him shook the bed and Logan's body slipped farther up the mattress with each powerful thrust.

Dom snarled and lowered his arms so that he was gripping Logan's thighs, the move lifting his ass off the bed. And Dom held him like that as he began lunging in and out of him, the brutal strokes burning and stinging as the thick cock flayed him alive from the inside out. The heat was overwhelming and sweat began to drip into his eyes. But Logan couldn't move – he could only lay there as Dom commanded his body and the sensation built under his skin and fired along all his nerves. He grunted over and over as Dom surged into him and then he felt Dom's hand grip his cock. He was so sensitive that it almost hurt as Dom stroked him.

Logan shook his head as everything started to go dark. It was too much and still not enough. And then it was. There was no warning as Dom sent him over the edge and light flooded behind his closed eyes. Sensation rocked through him as his body began jerking and thrashing. And then he was floating as liquid heat hit his belly and the orgasm spread its endless pleasure along his arms and legs, down to his fingers. Even his fucking toes curled before relaxing. His brain shut down and the sounds of his own moans and the slapping of skin on skin disappeared as he floated away into nothing.

He wasn't sure how long he lay there like that for, but soft, warm kisses along his face and jaw had him sighing and he wanted to just stay there like that forever. But his ass was still stuffed full and he could feel Dom's hard abdomen pressed against his now flaccid dick. His whole body felt like jelly and he knew he should at least offer to jerk or suck Dom off so he could find his release, but he didn't have the energy for that either.

"You're so beautiful when you come," Dom said as he brushed his lips over Logan's. Then that amazing tongue was inside his mouth, worshipping him like it always seemed to be doing.

He winced when Dom shifted. His ass hurt like a mother.

"Dom, I can't," he began, but Dom cut him off with another kiss. It went on for several minutes and Logan found himself following Dom's tongue back into his mouth, reluctant to let him go just yet. His arms ended up around Dom's shoulders and he explored the slick skin beneath his fingertips. Dom managed to pull his mouth free, but an instant later that seeking tongue was exploring Logan's ear, then dipping inside. It was an erogenous zone he didn't know he had and he felt a zap of energy go through him as Dom played with him. Then Dom's hands were moving, those blunt fingertips pressing into his skin.

As his body began to come back to him, he realized that at some point he'd wrapped his legs around Dom. He felt Dom's hands travel down to his hips and then he was gripping Logan's ass. He pressed up at the same time that his hips pushed down and Logan groaned at the feeling of Dom's hard cock sinking further into him. It burned and ached, but amazingly, it didn't hurt. Dom did the move again and again and then his lips were back on Logan's as his tongue mimicked the move. Logan's body started to thrum with anticipation every time Dom slid into him and soon the short strokes weren't enough anymore. He pulled his legs back every time Dom pumped into him until he felt the other man's balls press up against his ass when he was buried as deep as he could go. Dom moaned and tore his mouth free and buried it in Logan's neck. They stayed there like that for a long time until Dom took a deep breath and then started moving again.

∼

Dom's control was hanging on by a thread and when Logan lifted enough so that he could sink all the way inside of him, he had to release the other man's mouth so he could bite his lip instead while he fought the urge to pound into Logan without mercy. He knew Logan's ass had to hurt, but he needed him too much and couldn't force himself to pull out. He pressed his mouth against Logan's neck and once again felt that rapid pulse beneath his lips. It was a harsh reminder of the day he'd pressed his fingers to Logan's neck and that pulse hadn't been there. He tightened his hold on Logan and then began moving his hips, his cock easily gliding in and out of Logan's slick channel. He felt Logan's fingers biting into his back as he increased the pace and he lifted his head and searched the younger man's eyes.

He didn't see any pain, but he asked, "Am I hurting you?" anyway.

Logan seemed overwhelmed by what was happening between them and only managed to shake his head. Dom couldn't resist Logan's slightly parted lips and leaned down to kiss him again. He would never get enough of this man's mouth for as long as he lived.

Dom's whole body drew tight as his need for relief clawed at him and he began to lunge in and out of Logan desperately, his head dropping as he buried his face back against Logan's neck once more. He was glad when he felt Logan's cock stiffen beneath him because he wanted them to go over together this time and he hadn't been sure if he would be able to hold out long enough for Logan's body to recover from his first orgasm. It had taken everything in Dom not to come when Logan did, but it had been so worth it to be able to watch Logan come apart in his arms, to feel his body as it reacted to the sensation that'd flooded it. And when it appeared that Logan had actually blacked out from the pleasure, Dom had been arrogantly pleased.

"I love you, Dom," he heard Logan whisper in his ear and that was enough to end him. He shouted as his orgasm suddenly washed through him and his semen flooded Logan's insides. Logan jerked beneath him a second later and he felt teeth clamp down on his shoulder as Logan stifled his groan of pleasure. Dom kept thrusting into Logan as the aftershocks went through him and Logan's body milked the last drop of his release from him. Logan went limp beneath him and didn't complain when Dom dropped his weight onto him, his own body too sated to move. He barely managed to pull out of Logan before he was out cold.

CHAPTER 13

"Merry Christmas, Dom."

Dom smiled as the words were accompanied by a gentle stroke over his head. Logan really had a thing with touching him there and he had to admit, it felt pretty fucking amazing. Especially when there was a hard chest beneath his head to use as a giant pillow. The petting continued and Dom shifted so he was facing Logan. He wasn't sure how he'd ended up draped across Logan or how the man had managed to get them up by the headboard, but it was his new favorite sleeping position as far as he was concerned.

"Merry Christmas, Logan."

Logan's stomach picked that moment to growl and Dom chuckled as he started to sit up. "Let me make you something-"

But Logan grabbed him before he could move too far and said, "Not yet." He gently pushed Dom back into the position he'd been in and said, "Not yet," again. Dom settled back down and Logan started stroking him again.

"When did you last eat?" he said softly.

Logan shrugged. "Don't remember. Shane's mom put together a big dinner, but I'm not sure if I ate anything before I ruined everyone's night."

"What happened?" Dom asked softly, hating to see the pain return to Logan's eyes.

"I went off on them – all of them. Admitted I was having trouble trusting them. Told my sister how much it hurt that she hadn't come to me with everything. Then I pretty much outed myself right there in front of Shane's parents."

Dom grabbed Logan's free hand in his.

"I was surrounded by all the people that love me in this world, but all I wanted was you." Logan played with Dom's fingers, twining and untwining them with his own over and over as he spoke. "It felt like I was dying right there at that table as everyone laughed and ate around me. Part of me was missing and I was bleeding inside and I couldn't stop it," he said softly.

Dom pulled their joined hands to his mouth and kissed the back of Logan's. "I'm sorry," he said, his heart aching for Logan. But he knew exactly what Logan was talking about.

"You felt it too," Logan said.

Dom nodded.

Logan leaned back against the headboard and resumed his play with their hands. "Shane's dad was the one who told me I needed to tell you how I felt. He said that second chances aren't guaranteed… I've been so lucky because I've gotten a lot of them – second chances." Logan released his hand and brushed his fingers over Dom's mouth. "I'm so glad you decided to give me another," he said.

"Always," Dom said and lifted to meet Logan's seeking mouth. They kissed for a while until Logan's stomach growled again.

Dom pulled back and said, "Shower, breakfast, more fucking – in that order."

~

Logan watched Dom wince as he bent down to look for something in the fridge. They hadn't done things quite in the order Dom had dictated. Yes, the shower had happened, but the fucking had started within minutes of them cleaning off the remnants of last night's lovemaking from each other's bodies. And since there wasn't a bench in the shower, they'd ended up on their knees on the hard tile floor. Only it had been Dom bent over this time as Logan reamed in and out of him. He suspected they'd both have bruises on their legs to show for the adventure, but judging by the way Dom was walking, he'd have a few extra pains to deal with. Of course, after what had happened between them last night, Dom wasn't the only one sporting a well-used ass.

The omelet Dom dumped in front of him moments later had him drooling and he was more than halfway done before Dom sat across from him at the kitchen island and began working on his own food.

"How'd you get here last night?" Dom asked between mouthfuls. "You couldn't have made the last ferry."

Logan looked at him sheepishly before taking another bite of egg. "I kind of commandeered a plane," he answered.

Dom stilled, his full fork hovering in mid-air. "Am I going to need to come up with some bail money?"

"Fuck you," Logan said with a chuckle. "I chartered it. Even though the guy doesn't actually run a charter company."

"Start at the beginning."

"When I found out you weren't at your apartment, I knew I was screwed because there was no way I was going to be able to catch the last ferry out of Anacortes. I was pretty upset," he admitted, dropping his eyes to the plate in front of him as he remembered the heartbreak he'd felt when he'd discovered Dom wasn't in town.

He felt Dom's hand close over his briefly, a reminder that life was as it should be.

"I suppose your Concierge must have felt sorry for me or something, because he told me where you were. I guess since I'd been there before, he figured I wasn't some creepy stalker."

Dom chuckled at that, then began eating again.

"I tried calling a couple of places to see if they had any boats that would bring me up here, but everyone was closed. The Concierge finally stepped in and gave me the number of a guy with a float plane.

It took a little bit of haggling, but I got him to agree to my terms and he dropped me off at the public marina on the point and I walked here."

"You walked here in the middle of the night?" Dom asked angrily. "Do you know what could have happened to you?"

Logan smiled as Dom's protectiveness kicked in and he just listened in pleasure as Dom ranted and raved at him about needing to be more careful. It felt good to have this man worry about him.

"…and thank God you had the sense not to hitchhike - wait, terms? What terms?"

"What?" Logan said, when he realized Dom had stopped talking and was waiting for an answer from him.

"You said you got the guy who flew you here to agree to your terms. What were the terms?"

"Right, terms," Logan hedged.

"Logan," Dom warned.

"I wasn't exactly carrying a lot of cash with me so I gave him what I had which was like fifty bucks. I told him to bill you for the rest," he admitted.

Dom didn't seem to care about that part. Instead he said, "And he agreed to that?"

"Not quite. I had to sign over my car as collateral."

"Your car's a piece of shit," Dom said.

"Fuck you. It's a classic," Logan responded. "I had to give him my watch too."

Dom chuckled. "We'll get your watch back," he said with a smile.

"The car too."

Dom laughed again. "The car too."

~

Dom handed the valet his keys as Logan pulled their bags from his trunk. He took his bag from Logan and put it in his left hand and used his right to grab Logan's hand. He stopped when Logan didn't move and saw that his eyes were locked on their joined hands. It was then that Dom realized what he'd done and he dropped Logan's hand like a hot potato. People milled all around them, but he hadn't even considered that when he'd pulled Logan's hand into his own. They'd spent the last two days wrapped so tight around each other that it had become second nature for him to always have some kind of contact with Logan. He'd forgotten that things wouldn't necessarily be the same in the real world.

"Logan, I'm sorry," he said as he glanced around. "I don't think anyone noticed."

Logan watched him for a long, pregnant moment and Dom panicked because he couldn't figure out what was going through the other man's head. But before he could dwell on it further, Logan was kissing him, his tongue sweeping inside of Dom's mouth. All his fear disappeared as Logan made love to his mouth right there in front of his building as the occasional person moved past them. He was sure they got some strange looks, but he really didn't give a shit. And when Logan finally released him and took his hand back in his own, he realized he wasn't quite done and he yanked Logan back to him for another quick brush of their mouths.

They grabbed their bags and headed inside, but when Logan started for the elevator, Dom said, "Hold up a second." Logan followed him up to the front desk where a single receptionist smiled at him and then handed him the small white envelope he was looking for. "Thank you," he said as he released Logan's hand to take the envelope before crossing the room to where the Concierge desk was.

"Good evening, Mr. Barretti," the well-dressed man behind the small counter said. "Mr. Bradshaw," he said, nodding at Logan.

"Good evening, Harrison. I understand you're a bit of a football fan," Dom said.

The slim, silver-haired man colored slightly because between his well-dressed appearance and proper etiquette, he seemed more like someone who belonged in the balcony of a sedate opera rather than the crowded stands of a football stadium.

"I am," he said.

Dom handed him the envelope. "Thank you," he said solemnly as he took Logan's hand back in his. The older man looked at their joined hands, then smiled and nodded.

"You're welcome, Mr. Barretti," he said.

Dom tugged Logan towards the elevator. He heard a shout behind him and smiled.

"What did you give him?" Logan asked as he turned back to glance at the man who was now covering his mouth after his uncharacteristic outburst.

"Season tickets to the Seattle Seahawks along with a couple of passes to meet the team and an invitation to sit in the owner's box for the first home game." He heard Logan chuckle behind him.

By the time they were on the elevator and Dom had entered the code for his floor, they were on each other again, their mouths fused as Dom pressed Logan back against the smooth wall.

"Do you think it's always going to be like this?" Logan asked, as Dom sucked hard on his neck, then soothed away the sting.

"Yes," he answered without hesitation. He knew without a doubt that the need he had for this man would never go away.

They barely made it inside the door before Logan was working at the buttons of Dom's shirt. A discrete cough had them jumping apart.

"Vin," he breathed when he saw his brother standing in the living room, his obsidian eyes flickering from him to Logan. The relief at seeing his brother was instant and it took him only a few strides to reach his older brother and drag him into his arms. "Where the hell have you been? You said you were coming home two weeks ago!" Dom growled into his ear.

He and Vin had the same build and Vin only had about an inch on him in the height department. But life had been harder on Vin between trying to take on the responsibility of being the family patriarch at the tender age of eighteen and carving out a life after a bullet had taken away his career as a SEAL. The search for Ren had only heaped more weight on his brother's already crowded shoulders.

"Yeah, well, we got hung up in a little turf war that was going on," he muttered as he returned Dom's hug. "Then Banner broke his fucking ankle..." he said. "Merry Christmas, little brother," Vin finally said softly before releasing him.

It took Vin's shifting eyes to a place behind him to remind Dom of Logan and he turned to see his lover standing stiffly by the door with a deer-in-the-headlights look. He instantly dismissed Vin and went back to Logan, his hands going to the other man's face.

"Logan, baby, look at me." Logan tore his eyes from Vin, then focused them on Dom and relaxed. "We knew this would be the hardest part," he reminded him and Logan nodded. "You come first... no matter what."

He felt the rest of the tension drain from Logan's frame and he didn't give a shit that his brother was watching as he leaned down to brush a kiss over Logan's lips.

Logan bent down and grabbed both their bags. "Why don't I give you two a few minutes while I go put our stuff away?" he said.

"Come meet Vin first," Dom said.

Logan nodded, then stepped past Dom and extended his hand to Vin.

"Logan Bradshaw," he said as Vin accepted the greeting.

"Vin Barretti," he countered and Dom bristled at the way Vin seemed to be trying to dissect Logan.

"Welcome home," Logan said. "I've heard a lot of great things about you," he added before he retrieved their bags from where they sat next to Dom. Dom felt marginally better when Logan squeezed his hand as he walked past him.

He turned his attention back to Vin who was making his way to the kitchen. He pulled out three beers and handed one to Dom. Vin screwed the top off the other one, then took a long drink. He handed the third beer to Dom.

"For when he comes back out," Vin said as he motioned in the direction Logan had gone.

Dom was pleased that his brother wasn't freaking out, although he could see the questions lingering in his eyes. His attraction to men wasn't something he'd shared with any of his brothers and Vin had already been deployed by the time Dom had done any exploring. By the time Vin had come home, Sylvie had already become a permanent fixture in his life. He felt a twinge of pain go through him as he remembered the first time Vin and Sylvie had met.

"What is it?" Vin asked.

Dom chuckled. His sharp-eyed brother never missed a thing. "I was thinking about when you and Sylvie met for the first time."

Vin laughed. "Man, was she a little firecracker. She looked like this sweet, innocent young thing, but you couldn't pull one over on her," he mused.

"I miss her," Dom said.

"I wish I'd been here for you," Vin said. "Is he one of the people you had?"

Dom looked up at him in confusion.

"When I called, you said you had people that were helping you get through it. He one of them?"

Dom nodded. "His family too…but mostly him."

Vin chugged down some more beer.

"You think it's too soon," Dom said. "Sylvie hasn't been gone long enough for me to be in love with someone else."

Dom nearly jumped when Vin slammed his beer down. "Don't put bullshit words like that in my mouth!"

The outburst was unusual for someone as calm and controlled as his brother. "You get a chance for anything like what you had with Sylvie, you fucking take it, do you hear me? Not everyone even gets one chance, let alone two. And there sure as shit isn't some magic number out there that says how long you have to live with the loss of one love before you're allowed another."

Dom watched in stunned silence as Vin swallowed the rest of his beer. He couldn't ever remember a time his embittered brother had spoken about love before, let alone defended it so passionately. The man was notorious when it came to his own bitter attitude towards women. Dom knew it had started with their mother and her betrayal of her vows to their father. But a subsequent, doomed relationship with a cruel, heartless woman who'd claimed to love Vin even as she'd fucked an endless line of men behind his brother's back had ended any romantic notions Vin would ever have towards the opposite sex.

"Go get him," Vin said as he searched out another beer. "I want to meet the guy who was lucky enough to snag my baby brother's heart."

CHAPTER 14

"I need to go home," Logan said as Dom shifted on top of him so their cocks were lined up. Even through their clothes, he could feel the extreme heat that Dom's body always seemed to give off.

Dom stilled at his comment. "Why?" he asked almost suspiciously and he thought he saw a little bit of fear there.

"Because I can't walk around naked while I'm waiting for the single pair of jeans I have to run through the wash cycle in that big-ass fancy machine you call a washer."

"Who says you can't walk around naked?" Dom asked as he kissed him again.

Logan thrust his hips up so he could increase the pressure of Dom's length on his own. Dom humped against him and Logan used the moment to roll Dom underneath him. He ground against him once, then stopped and said, "I'll come right back." He felt the tension in Dom and knew he'd guessed correctly that Dom was worried if Logan left the safety of Dom's apartment, that he'd get cold feet and do a one-eighty like he'd already done once before. "I'll come back," he said again and Dom nodded.

"I'll go with you," he offered.

"You have to go back to work. And I have to find work. We need to get back to normal, Dom." Dom tried to push up, but Logan pinned him by the wrists and settled all his weight on the other man. They both knew Dom could easily unseat him, but he didn't. Logan released his wrists and joined their hands instead. "A normal that includes this," he said as he sipped at Dom's lips until the man was squirming beneath him. "I'm not running," he murmured. "Never again," he whispered as he settled his mouth fully on Dom's.

The visit with Vin had gone better than Logan had expected and he'd ended up liking Dom's brother a lot once Logan had gotten past his fear of being judged for being a part of Dom's life so soon after Sylvie's death. He also wasn't sure what to expect from Vin in terms of seeing his brother with another man. But that hadn't stopped Dom from holding his hand or resting his big palm on Logan's thigh as Vin had told them about his attempts to find Ren. When Dom had heard the details of yet another failed effort to bring Ren home, Logan had been the one giving comfort in the form of soft touches. And if it had bothered Vin in any way, the man hadn't shown it. After Vin had left to return to his waterfront home just north of the city, he'd held a somber Dom in his arms as Dom had shared memories of his childhood before his parents had died.

They'd spent the next few days just exploring each other's bodies and lives with no talk of the future, but Logan knew it was time to figure out how to be together when things weren't so safe and easy. He pulled back from Dom and started undressing him.

"I can't lose you too," he heard Dom whisper.

"You won't," he promised, then proceeded to back up his words with his body.

~

Dom heard his phone ding and saw the text from Cade that he and Logan had left Logan's apartment. His tension eased knowing Logan would be waiting for him when he got home, but he also felt guilty for still even worrying that Logan would freak out and walk away from him again. He knew that fear would ease over time and he just hoped his anxiety wouldn't cause strain on their newfound relationship.

His intercom beeped and Cecile's voice came over the speaker as she said, "Detective Hale is here to see you, Mr. Barretti."

Dom sighed and said, "Show him in please." Declan shuffled in and Cecile closed the door behind him. The big man looked like shit and Dom's initial anger faded as he remembered how much Declan had cherished his sister. Declan had just turned twenty-two when Sylvie had gotten sick the first time and he'd taken a leave of absence from his new job as a police officer to take care of her. He'd been there each time the cancer had come back and when Sylvie had slipped away, Declan had been there to hold her hand just like he had when she'd been little. Logan had told him of Declan's visit, but Dom wasn't completely sure of Declan's motives. He hated not being able to trust the other man, but he wouldn't risk his relationship with Logan for anything.

"I don't have anything new," Declan said as he stood in front of the desk. Dom nodded towards the chairs on the other side of his desk and Declan finally sat.

"What do you want, Declan?"

"Besides my sister back?" the man said bitterly. He ran his hands through his hair and seemed to try and shake his anger off. "Sorry," he muttered. He sat back in the chair and studied Dom. "It was hard to see you like that," he began. "He walked into the room and you lit up. Like you did whenever Sylvie came into the room."

Dom didn't respond. After all, what could he say? What Declan said was true.

"I know you didn't betray her. Not then, not ever."

Dom sighed. "I love him the way I loved her, Declan. The way I still love her," he said. "If you're asking me to choose-"

"No," Declan interrupted. "No, I don't want that."

"Then what do you want?"

"I want someone I can keep her memory alive with...someone who will help me remember all the good things when I can't," he said quietly. "I don't want to just remember her when she was sick or hurting. But that's all I see right now. What if I never see anything else?" Declan whispered.

"You will. Like the time she stole your police badge so she could show it off to her friends at school. Like when she made you take her and her friends to that princess movie and you had to go dressed as a prince because it was her birthday."

Declan smiled at that.

"Or when you walked her down the aisle – you nearly broke my hand when you shook it before you gave her to me."

"If the priest hadn't been so close, I would have threatened to kick your ass if you didn't treat her right," Declan admitted.

Dom laughed. "We won't forget her, Declan. How could we?" he asked. "She was anything but forgettable," he murmured.

Declan nodded, then stood. He reached his hand across the desk.

"Fuck that shit," Dom said as he got up and went around the desk and pulled Declan into his arms.

"I'm sorry, Dom," came the muffled words.

He slapped Declan on the back and said, "It's okay, Declan. Everything's going to be okay."

~

"Riley's on her way up," Logan said from behind him. Dom looked over his shoulder to see Logan coming out of the bedroom, his hair still damp from his shower and his phone in his hand. Dom glanced at the clock on the stove as he flipped the last pancake. It was barely eight. He felt Logan wrap his arms around him from behind and then kiss his neck. "She's got Eli with her – she said he wanted to show you something."

Dom turned off the burner as he let the food finish cooking, then turned to greet Logan properly. Their kiss grew heated quickly and Logan finally broke free and shook his head. He went to the refrigerator while Dom stacked the final pancake on the huge stack he'd already cooked and put the whole plate in the microwave.

"What are she and Eli up to today?"

"Shopping, I think," Logan said.

Dom flinched at that, remembering his last attempt at taking the kid shopping. He'd checked in on Eli and his mom, Mariana, a couple of times and the pair seemed to be thriving. Eli was set to start school in January and with the help of a tutor, everyone was hopeful he'd be caught up with his grade level by the end of the year. Mariana had been thrilled at the prospect of working in the billing office for Dom's firm and was slated to have her first day on Monday.

"You talk to your sister?" Dom asked.

"Yeah. She's going stir crazy – she really wants to come home and get back to work." Logan came to a stop next to him, a glass of orange juice in his hand. He took a sip, then handed it to Dom who took a quick drink before handing it back. Sharing a glass was such a domestic thing to do and it was ridiculous how much Dom loved the little things like that that had become a part of his and Logan's routine in the last week.

"You tell her it's not safe yet?" Dom asked.

"Yeah. But it's hard, especially since we don't have any new leads."

Dom's trip to Portland a few weeks ago hadn't turned into anything and the trail had gone stone cold since then. If Sam was out there, he was damn good at hiding.

"Did you guys talk?" Dom asked, emphasizing the last word. Things between Savannah and Logan had been stunted since their conversation at Christmas. Dom suspected the distance wasn't helping the situation, but he also knew that Logan was struggling with some of the things he'd said to his sister and his extended family.

Logan shook his head and when Dom forced his eyes up from the juice he'd been staring just a little too hard at, Logan sighed and said, "We will."

Dom nodded and released him as the doorbell rang. He went to the door and opened it and Eli walked in unabashedly. "I found this," he said as he held out a piece of paper in his hand.

Riley smiled as she followed Eli in, then hugged Dom – one of her big, all-in hugs that Dom was coming to love. "Hi, Dom," she said before she trotted into the kitchen to throw her arms around Logan as well. Dom sent a quick nod to Raul who stood near the elevator before he shut the door.

Eli waved his hand in front of Dom, the small scrap of paper barely missing his nose as Eli thrust it at him.

"What is it?" Dom asked as he took it and turned it over. It wasn't actual paper, but a receipt. There was a number scrawled on the back and he stiffened when he saw the name "Cy" written above the number.

"Where are you guys headed?" he heard Logan ask Riley.

"I told Mariana I'd help Eli pick out a few things for school while she goes to the salon to get a haircut."

Eli piped up. "After that, Riley's gonna take me to her work so I can see all the dogs and cats. She says she might be able to get me a job there a couple days a week after school," he said happily.

"Eli, where'd you get this?" Dom asked, careful to keep his tone even.

"Mama and I found it when we were going through Elena's stuff. Mama still thinks she's coming back," Eli added sadly.

Riley put her arms around him and said, "Come on, Eli. Let's go find you some clothes. We can grab some donuts on the way. How does that sound?"

"Then we get to see your work?" he asked.

"Absolutely," Riley replied as she herded Eli out the door. "Bye guys," she called as she pulled the door closed behind her.

"What is it?" Logan asked as he looked over his shoulder at the receipt.

"It's a fucking receipt," Dom said, smiling as he handed it to Logan. The other man's eyes widened when he saw the name Sam had used around Elena and then the number below.

"It's Sam's number," he said. He turned the receipt over. "It looks like it's for a gas station. He paid cash though," Logan said.

"There's an address," Dom said as he pulled out his phone. "Desi? Hey, it's Dom. I need you to run an address for me, then check that against a topographical map." He glanced at the receipt and read the address to the woman on the other end. "Check the surrounding area for properties with a hill that overlooks a lake. Also check for any property owned by someone named Cy or any variation of that. Yeah, thanks." He kissed Logan hard and said, "We just got our new lead!"

~

Logan fidgeted as he leaned back against the car and waited for Dom to come out of the gas station. It had taken them less than two hours to get to Summer Hill, a small town between Seattle and Portland. Vin had met them on the road and his big black SUV was parked behind Dom's Mercedes. Vin was pacing, clearly not happy about Dom's insistence that only one of them question the clerk so he wouldn't clam up. That had been almost ten minutes ago and Logan was nearing his breaking point. The possibility of being so close to finding Sam – no, Cy – was nearly too much. The lust for vengeance was eating him from the inside out.

"We'll get him," he heard Vin say as the man stopped next to him. He was wearing some type of holster under his suit jacket because Logan could see the butt of the gun. He'd watched Dom pull a couple of guns from a locked cabinet in the living room before they'd left and the reality of the danger they were facing was starting to dawn on him. It wasn't just his or Savannah's life on the line anymore. An image of Dom on the receiving end of a bullet like the one that had nearly killed him had Logan sucking in a harsh breath.

"Logan," he heard Vin say and he snapped out of the dark haze he'd been in. "He'll be okay. He knows how to take care of himself and he's got someone worth coming home to. He's not going to take any risks."

Logan forced himself to nod, then tried to push away the cold feeling that had settled in the pit of his stomach. They'd told Vin about Sam the night Logan and Vin had met. Dom's brother had been on instant alert when he'd learned of Savannah's assault and then raging when he'd been told about the fire and shooting. He'd asked them a barrage of questions about the investigation and the security measures Dom had taken. Between Dom, Vin and the men on their team, Logan knew he couldn't have asked for a better group of people to keep him and his family safe.

Dom came out of the gas station. "He says Reynolds has been in here almost every week for the past couple of years, but stopped suddenly a few months ago."

"After he was injured in the fire," Logan said.

"The fucker was here this morning," Dom said with a smile.

"We're close," Logan said, relief mixed with anticipation.

Dom closed his arm around Logan's shoulder to give him a comforting squeeze. "I'll check with Desi to see if she's made any progress." Dom reached for his phone, but before he could dial, it rang in his hand. Logan glanced at it and then froze when he saw Shane's name come up. Dom looked up at Logan, then answered the phone, putting it on speaker.

"Shane?"

"Dom?"

Logan felt his heart drop when he heard Savannah crying in the background. Shane's voice was filled with fear.

"What's going on Shane?" Dom asked, his voice calm and firm. All three of them huddled around the phone so they could hear.

"He's got Riley, Dom. Sam's got Riley!"

CHAPTER 15

Dom heard a choking sound escape Logan at Shane's words, but he forced himself to ignore him and said, "Talk to me, Shane. Tell me what happened."

"Jesus," he heard Shane say as he tried to collect himself. His breathing was harsh. "Um, he sent Savannah a picture. I don't know how he got her fucking number!" Shane nearly shouted.

"Tell me about the picture," Dom commanded.

"It's a picture of Riley and some kid."

Dom's heart sank and he saw Logan bend over like he might be sick.

"They're both tied up or handcuffed or something."

"Send me the picture now."

"Yeah, okay," Shane said as he fumbled with what Dom assumed was Savannah's phone.

Dom looked up at Vin. "Call Desi and see if she can trace the number that sent the picture. And find out what the hell happened to Raul – he was covering Riley and Eli this morning! Logan," he said. He watched as Logan pushed back his fear and emotion and swiftly stood. "Give Vin Savannah's number."

SLOANE KENNEDY

Dom turned his attention back to the phone and saw the message come in from Shane.

"I...I sent it," Shane stammered.

Dom pulled up the picture and forced down the fury that went through him at the sight of Riley and Eli bound to some kind of pole. They were sitting on what looked like a cement floor, their arms secured behind them. Their terror was clear, but they appeared to be uninjured otherwise.

"Jesus," he heard Logan say as he looked at the picture.

"We got it, Shane. Where's Gabe?" he asked.

"I don't know," Shane said. "We got the picture and called you." They could hear Savannah's sobs grow closer and Dom assumed Shane was moving back towards her.

"Savannah!" Logan yelled as he took the phone from Dom.

"Logan?" she cried.

"We'll find them!" he said. "I swear to God, we'll find them."

"This is my fault," he heard her cry.

Dom took the phone back from him. "Savannah, you listen to me! This is not your fault. Do you hear me?" He heard Savannah sniff, but she didn't respond. "Honey, I need you to calm down, okay?"

"Okay," she managed to force out.

Vin returned, his dark eyes grim.

"Shane, hold on a second, okay?"

"Yeah," Shane said.

Dom muted the phone.

"Desi's seeing if she can trace the phone. I talked to Cade. He said that Raul was escorting Riley and Eli back to the car near the shopping center. He must have seen the bomb strapped to the exhaust before they got in and managed to cover Riley and Eli with his body when it was detonated."

"Fuck!" Dom yelled, his control snapping. Logan closed his hand around Dom's arm.

"Is he okay?" Logan asked.

"He's in surgery – he got hit with a lot of shrapnel. After the bomb went off, it was complete chaos. A witness said Riley and Eli were both dazed by the blast and he saw what he thought was a Good Samaritan helping them. This shit happened almost two hours ago, Dom. Cade just got the news when the cops discovered the car was registered to us."

"Oh God," Logan said. "He's had them for two hours?"

Dom felt the panic gnawing at him and he struggled to think. He took the phone off mute. "Shane, you still there?" he said.

"We're here," he said quietly. Soft cries came from nearby then suddenly there was a loud ringtone coming through the phone.

"Oh my God," Dom heard Savannah cry.

"Fuck. Oh God, fuck," Shane said. "It's him. Dom, it's him. He's calling Savannah's phone. He's trying to video chat with her!"

"Get Desi on it," Dom snapped at Vin, but he was already dialing and stepping back.

"Shane, Savannah, listen to me. You have to answer it. Savannah has to answer it and keep him on the line so we can track him!"

"No!" Shane yelled.

An instant later he heard Savannah say, "I'll do it!" and he heard them scuffle.

"No fucking way!" Shane said again.

"Shane, listen to me. I know you want to protect her, but we need her to do this!" A few long seconds passed.

"Tell her what she needs to do, Dom," Shane said quietly.

"Savannah, draw him out. Keep him talking. Make sure it's only you in the frame. Answer now before he hangs up."

"Hello?" he heard Savannah say.

Vin reappeared and Dom muted the phone once more. Vin held up his phone and Dom sucked in a breath at the sight of Riley and Eli crying as they sat huddled together. They could hear Sam's voice as he screamed at Savannah. He felt Logan's hand grab his arm for support.

"Desi was able to tap into Savannah's phone. We can see everything, but they can't hear or see us. She started the track on his phone."

"You fucking bitch!" they heard Sam yell.

"Sam," Savannah tried to say, her voice shaking.

"Look what you made me do!" Sam shouted as a beefy finger came into the shot and pointed at Riley and Eli.

"Please Sam, don't hurt them!"

Logan's nails were biting into Dom's arm where he still held onto him and all the blood had drained from his face.

"Dom, we got it!" Vin said as a message popped up on his phone with coordinates.

Sam was still railing at Savannah as the three of them climbed into Vin's SUV and tore out of the parking lot. Dom pulled up the location on his phone. "Three miles," he said to Vin. "Turn right up here."

"You fucking bitch! Do you know what I did for you? How I looked out for your brother for you?" he screamed. "That piece of shit bar was nothing until I showed him how to run it! I did that for you!"

Dom looked at Logan who was sitting in the back seat. His elbows were on his knees and he was cradling his head in hands as if he was in physical pain.

"And then you let that pretty boy fuck you!"

The video stayed on Riley and Eli, but the image started to jump more and more as Sam's agitation grew.

"Do you like having him fuck that tight little cunt of yours, Savannah? Does it feel as good as when I was inside of you?"

"Fuck," he heard Vin mutter.

"Next left, Vin," Dom said. "Hang in there, Savannah," he whispered, though he knew she couldn't hear him.

"I'll come home, Sam. I swear. I'll get on a plane right now and I'll meet you anywhere you want."

"Liar," Sam said, his voice dangerously calm now.

Suddenly the phone shifted and they heard Eli shout "Don't you fucking touch us!" A second later Riley cried out in pain. The image went back to her and Eli, but Riley was lying on the floor, her eyes closed, blood dripping from a gash over her eye. Eli was cursing Sam as he struggled to get free.

"Lie to me again Savannah, and I'll kill them before the words even finish leaving those pretty lips of yours."

Dom heard Savannah start sobbing again. "I'm sorry, Sam," she said. "Tell me what you want."

"I want you to answer my question," he snarled.

"No, Sam. It doesn't feel as good as it did when it was you," Savannah said shakily. She added. "You were my first, Sam. You remember that, right?"

Dom cast a glance at Logan who was rocking back and forth now and he could see the tears on his face. He was going to rip Sam limb from fucking limb when he found him.

"This is it, Vin," he said, pointing at the gravel driveway.

"I remember," Sam whispered, his voice softening as if he were talking to lover. Dom knew at that point the man had snapped and his unpredictability made him more dangerous than ever. Suddenly the image changed and they saw Sam's face as he swapped the screen so Savannah would be able to see him instead of Riley and Eli. "I miss you, baby," he said.

Vin slowed the SUV as the house came into view. It sat near the base of a slight hill and just as Sam had told Elena, there was a lake behind the house. The white farmhouse was completely dilapidated, its paint faded in some spots, completely stripped in others. There was a wraparound porch that had probably been a pretty place to sit at some point in the past, but now it was covered in thick vines and the stairs leading up to it were torn or missing. Nearly all the windows were boarded up and the only one that wasn't had what looked like a sheet covering it.

Next to the house was a big shed, the bright red vinyl siding a stark contrast to the house. It looked nearly new and in front of the sliding door was a broken-down van. The side door was open.

"There," Dom said.

Sam was still talking to Savannah, but his tone changed suddenly and he said, "He's there with you, isn't he, Savannah?"

Dom didn't wait for the young woman to answer as he grabbed his gun from the waistband of his pants, then the second one he had strapped to his ankle.

"Logan!" he shouted and the other man instantly snapped his eyes up. He shoved the second gun into Logan's hand. "We need to go now!"

All three of them climbed out of the SUV. Dom pointed at the gun. "Safety's off. That fucker comes towards you, you point this at his chest and pull the trigger until the gun is empty." He didn't give Logan a chance to respond before he was running up the driveway, Vin several yards ahead of him.

"I told you not to lie to me," he heard Sam yell and then everything went silent as the call disconnected. Adrenaline flooded his system as he heard what sounded like Eli screaming, then silence. He managed to catch up to Vin as they reached the shed door. They cleared the first section where another car sat, then moved to a smaller room in the back. Logan was right behind him as they pulled the door open. They could hear what sounded like metal striking stone.

The first thing Dom saw when they breached the door was the blood splattered on the walls. His heart dropped at the sight, then relief went through him at the sight of Eli still struggling against his bonds. Riley remained on the floor, but he didn't see any additional injuries.

"Jesus," he heard Vin mutter and then the man was moving.

Sam's body lay lifeless on the floor, blood pooling beneath him from what used to be his face. A young woman stood above him in a yellow dress, her long red-brown hair shifting up and down her back as she brought a metal pipe down over and over on Sam's crushed head. She was covered in blood spatter and gore, but she kept striking Sam, even though he was long gone.

"Stop," he heard Vin say as he grabbed the young woman's arm and pulled the pipe from her hands. She struggled against him as he gripped her arms, then suddenly passed out.

Dom ran to Riley's side and dropped down to check her injuries while Logan checked on Eli.

"Vin, cuffs!" Dom said to Vin when he saw the handcuffs on Riley's wrists.

Vin shifted the girl in his arms and searched Sam's pockets, then tossed him the key. He released Riley from the cuffs, then threw the key to Logan. He checked Riley's pulse and sighed in relief at the flutter beneath his fingers. The injury over her eye looked nasty, but it wasn't life threatening.

"She hit her head," Eli said as Logan worked to get him free of the cuffs. "He was trying to hit me! She was protecting me and she got hit instead and she fell," Eli cried as tears streamed down his face. "Is she okay?"

Logan got the cuffs off and Eli scrambled to Riley's side.

"Logan, call 911. The address is 510 Sycamore."

Logan was dialing before he even finished saying the address. Dom pulled out his own phone and hit the speed dial. As the phone rang, he carefully moved Riley's head to check the other injury. There was a wound just above her temple and blood dripped slowly out of it.

"Cade," he said when the other man answered.

"Yeah."

"We found them. Get Gabe down here as soon as you can. Tell him she's okay," he said.

"Is she?" Cade asked quietly.

"Not sure. She's unconscious. But don't tell him that," he said.

"Got it."

"Have Trevor find Mariana – Eli's okay, but he'll need to get checked out at the hospital. I'll call you once I know where we're headed."

"On it." The line disconnected.

Dom looked at Logan who was finishing up with 911. "Call Savannah and Shane. Tell them they're okay, but nothing more," he said and Logan nodded stiffly, his eyes flashing with pain as he looked down at Riley. "Make the call, Logan," Dom said softly.

"Vin, how is she?" Dom asked his brother.

"She's still out, but her breathing's good. Marks on her wrists and ankles – he may have had her tied up too."

"He called her Mia," Eli said. Dom and Vin both looked at him.

"Sam did?" Dom asked.

Eli nodded as he dashed at the tears that were finally starting to slow. "He was pointing his gun at us. None of us saw her come in, but when he pointed the gun at us she hit him with the pipe. He seemed surprised and called her Mia and then she hit him again. And then she just kept hitting him," he finished, his voice wavering when his eyes fell on Sam's gruesome remains.

"Mia," he heard Vin say as he tried to rouse her. A second later he heard Vin curse. "She's got some type of collar on her."

Logan ended his call and reached down to touch Riley's face. "I'll stay with her," he said as he motioned to Vin. Dom was insanely proud of the strength in Logan's voice and wished he could just put everything on pause so he could take him in his arms. Logan seemed to sense his thoughts because he sent him a small smile.

Dom sidled up to Vin. "He's rigged it somehow," Vin said as he fingered the collar. The buckle had been soldered so that it couldn't be easily removed. "Hold her," Vin said as he pulled out a knife and carefully worked it through the plastic. The collar broke and Vin gently pulled it off to reveal a long, infected lesion that went around her whole neck where the plastic had dug in. Two small, circular wounds that almost looked like burns were on one side of her throat.

"What the hell?" Vin said and then he froze and suddenly turned the collar over. Two small metal prongs stuck out from a square shaped box. "Fucking son of a bitch! It's a shock collar," he snarled. "The kind they use on dogs to keep them from crossing an invisible fence or barking too much!"

Dom closed his eyes and wished to God the woman had left Sam alive so that he could wrap his hands around the man's throat and watch the life seep out of him. He felt Vin take the woman back in his arms and then he pulled her against his chest as he stood. His brother eyed Sam's body for a moment before he left, taking the girl outside.

He heard sirens and within minutes, paramedics were there and strapping Riley to a backboard. She still hadn't woken up and he and Logan shared a silent look as she was rushed from the room.

CHAPTER 16

"Logan?"

Logan snapped his head up at the sound of Riley's voice. He jumped out of the chair he'd been sitting in and rushed to the side of the hospital bed and took her hand. She looked at him in confusion, then around the small room.

"Where…where are we?" she asked, her voice scratchy. "Where's Gabe?"

"He's on his way, Riley. He'll be here really soon, okay? You're in the hospital."

"Hospital?" she asked as she tried to sit up, then winced.

Logan put a hand on her shoulder to keep her from trying to move again. "Stay still, honey. You hit your head pretty hard. You've been out for a while," he said.

Dom came in, two cups of coffee in his hand. Logan looked up and said, "Dom, she's awake. Get the nurse."

Dom nodded as he rushed back out of the room.

"What happened?" Riley asked.

"It's not important right now. Just rest," Logan said.

Her eyes narrowed in confusion and she put a hand to her head.

"There was an explosion," she said. Her brow furrowed as she was trying to remember. Then her eyes flew open wide. "Eli! Raul!"

"They're fine, Riley," Dom said as he came back into the room, the coffee gone now.

"That man! He took us!" Riley shouted as she tried to sit up again. Dom and Logan both held her down carefully and Dom grabbed her face.

"Riley, listen to me. Eli's fine. A little shook up, but fine. Raul too – he got out of surgery half an hour ago and the doctors expect him to make a complete recovery." She calmed at Dom's words. "Sam's dead – he can't hurt you or anyone else ever again."

Tears pooled in her eyes and she nodded her head as she tried to catch her breath.

"Miss Sinclair, how are you feeling?" the nurse said as she rushed into the room and began checking Riley's vitals. Dom stepped out of the way, but Logan didn't move as Riley's hand clung to his.

"My head hurts," she said as she wiped at the tears that leaked from her eyes.

"I'll check with the doctor to see what we can get for your pain," she said as she checked the abrasions on Riley's wrists where the handcuffs had bit into her skin.

"Riley?!" they heard a loud shout from the hall, then Gabe was there and Riley sobbed as he gathered her in his arms. "Oh God, thank you," he whispered as he clutched her against him.

"Gabe," Riley cried as her hands clutched his shirt. "I was so scared, Gabe."

"I know, sweetheart. You're safe now," he whispered brokenly as he kissed the top of her head.

"The doctor will be right in," the nurse said to both of them, but Logan wasn't sure if they heard her.

Dom took his hand and led him from the room so they could give the couple some privacy. Once they were in the hallway, Logan felt a sob overtake him as the relief that it was finally over sank in and he felt Dom's arms go around him.

"It's over, baby," he heard Dom whisper.

Logan nodded, but was too overcome with emotion to speak. Between the torment of hearing his sister being verbally tortured while they'd all had to sit and listen, helpless to stop it, and the sight of Riley unconscious on the cold floor of that shed, he was completely worn out, mentally and physically.

"She okay?"

Dom released him and Logan saw Cade striding down the hallway.

"Yeah, she's awake," Dom said.

"And the kid?"

"He's good – they're going to keep him overnight for observation just to be sure. His mom should be here soon and Vin's with him now."

Cade nodded, then smiled in relief. "I'll go check in on him," the man said and Logan hid a smile. Cade had acted like he didn't like the kid, but the guy was a big softie at heart, despite the hard exterior.

Dom must have been thinking the same thing because a whisper of a smile ghosted his lips before he told Cade which room Eli was in.

Cade hurried off and then a doctor was pushing past them and into Riley's room. They followed and stood near the door as the doctor greeted Riley and Gabe who still clung to one another.

"How are you feeling, Miss Sinclair?" the doctor asked as he pulled up Riley's chart on the computer next to the bed.

"Better," she said as she looked up at Gabe.

"Good," the doctor said before performing a quick exam. He checked the wound at her temple, then the one on her face. "I'm going to put a couple of stitches in this one," he said as he checked the injury above her eye. "But the other one should be fine without anything – we'll just keep it covered with some bandages." He maneuvered around Gabe as he finished his exam, but didn't ask the man to move.

He went back to the computer and entered a couple of things.

"Everything looks good, but I would like to admit you overnight for observation in case you have a concussion," he said. "I'm also going to have OB take a look at you, but I don't expect there to be any problems with the baby."

Logan froze at that and he felt Dom tense next to him. A stunned

Gabe and Riley stared in shock at the doctor. The man seemed oblivious as he typed his notes.

"Baby?" Gabe whispered.

The doctor finally looked up from what he was doing and noticed everyone's dumbfounded expressions. "Miss Sinclair, you do know you're pregnant, don't you?"

Riley couldn't seem to find any words so she shook her head.

"I'm sorry, I just assumed you knew," the doctor mumbled. "It's standard routine to do a pregnancy test on any woman of child-bearing years who comes into the ER," he said.

"I can't be pregnant," she said numbly. "I'm on birth control pills."

"Did you miss any or are you taking any other medications or supplements?"

Riley shook her head, then stopped suddenly. "Yes. A friend at work suggested an herbal supplement for anxiety. We've been under a lot of stress the last couple months..." she said, her voice dropping off.

"That'll do it. It's rare, but certain herbal supplements can reduce the effectiveness of oral contraceptives."

"Oh God," Riley said. She looked up at Gabe and shook her head. "I'm so sorry, Gabe. I didn't know," she cried.

Suddenly, Gabe kissed her long and hard. "A baby, Riley," he whispered in awe. "We're going to have a baby," he said as he kissed her again. "I love you so much."

Gabe held her as she cried against him and then they were both smiling as they finally focused their attention back on the doctor. Logan felt Dom's hand close over his.

The doctor smiled kindly at them. "So, I'll have OB come down and take a look at you and they'll determine whether or not to do an ultrasound. My guess is that it may still be a bit early for that, but they'll be able to determine that for sure. Congratulations to you both," he said as he left the room.

Gabe climbed into the small bed beside her and she snuggled up against him as they spoke softly to each other. Logan followed Dom from the room.

"We were so lucky," he whispered to Dom as he closed the door to the room to give Riley and Gabe privacy. "If that girl hadn't been there," he began, before he shook his head. They both knew that Sam had been on the verge of pulling the trigger and none of them would have been able to reach that shed in time to stop him. "Is she awake yet?" Logan asked.

"No," Dom said. "She's in pretty bad shape. Dehydrated, underweight. The injury from the collar she had on is infected, so she's spiked a fever."

"We need to find out who she is – help her if we can," Logan said.

"We will," Dom said. "Whatever it takes."

∼

Dom glanced at his watch as he made his way down the hallway towards the hospital room the nurse had told him the young woman was in. It was nearly midnight and he wanted to check on her before he and Logan headed to the hotel nearby to get some much-needed rest. The adrenaline spike that had kept him going all day was finally starting to wane and he felt like he could crash at any moment.

Shane and Savannah had arrived an hour ago after Dom had called in a favor and one of their firm's wealthy clients had agreed to fly the couple out on his private plane since no seats had been available on any commercial flights. The pair had been a mess when they'd arrived, but seeing Riley had done wonders for them and the tight-knit family had gathered around her as they'd shared in the joy of the pregnancy news. Eli had been allowed to come and visit with Riley before being herded up to Pediatrics to spend the night and the staff had found Mariana a cot to sleep on so she wouldn't have to leave her son.

Relief flooded him as he realized it really was all over now and he and Logan could start to build their life together.

"Sir, you need to leave those on," Dom heard a woman say from the room he was about to enter. "Sir, I'll have to call security!"

Dom tensed at her words and quickened his pace.

"Then call them," he heard Vin say and he slowed as a pissed off nurse hurried out of the room. Dom came to a stop in the doorway of the young woman's room and took in the sight before him. His brother was removing the second restraint from the girl's wrist. The first one already hung loosely from the railing of the hospital bed. She was still unconscious, but moving and thrashing in the bed as she seemed to be fighting off some nightmare.

"Shhh," he heard his brother say as he sat on the edge of the bed next to her and took her hand in his, his fingers gently rubbing the abrasions on her wrist that had been caused by whatever Sam had used to restrain her with. Between the inhumane collar and the proof that she'd been recently bound, they could only assume she was another one of Sam's victims – one that he'd left alive for some reason.

Dom watched as Vin stroked the girl's cheek gently and she settled under the touch. "How is she?" he asked, as he entered the room.

Vin stood quickly, but to Dom's surprise, he didn't release the hand he was holding. In fact, his thumb was rubbing back and forth over her fingers as if trying to soothe her and Dom wondered if Vin even realized he was doing it.

"She's been in and out. The fever's down, but every time she wakes up, she freaks out and these assholes seem to think that tying her up will fix that," he said angrily. As he spoke, the nurse reappeared with a burly looking orderly who stepped into the room and headed for the bed.

"Sir, I'm going to have to ask you to step out," he said to Vin as he reached for one of the restraints.

"You touch her and I will fucking take you apart," Vin said quietly, coldly. Dom knew that tone and stepped forward before the orderly could do anything.

"Get whoever's in charge in here right now," Dom said. The orderly opened his mouth, but another look at Vin had him snapping it shut again and then he left the room.

Dom turned back to Vin who was studying the woman who now lay peacefully in the bed. She was a pretty thing, but painfully thin and pale. The staff had managed to get her mostly clean, but some of her long, auburn hair was threaded with dried clumps of blood.

"The cops stopped by to try and talk to her," Vin said. "They found a room in the house that may have been hers." Vin looked up at him. "It was bad, Dom, what they found. And cadaver dogs are hitting all over the property."

Dom knew Elena would probably be among the bodies that would be dug up and he dreaded having to tell Eli and his mother. He nodded towards the girl. "Do they know who she is yet?"

"They found some notebooks in the room – like the kind kids use in school when they're little."

"Composition books," Dom supplied.

"Right. The name 'Mia Hamilton' was written in them."

"Eli said Sam called her Mia."

Vin fell silent for a moment, then said, "The cops discovered some paperwork in the house too. It belonged to Cyrus Hamilton."

Cy. The name Sam had used with Eli's sister. Shock went through him when he connected the rest of what Vin had said.

"They think she might be his daughter, Dom."

"Shit," Dom said as he looked down at her.

"They're going to test her DNA against his." Vin finally put the woman's hand back down on the bed, though his fingers lingered on her skin for a few more seconds. "There's a new lead on Ren." Normally that kind of statement would have been said with excitement and hope, but the way Vin had said it made Dom realize that his brother was starting to lose faith in the belief that Ren might still be out there.

"Go," Dom said. "Find him." Dom ached to have Vin back in his life as a permanent fixture, but even if there was the slightest chance of finding Ren alive, they had to take it. "I'll take care of everything here," Dom added as he motioned to the woman between them.

Vin glanced at him, then looked at Mia again. He nodded, then went around the bed and pulled Dom into a quick hug before releasing him and heading towards the door.

"Don't let them fucking tie her up again!" he said as he left.

"I won't," Dom promised as his eyes went back to Mia. The woman had earned every protection his money and reputation could buy, and then some.

I was so proud of you today, Savannah," Logan said as his sister leaned into him and he closed his arms around her. They were sitting on one of the benches in the waiting room. Her eyes were puffy and red from the crying she'd been doing on and off since she and Shane had arrived at the hospital. They'd stayed in Riley's room until the young woman couldn't keep her eyes open anymore. Gabe hadn't left her side for even a minute and Logan guessed that between the scare he'd had today and the news that he was going to be a father, it would be a long while before Gabe slept. Shane had gone to load their bags into Dom's car while Dom checked on the young woman who had saved all their lives today.

"I was so scared," she admitted. "Scared that I'd say the wrong thing…" She shuddered in his arms and he kissed the top of her head.

"You kept him talking – you were amazing," he responded.

"Are we going to be okay? Me and you?" she said as she sat back and looked up at him.

He nodded. "Yeah, we are."

She leaned back into him. "You don't hurt anymore, do you, Logan?"

He leaned down and kissed the top of her head. He saw Dom coming around the corner and their eyes locked. "No, sweetheart, I don't."

"*G*o to sleep," Dom murmured.

"Can't," Logan said as he watched Dom's eyes open. They lay on the hotel bed facing each other. Enough light filtered through the curtains so that he could see the outline of Dom's face.

"Why not?" Dom said, his arm folding under his head.

"Just not ready yet," he said. They were both bone tired and had barely managed to even drag themselves into the tiny room before crashing on the bed. "Sylvie wrote to me again," he said. Dom inhaled deeply at that. "I got the letter after I accused you of paying my hospital bills," Logan told him.

"I remember," Dom said and Logan saw the outline of his smile as he remembered the other events of that encounter in his office. Logan instantly hardened as the memory flashed through him of watching Dom suck him deep as he was pressed up against the cold, smooth glass of the window.

"Stop that," Logan admonished. Dom laughed. "She told me not to pay back the money. She said I should pay it forward."

"Smart woman," Dom said softly, a warm tinge in his voice.

"I was thinking about maybe opening a center...a crisis center or something. For kids like Eli," he began. "A place where they'll feel safe – where they can get the support they need." Logan stroked Dom's cheek. "You saved that kid, Dom. You got him off the streets, gave him a place to stay, found his mom...I want to bring people like you together with the kids who need them," he said. "If my parents had had just a little less money, that could have been me and Savannah out there. We could have ended up like Eli and his sister."

Dom was quiet for so long, Logan was getting nervous. "I think Sylvie would be proud, Logan," Dom said as he leaned over and kissed him. "I know I am," he said as he shifted closer. "You're so much stronger than you ever gave yourself credit for."

Logan lay flat as Dom leaned over him. He shivered when one of Dom's big hands clasped the side of his face. "I love you and I will thank God and Sylvie every day for the rest of my life for bringing you to me." Dom's lips covered his own and Logan sighed in relief as everything in his world righted itself. He was finally exactly where he belonged.

EPILOGUE

Dear Sylvie,

I've been trying to write this letter for a long time, but I find that every time I sit down to do it, the words I put down on paper seem too simple, too trivial. Saying thank you isn't adequate – isn't enough for all you have given me.

Gabe told me once how Shane saved his life by not letting him walk away from Riley. It didn't make sense to me at the time because in my mind it was simple – you love someone, you don't leave them. But I didn't know what love was then. Like everything in my life, I had this image in my head that love would come in a certain package at the right time in my life. It would be straightforward and easy and obvious...and it was guaranteed.

But it hasn't been any of those things and I will be forever in your debt because you saw something in me that I couldn't. If you'd torn up that first letter like you'd considered doing, I probably would have ended up okay. Maybe I would have even met a nice woman someday, gotten married, had kids...the whole white picket fence thing. But I would have done exactly what you made Dom promise not to do...I would have just existed, not lived.

Because in being with Dom, I know what life is now. It's like you said, being around him makes it possible to breathe. I didn't know what you meant by that until I let him go and nearly lost him forever.

One of my favorite things about Dom is that he can love us both in equal measure. I think that's what I was so afraid of...that maybe he'd never quite love me enough. I kept wondering why he would choose me over you and it took me a while to figure out that he hadn't chosen. That it was never about choosing for him. He loves you still. And like you, I have no doubt of his love for me.

We talk about you often and he always gets this certain little smile when he says your name – I call it the 'Sylvie Smile.' I mentioned that to Savannah once and she laughed because she says he has a smile for me too.

Shane and Savannah have found a new place, a small apartment not far from us. Savannah has returned to her teaching job and Shane is learning all about that computer gibberish that Dom loves so much. Gabe and Riley are getting married next weekend in a small, simple ceremony. Baby is thriving under Eli's care and Vin has assured us he will find us another dog once he brings Ren home. He has made us promise to give the dog a more manly name, though you'll be pleased to know I did have my fingers crossed behind my back when I gave my promise.

There is still no word on Ren and I can see that it haunts Dom, though he tries to hide it. He continues his search for Rafe as well, but with all the years that have gone by with no word, he's admitted that he doesn't have much hope left. It is a pain I wish I could take from him, but we both know he will never truly give up trying to protect those he loves most.

As for me, I have finally decided on what the next chapter of my life will look like. Construction begins tomorrow on my bar. Instead of selling it, I have decided to turn it into something that can help kids get the second chance they need. With any luck, 'The Sylvie Barretti Hope for Life Foundation' will be up and running within the next couple of months.

I doubt this will be my last letter to you Sylvie, since I will have so much I want to share with you over the coming years about Dom and our life together. So for now, I will leave you with these annoyingly inadequate words until I can find the right ones.

Thank you. Thank you for sharing him with me, for giving us the future that you should have had. I promise that I will love him enough for the both of us until we are all together again.

Logan

The End

ABOUT THE AUTHOR

Dear Reader,

As an independent author, I am always grateful for feedback so if you have the time and desire, please leave a review, good or bad, so I can continue to find out what my readers like and don't like. You can also send me feedback via email at sloane@sloanekennedy.com

Join my Facebook Fan Group: Sloane's Secret Sinners

Connect with me:
www.sloanekennedy.com
sloane@sloanekennedy.com

ALSO BY SLOANE KENNEDY

(Note: Not all titles will be available on all retail sites)

The Escort Series
Gabriel's Rule (M/F)
Shane's Fall (M/F)
Logan's Need (M/M)

Barretti Security Series
Loving Vin (M/F)
Redeeming Rafe (M/M)
Saving Ren (M/M/M)
Freeing Zane (M/M)

Finding Series
Finding Home (M/M/M)
Finding Trust (M/M)
Finding Peace (M/M)
Finding Forgiveness (M/M)
Finding Hope (M/M/M)

The Protectors
Absolution (M/M/M)

Salvation (M/M)

Retribution (M/M)

Forsaken (M/M)

Vengeance (M/M/M)

A Protectors Family Christmas

Atonement (M/M)

Revelation (M/M)

Redemption (M/M)

Non-Series

Letting Go (M/F)